God's Messenger – God's Victim

God's Messenger – God's Victim

A *Bildungsroman* Stockholm Syndrome Novel

E. E. "Doc" Murdock

H.O.T. Press
Publishing fine books since 1983

H.O.T. Press
Los Angeles, California
www.hotpresspublishing.com

ISBN: 0-923178-33-3
ISBN-13: 978-0-923178-33-8

Books by E.E. "Doc" Murdock

Novels

- **The Pain Artist:** An American Hikikomori
- **My Vietnam War**
- **A Psalm for Cock Robin**: A Harp and His (Dead) Mother Mystery
- **Crueltown**: A Drew Steele Los Angeles-Las Vegas Mystery
- **The End of the Civil War**: A Drew Steele Civil War Mystery
- **Who Owns Arizona**: A Drew Steele Civil War Mystery

Political Books

- **From Washington and Adams to Hillary and Trump:** The Stories behind the Story of Every Presidential Election, With Special Focus on the *Volatile* Presidential Election of 2016

- **Obama Won, but Romney Almost Was President:** How the Democrats Targeted Electoral College Votes to Win the 2012 Presidential Election

Textbooks

- **How to Write Fiction: Tools and Techniques**
- **Self Management: A Guide to More Effective Study**
- **Computers Today**
- **Computers the Easy Way**
- **Windows the Easy Way**
- **DOS the Easy Way**
- **HyperCard the Easy Way**
- **dBASE the Easy Way**

Acknowledgments

I am indebted to the members of the Ojai Writing Workshop who provided valuable feedback as I worked through the many drafts of this book. I would also like to acknowledge the help of all my students at California State University, Long Beach who taught me so much. And of course, in the end, it was Zoe that made this book happen.

For Zoe,
without whom this book would not exist,
and without whom I would not exist.

Jobe 1

Jobe is walking back to the trailer, feeling pleased with himself. He's been doing his duty, spending the entire day out in the cold finding food for Mother. Mother says he's probably about to turn seventeen, so it's time for him to grow up and act like a man. It says that in the Bible. Mother says all of the answers needed in life can be found in the Bible, and the Bible says that to be a good man in this world of sinners, you must be upright, fear God, and eschew evil. Jobe has been trying really hard to be upright, and he does fear God, and he sure does eschew evil. Therefore, he *is* being a good man, a man loyal to his mother and to God who is watching him, guiding him, from his throne up there in Heaven.

And he knows for sure God certainly has been guiding him on this day because he found two dark-colored, but still edible, bananas in a dumpster behind an ice cream store over on State Street. Not only that, he also spotted an apple high up in some rich person's tree, an apple that obviously deserved to be taken because it's winter now and nobody had bothered to pick it. Besides, as it says in the Bible, *Do not despise a thief if he steal to satisfy his soul when he is hungry.*

Jobe's stomach is telling him he is very hungry, but God wouldn't want him to eat any of the fruit, not even the dried-out, almost-flat apple. As the Good Book says, *It is a privilege to share in service to the Lord,* and that means he should bring the fruit to Mother. If he deserves any of it, she will give him some.

When he gets to the trailer park, Jobe doesn't go through the main entrance where somebody might see him; instead, he goes around to the back way and ducks under the sagging barbed-wire fence. He hurries through the tall weeds to get to the old trailer the little bald man is letting Mother live in. It's a pretty terrible place to live in, but that doesn't matter; it's a roof over their heads, no better and no worse than all those other terrible places he and Mother lived in before. He should be grateful to God, and to Mother, for providing it.

He pulls open the rusted trailer door and calls out, "Mother, guess what I found!"

She's lying on her back in the middle of the floor. She's naked. Nothing unusual about that: she must be sailing away on another one of her drug trips.

But then, Jobe notices that she isn't blinking, and the hypodermic needle is still hanging from her arm.

Jobe immediately knows what it means: Mother often told him that someday he would probably find her like this. All it would take, she said, would be for "some crazy man" to slip her a bad dose, and Jobe would come home and find her "deadern a doornail."

Jobe quietly closes the door and goes to sit reverently next to his mother's lifeless body. If it wasn't for her unblinking eyes, she could be sleeping. But her face is not the peaceful face of someone asleep—it's drawn tight, as if in anguish. Jobe realizes she must have died angry. Mother was often angry. It makes Jobe feel sad that she had to be angry and unhappy when she died. But he knows Mother would not want him to be sad. No point in crying about bad things, she always said—what's done is done, and there's not a damn thing we can do about it. She'd say if God decided to call her up to His side, well then, our Lord knows best.

Jobe pulls the hypodermic needle out of her arm and throws it into the corner. He feels angry at that hypodermic needle, and maybe even a little bit angry that Mother had to like drugs so much that it made her die. But again, he knows what she'd say: it doesn't matter how a person dies, dead is dead, something that's gonna happen to us all sooner or later.

He thinks about covering her up with a blanket, but decides against it; Mother never did like anything between herself and God above. She always said God sees us as we really are, and it's folly to pretend otherwise.

Jobe stares at Mother's body. Why had she gotten herself so thin? Even her once lovely face is too thin now, her dark eyes now withdrawn back deep into her head. Her wrists are now bird-thin, and her hip bones and rib bones are obvious, as if by the time God called her up to Heaven she was not much more than a skeleton, bones barely covered by skin. Lately, she'd been complaining about how thin she'd gotten: she said men liked thin, but not this thin.

Jobe realizes he has never seen death before. Many times he's seen Mother lying naked on the floor, and sometimes she was so unconscious from injecting her drugs into herself it made her look dead. But all those times before, he could see the slight movements of her chest that proved she was still breathing. Now, there is no movement, none at all.

Jobe wonders how God would want him to think about death. He closes his eyes and searches for an answer. Soon, the familiar voice from inside his head provides words from the Bible: *He will wipe away every tear from their eyes, and death shall be no more, neither shall there be mourning, nor crying, nor pain anymore, for the former things have passed away.*

Jobe opens his eyes. God's words make sense: the Lord has wiped away every tear from Mother's eyes, and she will feel no more pain. It means Jobe should also wipe away the tears from his own eyes. He should not mourn her passing. God has taken her for His own reasons, and God's actions are not to be questioned by mere mortals.

But when God takes a person's soul away, what happens to the body that is left behind? Mother told him this could happen, but she didn't say what to do if it did.

Jobe reaches out to move a strand of her pretty hair that seems to be sticking right into one of her staring eyes. He knows she's beyond caring about such things, but he also knows she always liked him to touch her hair. She was very proud of her nice long dark hair, and she often asked him to brush it for her. He liked doing that, and she would usually let him do it for a long time.

Jobe looks toward the door. Mother's death means this is the end of this phase of his life. But what will the next phase be? He usually prefers not to think about the details of life's phases, but now he has a problem: without Mother there to trade her "favors" for the rent, the little bald man who owns the worn-out old trailer will demand actual money. Job has no money, so the man will make Jobe leave.

And there is Mother's body to think about. Jobe knows about cemeteries: Mother told him it's where people get buried in the ground after they die. But it probably costs money to be put in a cemetery, and he doesn't have a single cent. And Mother didn't have any money either; she always spent what little money she got from the men on her drugs.

Maybe it would be better to just get away quick, before anybody finds out she's dead. Somebody will come, and they will know what to do with her body.

Jobe again looks toward the door. If he walks out that door, it means he'll be facing a whole new reality. It means he'll be on his own. Jobe has never been without Mother. About seventeen years ago, God placed him inside of her unexpectedly, and they had been together ever since. Many times she told him the story of how he never should have been born, how she often regretted getting up and walking out of the waiting room in that abortion place so she wouldn't have to drag a "damn kid" around with her all the time. But then, she'd always relent. She'd reach out and muss up his mop of blonde hair and say that now she was actually glad he had been born, even if it did have to happen lying on the floor of a filthy public restroom.

Should he go, or should he stay? Jobe decides he should let God decide. Even though it is very cold inside the trailer, Jobe sits quietly, not moving at all as he waits for God to tell him what to do. He's sure time is passing, but for some reason, no message from the Lord is coming. Has God stopped talking to him? Now that He has called Mother up to His side, is He going to stop listening?

No, that could not be. Maybe God is trying to teach him a lesson, a lesson about death. As it says in His Holy Book, *The dead know nothing, and they have no more reward, for the memory of them is forgotten.*

Jobe suddenly understands what that verse from the Bible means: without a soul, the body is nothing. A useless shell. There is nothing to be done. There is nothing that *can* be done. It means this phase is over, and he must leave all the things from this phase behind.

He stands up and goes to the window. Soon after they moved into the trailer, Mother covered all the windows with taped-on newspapers, but he can tell it's starting to get dark out there.

That makes him think about how different the world outside will be. Inside, the world he is used to, is this shabby room with its water-stained fake-wood walls and the smoke-colored area around the hole where the stovepipe goes out. There is the one single bare bulb hanging down on a twisted wire that's half torn out of the sagging ceiling—an indication of Mother's frequent anger. Jobe stares at the hanging down bulb. Why have a light bulb if there is no electricity? Why didn't the electricity ever get turned on?

And why are those dirty dishes piled in the dented and corroded metal sink? Those dishes are so caked with grime, they must have been there in that sink almost since the day they moved into this terrible place. Mother must have decided there was no reason to bother washing dishes because she knew they would soon get kicked out, just like they'd gotten kicked out of all those other places. Mother was good at finding them free places to live, places provided by men who would make Mother moan and cry in the night. But eventually those men would decide Mother was too weird for them, and he and Mother would get kicked out. But as bad as the places they lived in were, at least Mother almost always provided a roof over their heads. Now that aspect of Jobe's reality is also about to change: once he walks out that door, he will have nowhere to come home to. He'll be outside, and the outside is unknown.

Why hadn't Mother prepared him for this? His reality has always been whatever reality she could scrape together for them. But now he sees he's going to have to learn how to create his own reality. God must be telling him it's time for him to go out into the world and find his own path. Jobe knows he must obey. As the Bible says, *Meddle not with them that are given to change.*

But what if the Devil is out there waiting for him? Mother never let him forget that the Devil is always lurking out there in the world, watching and waiting for an opportunity to steal your soul.

But the Bible says *Submit to God and resist the devil and he will flee from you.* That has to mean God is telling him he must go out and confront the Devil and defeat him. The Lord is promising to guide him through such dangers. The Lord will guide him, as long as he remains faithful and remembers the words of the Bible.

That thought makes Jobe wonder where Mother's Bible is. She was never without it, so it must be nearby. He looks for it under the piles of discarded, balled-up clothes and the stacks of old newspapers and magazines. But it isn't there. Could it be that in her last moments of hopelessness she threw it away, as if her last act was to reject the words of our Lord? No, that could not be. Even in desperation, she wouldn't do that.

He looks down at Mother's body. "What did you do with your Bible, Mother? Shouldn't it belong to me now that you have risen up to meet God?"

She doesn't answer, but a voice inside of Jobe's head tells him that Mother would have never taken the final step toward her ascension without that Bible in her hand. It means she must have been holding the Bible in her hand just before she injected that last shot of whatever kind of drug it was.

And that tells Jobe where the Bible must be.

He rolls Mother's body up onto its side, and sure enough, there is the little black Bible. It was under her body the whole time. It is very beat up from all those times she threw it against the wall, but every time, she'd pick it up again and hold it close to her chest, eyes closed, whispering prayers, begging for forgiveness.

Jobe reverently picks the Bible up and lets Mother's body roll back down. Now, with the Holy Bible in his hand, he's armed against the Devil. The big world is out there waiting for him,and he must go out and learn about it. God has commanded it, so it must be done. Jobe knows the Devil will be out there somewhere, and he knows the Devil will try to capture his mind and his soul, but he now understands that overcoming the Devil's temptations must be a necessary part of his new path of learning. God is testing him, and Jobe knows this is a test he must pass if he is to trod the road to salvation. He will go forth and defeat the Devil. Mother's passing means the Lord has confidence in him. With the Lord at his side, Jobe is sure the Devil will be no match for him. He will defeat the Devil, and in so doing, he will be transported to a higher domain of knowledge.

With that hopeful thought, Jobe opens the door and steps out into the night.

Chrissy 1

This is my secret diary. I'm starting it right now. They won't let me have a real diary, so I'm going to keep track of everything that happens to me in this way, inside of my head, as if I'm writing it down on paper with a pencil.

I know it's going to be hard to tell about what happened to me today, but if this is going to be like a real diary I should start out with what happened this morning and tell it from the beginning.

This morning, when all the other kids were outside working in the gardens, I snuck off to the girls' bedroom and got my Annie doll from her hiding place behind the big dresser. She was a little bit dusty, but as soon as I blew the dust off of her beautiful red hair, she was as happy as ever. I sat on the floor between two of the beds and got Annie set up as if she was on a stage about to perform in a dancing contest. But I barely had her starting her dance routine when the bedroom door opened. Darn, it was Mother Vicki. I ducked down, but it was too late. She'd spotted me. She asked me why I was hiding in the bedroom instead of being outside working in the gardens along with all the other kids.

I told her I was about to go out, and with my foot I slid Annie under the nearest bed.

Mother Vicki shook her finger at me and said I shouldn't be shirking my duties. Then she said she suspected I'd been playing with that red-haired Annie doll again, and she reminded me that the Prophet had banned any toys with the color red on them.

I said I had red hair too, but she said that was different because I couldn't help it. She said I was too old to be playing with dolls anyhow because I was almost a teenager now.

I said I'd hardly ever got to play with dolls when I was younger because they make us work so hard out in the fields all day.

She didn't care about that. She said I had to give her my Annie doll.

But I wasn't about to give it to her. I told her she wasn't my real mother, so I didn't have to do anything she said. Besides, even though she was married to my father, she wasn't really all that much older than me, so what gave her the right to tell me what to do?

That made her real mad. She said she was going to report me to the Prophet for having a red toy and for talking back to her.

I knew I'd better try to talk her out of that. The only one of the other kids in my family that ever had to go in to see the Prophet was my oldest brother, Carl, and he got kicked out of the community right after that. Now, none of us even knows where he is. Maybe Dad does, but he refuses to talk about it. It's as if Carl died, not just got sent away.

I real quick told Mother Vicki that I was real sorry, and then I told her maybe she was right, maybe I should give up my Annie doll. I reminded her that tomorrow would be my thirteenth birthday, and I said that maybe if I got something different for my birthday, I'd be willing to give up my doll. I told her I'd been thinking that I'd like to start keeping a diary. I asked her if she would get me a little notebook for my birthday, that way I could keep a diary and write in it all the things that happened in my life.

She opened her mouth and got all red-faced. It was as if I'd slapped her. She even took a step back, like there was something wrong with me, like I was the devil or something. She went back to shaking her finger at me, telling me that a diary is the very essence of vanity and self-centeredness. The Prophet had warned us all against that.

She said that settled it, she was going to have to report me to the Prophet. She turned and stomped out of the room.

That got me worried. She's one of the Prophet's daughters, so maybe he might really listen to her. But then, the Prophet has a whole lot of daughters, so I hoped that maybe he wouldn't listen to her. After all, she's not a boy.

At lunch, Mother Vicki waited until my real mom and two of my older sisters had gone out to the kitchen to start washing the dishes, and then she said I had to come with her to see the Prophet. The little kids were all staring at me, and for a minute I liked being noticed for a change, but then I realized they were looking at me like that because they were scared for me. That got me kind of scared too.

Mother Vicki dragged me all the way up to the big house, and she didn't say a word to me all the way. She just pushed me into the Prophet's office and closed the door behind me.

The Prophet was sitting behind a big desk, writing something in a notebook. At first I had the hope that he might have heard about me wanting to start a diary and he was going to give me that notebook. But after making me stand there for a long time, he finally closed his notebook and came to stand in front of me. He wasn't as tall as he looks on Sundays when he's up on the stage in the chapel telling us what the Lord told him to tell us, and his really-black hair had some gray in it that you can't see when we're all way down in the audience. In fact, close up, he seemed so fat and old that I had to quickly look away, afraid of what my eyes were seeing.

What happened after that I haven't told anybody about because I'm pretty sure nobody would believe me. He started out by telling me I was almost a grown women now and should act my age. He said a young woman like me should be starting to think about marriage.

I hadn't ever thought about myself like that, and I kind of liked it that the Prophet, the most important person in the world, would think that about me.

But then he told me to take off all of my clothes. I almost couldn't believe he'd said that. If I took off my clothes, that would mean he'd see me naked, and we girls are all taught that boys and girls aren't ever supposed to ever see each other naked. But then he said it again. He said it was an order from him, the Prophet.

I started crying, but he didn't care. He said if I didn't take off my clothes this very minute, he would tear them off of me.

I didn't want to get my nice new blue dress torn, so I finally did it. I took off everything but my underwear, but right away he said I had to keep going and take off everything. I did it, but after I dropped my panties to the floor, I tried to cover myself up with my hands. He pulled my hands away and made me stand there all naked while he walked around me, looking me over.

I didn't dare even look up at him, but I was wondering what he was thinking. Did he think I was pretty? A boy in school once told me I was pretty, but nobody else ever said that kind of thing about me.

He kept on looking me over and I wondered if he was sizing me up to figure out what kind of wife I would make for somebody. We girls had always been taught to do whatever a male tell us to do, even boys our own age. They said the Bible makes it clear that men are to rule the women and the women are not to complain. Besides, he's an adult and in church they're always telling us kids we have to do whatever any adult tells us to do, even if the adult is not in our own family.

Then, he sat down in a chair and said I should come over and sit on his lap.

I really, really didn't want to do that. Having a grown man look at me while I was naked was bad enough, but having to sit on his lap while being naked would be a whole different thing. Wouldn't doing that be against all the things we girls had been taught in school, about keeping ourselves pure and clean in the eyes of God?

I was still crying, and I was looking toward the door wondering if I would somehow get away. But how could I go outside into the outer office where his employees were if I didn't have any clothes on? What would the people out there think had been going on in his office?

I was so scared I was shivering like I was cold, but when I tried to back away from him, he reached out and pulled me down onto his lap, real rough like. He told me to stop my ridiculous crying. He said a young woman like me, nearly old enough to be married, should not be crying like a child.

I tried to get away, but he was so strong I couldn't. He told me to sit still and keep quiet. He held me real tight against himself and started whispering into my ear about how fine and young and thin I was. Then he reached around and put his hand on my private girl part down there between my legs. I felt an electric shock kind of feeling, and I jerked, but that just made him hold me tighter. Then he put his fingers inside of me, and that made me so afraid and so confused I couldn't breath. I tried to squirm around to make his fingers come out of me, but he jerked me back against himself and told me not to move.

Then his hand started moving in his lap under me. I closed my eyes and tried not to think about what he was doing down there.

What he was doing with his fingers inside of me was real rough and it was hurting me. I couldn't stop crying, but he didn't care. He just kept on doing what he was doing to me and doing to himself. I tried to imagine I was somewhere else and this wasn't happening, but it didn't work because he was hurting me more and more, and it was also making me all hot and sweaty. I was afraid to tell him to stop because I was afraid of what else he might do to me. I couldn't figure out why the Prophet would be rubbing me down there when one day at school one of the elder women took us older girls into another room and told us never to rub ourselves down there. They said it was a bad thing to do. So why was the Prophet doing that to me? Was he trying to teach me something? Was he testing me in some way to see if I was ready for marriage?

He kept on rubbing on me down there faster and faster, and at the same time, he was doing something real fast to himself underneath me with his other hand. What he was doing to me was not only making me hot, it was making me dizzy and that made me even more confused. I tried to tell myself that what he was doing to me and what he was doing to himself couldn't be bad because this was the Prophet, the most important person we have.

He was breathing fast, and that made me realize I was breathing fast too. He whispered in my ear that I shouldn't worry about what he was doing because I was as safe in his arms as in God's arms.

But then he let out a little groan, and then he stopped doing whatever he was doing to himself. He pulled his fingers out of me, and his breathing started slowing down. He put his cheek close to my ear and whispered that he'd always take care of me and that he'd find a good husband for me pretty soon, or maybe, because I was so fine, he would take me for himself.

I thought about what it would be like to be his wife. He had a lot of wives, some of them about as young as me, and they all got a lot of respect and special privileges just because they were all wives of the Prophet. The youngest ones were always pregnant with babies inside of them, so they didn't even have to work out in the fields like the rest of us did. I thought maybe it would be good to be special like that, but then I realized that I didn't want to get married to a fat old man like him even it I did get special privileges. In fact, I was thinking maybe I didn't want to get married at all if this is what being married was like. I have to admit to you, my secret diary, that I wasn't having very nice thoughts about the Prophet right then.

But then all of a sudden, he pushed me off of his lap and told me to get dressed. He said it like he was mad at me. He was looking at me like he didn't like me anymore, like he was disgusted with me or something. He said I shouldn't tell anybody about what had happened or I would be in big trouble.

While I hurried and got dressed, he went back to his desk and started writing in his book again. He didn't say anything more to me or even look at me, so I just left. I tried to walk steady out past the people in the outer office even though I was shaky and hot, and I probably had a really red face. The women in the Prophet's outer office who are his assistants told me to get back to work in the community gardens along with all the other children, so I did that and tried to not think too much.

But I'm still very confused about what the Prophet did to me. Maybe someday I'll be able to figure it out, but I sure hope he doesn't pick me to be his next wife. I'm sorry to think about the Prophet like that, but it's true.

Jobe 2

Jobe pulls his sweatshirt hood up over his head and moves quickly away from the trailer. But then, he stops to look back at it for the last time. What a terrible old flat-tired thing that trailer is. Not a very nice place for Mother to die in. But maybe God doesn't care about things like that. Who can say what the Lord has in mind for us? Like it says in His Holy Book, *No man can know His will*.

Jobe hurries along the dirt path between the other trailers, hoping that it's too dark and smoggy for anybody to him leaving. He thinks it's weird that they even call this place a trailer "park." Jobe doesn't know much about the world, but he does know this is not a park; it's nothing but a scattering of old trailers that got dropped into the middle of what looks like a weedy garbage dump. Jobe doesn't normally allow his mind to take much notice of such things, but now he can see why Mother called it a bottom-of-the-barrel place, a place inhabited by lost people. Although Mother forbade him to associate with the neighbors —"wretched unbelievers," she called them—Jobe has been watching them, and a while back, he put them all on a special list in his mind. There is the hoarder woman with her piles of stashed treasures stashed away, layer upon layer, under her sagging plywood carport. Why does she keep all that worthless stuff? Doesn't she know the Bible would tell her *One's life does not consist in the abundance of possessions*.

Jobe hurries on and passes by the unpainted wooden trailer of the yellow-dress woman. She rarely comes out of her trailer, but when she does, she always looks sad, and she always wears the same faded yellow dress, and she always has the same sad little plastic yellow flower in her hair. Jobe understands that God has not smiled fondly upon that woman.

The last place he has to sneak past is the domain of the self-described car repair dude, the sour man with the greasy long hair. He never actually repairs any cars, but he continues to collect them. Jobe knows those cars will never get repaired. They're all up on cement blocks, and they're all permanently bound to the earth by thick cobwebs. The car repair man doesn't even have a trailer—he lives in the back seat of one of his cars, a huge old four-door Cadillac that seems to have once been yellow but has now turned mostly into a kind of rusted-out brown. The back seat is his bedroom and the front part, where there used to be car seats, is his kitchen where he burns his little wood fires all night. God must not like that man either.

Jobe heads for his secret break in the barbed wire fence, feeling confident that nobody saw him leave.

Out on the street, Jobe feels free from that old reality. No one saw him go, and no one will miss him. Someone will come and take care of Mother's body.

He hurries on, refusing to even look back. Mother's body may still be back there, but her soul has departed to be with God, and that's all that matters. Now, the part of his life that was being a son is over. God has commanded him to go forth and learn, so that is what Jobe will do.

But as he walks, a new truth comes into his mind: it's cold, too cold to be outside and all alone. Why isn't it spring yet? It's been winter too long. The snow has mostly melted, but the trees are still dead. Their limbs look like skeleton arms reaching down to grab him. And the grass is still brown, also dead-looking. Being out in the cold all alone makes him feel so unsure, he's almost ready to turn around and go back. But he knows he can't do that; with Mother gone, there is nothing for him back there. But what is ahead for him? Where should he go?

He decides all he can do is just keep walking and trust that God has a plan for him.

When he comes to the railroad yards, Jobe remembers how he often had to hang out there watching the trains being hooked up together while his mother "entertained" her men friends back at the trailer.

Jobe understands why she had to do that. It was because she needed the money to buy food for him, to pay for the wood to burn in the little wood stove so he could be warm, to pay for the lantern oil so he wouldn't have to live in the dark, to pay for her drugs so she could be happy, despite "having to drag a damn kid around" with her all the time.

But hanging out at the train place is in the past now. He needs to keep his focus on the future. He must follow the path God has laid out for him. But what is that path? Where is God leading him? He should ask; after all, the Bible says *Let him ask God, who gives generously to all without reproach.*

Jobe stops walking and looks up to Heaven. "Please, God, tell me what to do. The world feels too big for me."

He waits, but there is no answer. This must be part of God's test of him. He has to decide everything for himself.

Jobe begins walking again, simply going forward, hoping God is leading him in the right direction.

He shivers. Being out in the world all alone makes the night seem even colder. That means he should go somewhere to get out of the cold. But where? The stores he's passing are dark with signs on the doors that say "CLOSED." Why are they closed? Does every store in Salt Lake City close at night? Jobe has rarely been outside at night because Mother always said the Devil rules the night. Is that why all the stores close at night? Are they all afraid of the Devil?

He soon finds himself standing in front of a store that does have lights on inside. A sign on the front says it's a drug store. Jobe has noticed that store before, but he's never gone inside because he's afraid of drugs. But now, with it being so cold, maybe he should go in and look around. He doesn't have any money, but maybe they won't know that. He decides to go in, at least long enough to get warm.

Once inside, he discovers it *is* warmer, and he is grateful. There are long aisles with shelves full of small colorful packages. Jobe is about to take a chance and pick up one of those packages to see what kinds of drugs are inside, when a man in a uniform comes and tells him he has to leave.

Jobe doesn't ask why; he knows why. It's because people don't like him. It's always been like that. In the past, the few times he ever went inside a store, they would always look at him suspiciously, as if they thought he was going to steal something.

Back out on the street, it feels even colder than before. If stores won't let him go inside, where can he go to get warm? If he stays out here in the cold, he might freeze to death. There aren't any people around, and there aren't very many cars going by in the street. If he fell down on the sidewalk right now, would anybody stop to help him? Probably not. They would just let him die there. It's like Mother always said, nobody cares about anybody; they only care about themselves.

But that thought about Mother reminds him of something: on days when Mother had a man in for the whole day, Jobe would go way downtown to the indoor mall. It's out of the weather, and there is a bench in the wide hallway where he would sit and watch the people go by, imagining what their lives might be like. So he should go there. Downtown is a long ways away, but Jobe is good at walking, and walking fast will help him stay warm.

He hurries as fast as he can, and when he gets closer to the downtown area, he breaks into a run. Just thinking about being indoors where it's warm makes it worth running fast and getting out of breath.

When he finally makes it to the downtown mall, he runs to the big glass door and pulls on the handle. But the door won't open. He tries it again, pulling even harder. The door won't budge. Are they keeping him out? But why? They never kept him out when he came here before in the daytime.

He puts his face against the glass and cups his hands to see inside. It's dark in there. Strange. Why would it be dark? It's never dark in there. The mall must be closed. But why? Did they know he was coming and lock the doors against him? It could be a sign. Mother said the world is full of signs and omens, and he should always be watchful for the signs that will tell us what is going to happen next. Jobe remembers the words she read him from the Bible: *There will be signs of what things are about to be accomplished.* She also read him the part where the Bible says *Be watchful. Your adversary the devil prowls around like a roaring lion, seeking someone to devour.* Jobe knows he has to be on the watch for signs and omens, but what does this kind of hateful omen mean? Does the door being closed and locked mean the Devil is close by, trying to keep him outside in the cold so he'll freeze to death leaving his soul ready to be taken?

He looks at the writing on the glass. It says the mall is closed on Sunday. Maybe it means today is a Sunday, the day God takes care of the churches. That's even worse. Sunday is the most dangerous day, the day when God is busy doing Sunday things, leaving the Devil free to do whatever he wants. It means Jobe is in a very vulnerable situation: he's outside with nowhere to go, all alone on a dark and cold Sunday night when the Devil is on the loose. Jobe looks around and feels the panic building up inside of him. But he knows he must not panic. Mother always got mad at him when he panicked, and she'd hit him and keep on hitting him until he calmed down. Eventually, he learned he could calm himself down by hitting himself. He tries to remember that good feeling of hitting himself to get calmed down on the really long days when Mother had locked him in the closet while she went out to meet men. But Mother is not here to help him now, so what should he do? What would she tell him to do?

Jobe realizes she'd tell him to be logical. Mother's hitting taught him to calm down and be logical. And being logical always means he should wait for directions from God.

That's it! There's no reason to panic. He should be logical and ask God for help. God will guide him.

Jobe closes his eyes and waits for God's words to fill his mind.

He waits and he waits, but nothing is coming. Maybe on Sundays, God is so busy doing church things, her has no time for anybody who is not inside of a church. So maybe that means Jobe should also go to a church. He could go inside a church to get warm. That's logical. But Jobe has never been inside of a real church because Mother didn't like the "snobby people" in churches. She said they were all looking down on her. Once when he was little, Mother did take him into a basement of a house where people were praying out loud and dancing around and playing with poisonous snakes. But a big fat man there got bit by one of the snakes, and Mother said it proved those people didn't believe in God in the right way, so they left and never went back.

Jobe doesn't know where any churches are. That means he needs a sign from God to lead him to one. That's also being logical.

He opens his eyes and looks for a sign. Right away, his eyes are seeing pointed towers rising up out of the darkness. Jobe knows what those towers are: they're the pointed spires that are on top of the huge stone Mormon's temple that dominates the center of town. It's right across the street. Jobe thinks maybe that Mormon place is a kind of church, a really big church for Mormon people. God must be telling him to go to that temple church and maybe go inside of it to get warm. Jobe is not sure if the Mormons worship the same God as he and Mother do, but if that big temple across the street really is a kind of church, no matter what they believe, he should go in there to get warm.

Jobe crosses the street, but the closer he gets to the Mormon's temple, the more scary and threatening it looks. It's very tall, and he wonders why it has those sharp pointed spikes reaching up into the dark sky. Are the Mormons pointing their building's spires up toward Heaven to threaten God?

Jobe stops. Maybe this is a mistake. Maybe he shouldn't go anywhere near that place. It's a huge and forbidding building, and he doesn't know what goes on inside there. Once, a long time ago, he got very brave and tried to go inside, but a guard man told him he wasn't allowed in. Somehow, that guard man knew he wasn't a Mormon.

But now it's nighttime, and it's very cold outside. It will be warm inside that big temple, and after all, it must be a kind of church, so they'll have to let him in, at least long enough to get warm. Although Mother always called them "the weird Mormons" and told Jobe to stay away from them, this time it was God that led him here. That must mean it's okay to go inside.

He hurries down the block, following along next to the high iron fence. But when he gets to the entrance, the big black iron gate is closed and locked. Once again, it's as if somebody knew he was coming and locked the gate against him. It's another omen, maybe another sign of the Devil, and it scares Jobe. It's like the whole world has turned against him.

But maybe there's another way in. There could be a gate on the other side.

He hurries down the block and around the corner, and sure enough, there is another big iron gate. But even before he gets there, Jobe can see that it's also closed.

It means everything is closed against him, even this Mormon's temple. It has to be the Devil's doing. The Devil led him here to this Mormon church-type place as a trick, making him think he was being guided by the Lord.

He's about to run away as fast as he can when he sees a movement in the darkness. Is someone there? Is this the sign from God he has been expecting? Or is it another one of the Devil's tricks?

Staying close to the tall fence, he cautiously goes closer to the entrance.

He sees two people, a woman with a tight black hat covering her head and a skinny little girl with short dark hair. They're sitting on the sidewalk next to the gate. Why would they be sitting there? Are they waiting for the church to open? Or, could it be that they're waiting for *him*? Did they somehow know he was coming? God might have put them there to wait for him; otherwise, why would a woman and a child be sitting out here on this cold night?

He goes even closer, and then he sees them for what they are: beggars. The woman has a hand-lettered cardboard sign on her lap:

PLEASE GIVE - HELP DAUGHTER WHOS RETARDED

A paper cup is on the sidewalk in front of them.

Jobe wonders why God would have led him to beggars. Is the answer in the Bible? He holds Mother's old Bible up against his forehead and waits for an answer.

And then it comes to him: it's in the parable about a rich man clothed in purple and fine linen who feasted sumptuously while he let the hungry beggars outside his gate die in the cold. Maybe God led him here to help these two beggars. But Jobe has no money, so how can he help them? Maybe he's reading the signs wrong. Maybe God didn't lead him to these two people. In fact, it could be another one of the Devil's tricks. If so, he should run away fast. But how could a woman and a child be of any danger to him?

Chrissy 2

What I have to tell you, my secret diary, is that it's been a really long day and I'm really tired. I'm still out in the community gardens, and it's hard work, but it's giving me time to think about what the Prophet did to me. I keep wondering why he picked me to do that to. Was it some kind of test?

I have to admit to feeling resentful that I have to spend all day out working after what he did to me. I'd rather just be sitting quiet in my assigned seat at school.

But I've been getting bored at school lately anyhow because lately it's mostly been lessons by the Prophet's brother who spends all day warning us about Satan and evil and telling us how we shouldn't let ourselves get tempted. It's boring because I already know about the devil and temptation from Sunday School. Actually, about the only fun thing that happens in school is when our men teachers show us maps of the world and tell us how different other countries are from this country and how the people who live in those other countries are bad because they don't believe in Joseph Smith or the Book of Mormon or the Doctrine and Covenants or any of the other important things we know are true. But even if the people in those foreign places are bad, I'd still like to go there and see for myself. Maybe that makes me a bad person, but I can't see anything wrong with dreaming about it.

But it really is just dreaming, I never get to go anywhere. I've never been anywhere outside of our little village, except the couple of times I got to go into Saint George when it was my birthday. And Saint George isn't even that big of a town anyway.

But there's no chance of getting to go to school, not for a while yet. None of us kids have been anywhere near the schoolroom since the spring planting season began.

Every spring, the grown-ups gather together inside the big community greenhouses to get the plants started so they'll be ready for the planting, so it's up to us kids to get the dirt in the community gardens ready. It's a lot of work. Every kid has to help, even the littlest kids. We all dread the coming end of winter because getting the big gardens ready for spring planting is the hardest work we do all year. Weeding the gardens all summer is hard work too, almost as hard as the picking that has to be done later, but this is harder because the ground is still frozen and we have to dig it all up and make perfect rows out of it.

But I know it had to be done, so I just went to work alongside all the other kids without saying anything about what had happened to me. Even if I did tell anybody what the Prophet did to me, I don't think they would believe me. They might say it was me trying to get him to do that to me. But I don't think I did anything to make him do that. I was wearing the same kind of long dress every other girl in the community has to wear, and my mom braids my hair at the back of my head so it looks like all the other girl's hair. So how could it be my fault? But maybe I did do something wrong and didn't realize it.

Anyhow, whether I did anything wrong or not, it's too shameful to tell anybody about it. There must be something about me that would make him want to do that to me. Mother Vicki is always saying I don't fit in. She says the other kids don't like me because I think I'm too pretty. But that's not true. I don't think I'm as pretty as a lot of the girls. And I'm the only one with red hair. Maybe that's why they don't like me, because of my red hair.

Anyhow, I decided to just do my work and keep quiet.

Oh, and here's another thing. After a while, I realized nobody was working next to me. The other kids were avoiding me. At first, I thought maybe they somehow guessed what the Prophet did to me, but then I realized there was no way they could have guessed that. They just thought I must be a bad person if I got called in by the Prophet. They know my brother Carl is the only other kid lately that got called in by the Prophet, and he got banished from the community right after that. All the kids said he must have done something shameful to get banished, and they were glad he got thrown out of the community. But Carl told me all he did was kiss a girl he liked, and she liked him too. She was a girl his own age. It wasn't his fault that the Prophet had already promised that girl to some old man.

I realized I was working all by myself. Even my real little sister was staying away from me. When I went to her and tried to ask her why she was avoiding me, a boy from another family who is a little bit older than me came over and said I shouldn't be talking to her because I might taint her. That was the word he used, "taint." Maybe that means the other kids all think I'm going to get banished too. I sure hope that doesn't happen. Where would I go? Would they send me to where Carl is? That might not be so bad cause I'd get to see my favorite brother again. He was the only one in my family who ever seemed to like me, the only one who ever talked to me very much. I'd sure like to see him again, but I know if I got banished I'd really miss my real mom and all my brothers and sisters.

I'm glad I started this secret diary, but I wish it was a real paper diary. If I had a real paper diary, I could write down all the things that happen to me and wouldn't have to remember it all so careful like I'm doing now. It would help me think through things too, like why the Prophet did what he did to me and why everybody is treating me so mean now, like I'm not holy enough to be part of this community anymore. I don't think it's fair. Even though I did get called in to see the Prophet, I'm still the same girl as I was before. Sort of.

I know that now that I'm almost a teenager, I should try to be grown up and brave. I tell myself not to care about the mean things the other kids are saying about me because sticks and stones can break my bones but names can't.

Jobe 3

Jobe stays where he is, hiding in the shadows next to the Mormon Temple's tall iron fence. He watches the two beggars. How can they stand to sit so still when it's so cold? Both the woman and the little girl are wearing heavy coats, but it still must be very cold for them to be sitting there on that cold and hard sidewalk.

Jobe feels sorry for them, especially for the girl who seems to be just staring off into space.

But Jobe knows he has no way to help them, so these people must not be part of God's plan for him. Maybe running into them wasn't an omen after all.

Jobe is about to walk away when the woman spots him. She takes her hand out of her pocket and grabs the paper cup. She shakes it at him. "Hey, bub, hows about a donation? It's ta get treatment for my daughter here."

Jobe notices the woman is wearing thick gloves. He shrugs. "I'm sorry, ma'am. I don't have any money."

The woman again shakes the cup at him. "Don't give me that malarkey, kid. Everybody got money. Cough up a little at least."

"No, really," says Jobe, moving a little closer. "I don't have a dime." He pulls his pants pockets inside out to show her.

"Well, shit," says the woman, "then you ain't no better off than us." She turns to her daughter who is still staring straight ahead. "Well, Rosie, guess we might as well pack it in for tonight."

The little girl, who didn't seem to have been listening, immediately stands up and helps her mother struggle to her feet. The girl glances at Jobe, and that brief look makes him wonder if she might be older than he first thought. Something about her dark eyes, like they are very watchful. Jobe can see that she's a lot shorter than he is, and very thin. She looks to be only about fourteen or maybe fifteen, but those eyes, in that one quick look, seemed older. But after that one look, the girl quickly went back to staring at nothing. Jobe thinks about that word on the woman's begging sign: it says the girl is "retarded." Jobe has no idea what being retarded means, but it must have something to do with why she just stares at nothing and doesn't talk.

Now that the woman is standing up, Jobe notices that she'd been leaning back against a big black plastic bag that seems to be stuffed full of something. Clothes maybe? Or blankets? And she'd been sitting on a folded up thick blanket. Maybe this woman is better prepared for the cold than he thought. She's pretty big, not actually fat, more like . . . hefty. Maybe that means she can take the cold better than a thin person like him.

After stuffing her sitting-blanket into the plastic bag, the woman turns to Jobe. "Well, what you starin' at, bub? You got some kinda problem?"

Jobe shakes his head. "Sorry, ma'am. No, I don't have a problem. Or, I mean, I guess I do have a problem. I don't have any place to go and it's real . . . cold."

"No place to go? Why's that, kid?"

"Well, uh, my mother died today, and I can't go back there because I don't have money, and it's cold, so I just came here to—"

"Your ma died? Just today?"

Jobe nods and looks down at the sidewalk.

"What she do, overdose?"

Jobe looks up at her. How could this odd woman know that?

The woman nods. "Yep. See it all the time. Killer drugs. It's a Goddam epidemic. I'm tellin' ya, a Goddam epidemic."

Jobe winces at the woman's use of such unGodly language. "Uh, I'd rather you didn't use the Lord's name in vain like that, ma'am. I mean, if you wouldn't mind."

The woman grins at Jobe. "Ah ha! Yer one of them Bible thumpers, ain't ya? I noticed right off the bat you got yourself a little Bible there.

Jobe holds his Bible tightly in both hands to make sure this strange woman doesn't try to take it away from him. "This Bible was my mother's, and now I guess it's mine because—"

"Yeah, yeah. I get it. So your ma bein' dead means you got no home to go to anymore. Right?"

"I . . . guess so."

The woman turns to her daughter who seems to be interested in the street light above. "Well, what you say, Rosie? Should we help this dude out?"

The girl stares at Jobe, and then, without changing her blank expression, turns away.

"Okay, looks like we'd better take ya along with us. Just let me load up and we'll go.

She ties off the top of her big plastic bag and throws it over her shoulder. Then she nods toward her daughter. "My little Rosie ain't really retarded like my sign says." She holds up her cardboard sign and taps on the word "retarded." "They say it's only the autism, but as I hear it, that ain't much better. Still, she's a good kid, so I'm not about to let 'em lock her up in one a them places where she'll never see the light a day again and won't learn about the world like I can teach her about. Ain't that right, Rosie?"

The girl doesn't respond, and Jobe wonders if she's even hearing what her mother is saying.

The woman waves her hand at Jobe. "Okay, boy. Let's go." She starts off down the sidewalk, the girl following close behind her.

Jobe hesitates, then follows. He might as well go wherever they're going, at least until he learns what God's plan is for him. He hopes the woman has a warm place to go to.

"So, kid," the woman says over her shoulder, "what's your name?"

Jobe hurries up next to her and matches her pace. "Jobe."

The woman looks surprised. "Really? Like in the Bible?"

Jobe shrugs. "Yes, except in the Bible, it doesn't have an 'E' on the end. I guess my mother wanted to spell my name different. I don't know why."

"No 'E' eh. Fine with me. Jobe it is. With an 'E' on the end." She laughs.

Jobe isn't sure why she laughed, but he doesn't say anything.

"Name's Bella," the woman says. "Bella the bell. That's me. But most everybody down at the park calls me Momma B. I don't get why. I'm not even turned forty yet, and I don't got a spec of gray hair. You wanna see?" She pulls off her stocking cap to show him her greasy-looking dark hair, but then she quickly puts her cap back on, pulling it down over her ears. "And I only got the one kid, so I don't get the momma thing atal. I had me a coupla other kids once upon a time, but they kinda got lost along the way. Anyhow, now all I got is the one. She's a good kid. Helps me out a lot."

She turns to her daughter who is following along a few paces behind. "You help me out, don't ya, sweetie?"

The girl is looking down at the sidewalk as she walks and doesn't answer. Jobe wonders why the girl doesn't answer her mother. Can't she talk at all?

"Uh," says Jobe, "you mentioned a park?"

"Yeah. The park. It's not far. You'll see."

The woman quickens her pace and doesn't say another word until they come to a busy street. She points across the street. "The park."

Jobe knows the park she's pointing at. It's mostly dirt and patches of brown grass. It has a few big trees, but thay are still winter-bare. He's walked past that park before, but he's never gone in there because it seemed like it was a hangout for men that looked homeless. He wonders if it's safe there, especially at night.

"You never been to that park before, kid?"

"No, ma'am."

"Name's Bella. Not ma'am. Bella the bell, remember?"

"Oh, right. Yes, Bella, I've seen that park, but I've never been in there. It looks like a place for homeless people."

"Well, that's what you are now, right? Homeless?"

Jobe hasn't been thinking about it that way, but he realizes she's right. Still, he doesn't think being without a home to go to is the same as those people in the park. They seem like maybe they've been homeless for a long time.

Bella doesn't wait for the light to turn green. She leads Jobe and Rosie across the street, holding up her hand to make the cars stop. They do stop, but one of them beeps its horn at her. Bella holds up her middle finger and continues across the street and into the park.

Jobe hurries across, but then he hesitates on the sidewalk. The park seems cold and dark, and there are people all over the place, some of them in sleeping bags, but others only covered by pieces of cardboard. Jobe is not sure he wants to go into a place like this.

As if she's reading his mind, Bella comes back to grab his arm. "This place may look scary, but it's not really. You just stick close to me, kid, and you'll be all right. Long as ya don't go gettin' yourself involved with anybody. Talk to 'em, and they'll try to take your money. And when they find out you don't got none, they might even take those run-type shoes you're wearin'. You hear me?"

"Yes, ma'am. I mean, Bella. I'll stay close to you."

As Bella leads her daughter and Jobe across the dead brown grass, Jobe notices some tall metal bars with rusty chains hanging down. It must have been a place for swinging, but there are no swings there now. And there's a rusty slide too, but it looks like it hasn't been slid down in a very long time.

Bella drops her bundle next to a wooden wall. She knocks on the wall. "This old tennis wall may be fallin' apart, but it's good enough for stoppin' some of the wind when it comes from the west, which it usually does at night."

"What you got there, Momma B? New boyfriend?" The voice, a gruff man's voice, comes out of the darkness.

"Kiss mine," yells Bella.

"Okay, bring it over here," comes back the voice.

"You'd better hope I don't," yells Bella.

The voice doesn't come again.

Bella opens her bundle and pulls out a ragged blanket. She quickly spreads the blanket out on the grass.

Rosie promptly plops down on the blanket, turns onto her side, and pulls her knees up close to her chest.

Her mother sits down on the blanket next to her and pulls a heavy-looking quilt out of her big plastic bag. She covers her daughter with the quilt and looks up at Jobe. "Well?" She pats next to herself.

Jobe can see that she's inviting him to lie down next to her, but he holds back. Has God led him to a woman who wants to help him, or is it the Devil trying to tempt him? He *is* cold, but he can't quite imagine lying down next to a female, especially not when there are other people nearby that might see. It makes him realize he's never been that close to any woman, especially not while lying down, except for his mother that winter when they were forced to sleep right next to each other in the back of that old van. Jobe decides it might be all right to lie down next to the woman if this situation is like that one. Bella is probably just trying to help him stay warm like Mother did when she hugged him all night that time. And it really is way too cold to imagine spending the whole night sitting out in the open.

He joins Bella on the blanket and turns away from her. He uses Mother's Bible as his pillow, and that gives him some assurance that whatever happens, God will watch over him.

Bella pulls the quilt over him, and Jobe can feel Bella very close to his back. Maybe she's staying close to help him be warm.

But then he feels Bella reach around to the front of him. She puts her hand into his pants and starts messing with his private boy part.

Jobe isn't sure what to do. Is this part of God's plan to teach him about the ways of the world, things he never got to learn about in his seventeen years of living alone with Mother? After all, the Bible says,

An intelligent heart acquires knowledge, and the ear of the wise seeks knowledge.

But it could also be exactly the kind of temptation Mother warned him about, the Devil's work. Should he get up and walk away? Shouldn't he at least push her hand away? He desperately tries to think of something in the Bible that will help him decide what to do.

And then he finds it: *No temptation has overtaken you that is not common to man. God is faithful, and he will not let you be tempted beyond your ability.* It means this is a test. God wants him to prove that he can learn about the ways of the world without getting caught in the Devil's web. It means he should wait and see what happens.

He doesn't move at all, but what she's doing down there is making things respond the same way it happens when he uses his own hand at home to do it in bed at night. It feels almost the same, but Jobe knows it's different because this is another person doing it, and that other person is a female. But it doesn't *feel* like a bad thing, and Jobe is curious about what she'll do next. He remembers one place in the Bible that says *Even if the spirit indeed is willing, the flesh is weak.* That might mean he should tell her to stop. But there is another place in the Bible that says *Call to me and I will answer you, and will tell you great and hidden things that you have not known.* That means he should wait and see what God tells him to do.

He lies very still and listens for any message from above.

But it's hard to stay focused on listening for words from God when his mind wants to focus on what Bella is doing down there. It's very distracting. Maybe it's both a temptation and a test. Even though this woman has got him very distracted, Jobe does remember one thing the Bible says about temptation: *He will provide a way of escaping temptation so that you may be able to endure it.*

That must mean God is telling him to endure and learn from this experience. If he lies very still and doesn't actually participate in any way, it will only be something that was done *to* him, not something he did intentionally. That way, he can learn what he's supposed to learn and still pass the test against being caught in the Devil's temptations. He's determined not to be outwitted by Satan. The Bible says that when the Devil comes to present you with a fiery message, it is a test. It says *Do not be surprised as though something strange were happening to you. Each person is tempted when he is lured and enticed by his own desire and desire when it has conceived gives birth to sin.* That tells

Jobe if he avoids feeling any desire, then it's not a sin. As the Bible says, *Blessed is the man who remains steadfast under trial.*

Jobe closes his eyes, determined to remain steadfast.

But no matter how steadfast he remains, he can feel that things are now really starting to happen down there.

That seems to be a signal to Bella. She quickly pulls down the front of his pants and rolls over on top of him. She does something else down there with her hand, and then she starts moving fast and hard against him.

Jobe keeps his eyes closed and tries not to feel anything. He doesn't dare move because moving would be participating. He is not participating; all he is doing is lying still, not sinning at all, thinking only Godly thoughts.

But as determined as he is to keep God in his thoughts, his mind keeps on wanting to focus on the strong things he's feeling. He's never experienced anything quite like this. It's different, and maybe even a lot better, than when he uses his own hand to do it.

It doesn't take long for the usual thing to happen.

Bella seems to know right away, because she rolls off of him. "Well, Christ, Jobe, that was too quick for me to get anywhere."

"Sorry," he mumbles.

She snuggles up close to him and reaches down to again begin playing with his private boy part.

Jobe decides that this time, he'd better resist. Going along with Bella once was a learning experience, a lesson God wanted him to engage in and learn about, but the Bible says *Let the wise hear and increase in learning and obtain guidance.* It must mean engaging in that kind of thing once should be enough learning. Doing it again might actually be a sin.

She stops. "Jesus, kid. What's the matter with you? A strappin' young guy like you, already done for the night?"

Again, he whispers, "Sorry," and tries to not think about how it felt when she did that thing to him. Part of him wouldn't mind doing it again, but he knows he shouldn't. And besides, he suddenly feels completely worn out by everything that's happened since the start of this long day.

He turns away from Bella, hoping she won't push him out into the cold.

But she won't leave him alone. She pulls at his shoulder to make him lie on his back again.

"Don't make sense, young guy like you. But maybe it's just me. I bet if you were to hop over there on top of Rosie. I bet that'd get you goin' again, wouldn't it?"

Jobe isn't sure he heard her right. Was she really inviting him to do that same thing to her daughter?

"Well?" she asks and starts messing with his private boy part again. "How about it? Do me again, and I'll let you do her. Deal?"

Thinking about getting to do that same thing to her much younger and much prettier daughter, again brings his focus back to the feeling of what Bella's warm hand is doing to him. The same feeling as before is starting again, and before he can do anything about it, she's on top of him, and the same thing happens all over again.

When it's over, Bella rolls off of him. She sighs and pats his hip. "Well, that's better. Now you're actin' like a real man."

She turns away from Jobe, and it isn't long before she's asleep and snoring.

Jobe lies still, staring up into the darkness. He can hardly believe this is still the same day that he was out searching for food, and then he came home to find that Mother had been taken up to Heaven to sit with God. And then God led him to that Mormon Temple to meet this strange woman and her daughter. And now, he's lying right next to her and something happened that has never happened to him ever in his whole life. And she even suggested he could do the same thing to her daughter if he wanted to. Was she serious about that?

He sits up and looks over the top of Bella toward her daughter. It's pretty dark, but there's enough light to see the reflection of the girl's eyes. It means she's awake, and she's looking right at him.

Jobe lies back. He's a bit unnerved by the girl's staring eyes. Does she understand what her mother just did to him? She may not understand much, but she must know what *that* was all about. What must she think of him? What would a young girl think about her mother doing that kind of thing to a stranger?

On the other hand, maybe the girl is used to it. Maybe her mother does this kind of thing with strangers all the time.

He turns to look at the girl again, but she's turned away. Maybe she's gone to sleep.

Jobe again lies back to stare up into the darkness. He doesn't want to think about it, but his unruly mind wants to keep on thinking about what Bella said: would it feel different to do that same thing with Rosie? She's closer to his own age, and she really is kind of pretty.

Jobe knows he has to put an end to that kind of thinking. And he knows exactly how to do it. If he had a stick, he could whip those kinds of thoughts out of himself. That would show the Devil he's not about to be drawn in by his evil temptations. But even if he doesn't have a switch, he knows how to induce the pain of purity. He pulls his hands out from under the quilt and pinches the bottoms of both of his ears. He pinches them really, really hard like Mother used to do to him whenever she could tell he was having impure thoughts.

The pinching hurts. Actually, it hurts a lot, but he's used to that kind of pain. Mother often gave him that kind of pain to keep him pure and reverent. He squeezes the bottoms of his ears even harder, just like Mother used to do with her very strong fingers and her very sharp fingernails. It hurts, but he knows that if he keeps on pinching and keeps on thinking only about God's wisdom, sooner or later, the pain will go away, and at that moment, the Lord will show him the path away from such sinful thoughts.

The pain *is* strong and pure, but it doesn't seem to be working. He keeps on pinching, wishing his fingers were as strong as Mother's. What advice would the Bible give him in a situation like this? There must be an answer. He tries hard to concentrate, but it's almost as if the pain itself, instead of clearing his mind of impurity, is keeping him from figuring out what the Bible would tell him to do.

But then it comes to him, the words entering his brain as if from the Lord himself: *A sin a person commits is outside the body, but the sexually immoral person sins against his own body.*

It means Jobe has not sinned because he was not being sexually immoral. He didn't seek the sex that Bella did to him, nor did he take any action to cause it. It was all Bella's doing. But to do the same thing with the daughter, a young girl who may not understand what she is doing—well, that *would* be immoral. In fact, he should get up right now and get himself out of this situation.

He releases the pinching pressure on his ears and pushes the quilt down. He begins to edge his way off of the blanket.

But Bella somehow senses his movement. Even though she still seems to be asleep, she puts her arm around him and pulls him back close to her. Then she goes back to snoring.

Bella's body is very warm, and Jobe knows how cold it is out there. He decides there's no sin in just staying where he is until morning. He pulls the heavy quilt up around his shoulders and tells himself to just lie very still and wait. Surely God wouldn't want him to go out and freeze to death in the cold. He'll wait until morning and figure all this out then.

Chrissy 3

It's nighttime now, and the main thing I have to report is that it looks like I'm still going to get to go along to Saint George tomorrow on the big shopping trip. Every two weeks, the Prophet gives Dad some of the welfare money and government food stamps from the Law of Consecration pool. Then Dad doles it out to my mothers and the three of them get together at the kitchen table to make up the big shopping list. With Dad and three mothers and so many kids to shop for, it's a big deal.

Normally, my mothers go to town by themselves in Dad's big car, but if one of us kids has a birthday that week, that kid gets to go along and get ice cream. This time it's my birthday and nobody else's, so I'll be the only kid who gets to go along. I know all the other kids will be jealous, but so what? I'm the only one with a birthday, so only I get to go.

Somehow this year feels different from my other birthday years. Those other times, all I cared about was getting to go to town and walk around in the big Walmart store to see stuff and then getting to go to the ice cream store for my special treat. This time, I've only been thinking about how I might be able to find a way to get myself a little notebook so I could have a real diary. But I don't have any money and Mother Vicki won't allow me to have anything as selfish as a diary, so I don't know why I keep on thinking about it. It's impossible.

Actually, for a while, I was afraid I wasn't going to get to go. At supper, Mom and Mother Vicki got into a big argument about it. Both Mother Vicki and Mother Laura agreed that I didn't deserve to go, even though tomorrow will be my birthday. But Mom stood firm and said of course I was going to get to go because every kid gets to go to town and get ice cream on their birthday.

One of the best things about going to Saint George tomorrow is that I'll get a whole day off from being out in the community gardens getting blisters on my hands and nobody talking to me. But maybe it's good that nobody wants to talk to me because if they asked me about what happened when I got called in by the Prophet I wouldn't know what to say. I still haven't told anybody about what the Prophet did to me, not even my real mom. I'm scared to because I'm afraid that even my own mom won't believe me. After all, the Prophet was chosen by God to lead us, so whatever he does has to be all right, doesn't it? I have to remember that and stop thinking bad thoughts about him. Maybe for that reason, it's actually better that this is a mental diary and not a written down in paper diary where someone else might see it sometime.

Jobe 4

Jobe is jolted awake when Bella pulls the quilt off of him. It's starting to get light, and he's embarrassed to discover that his pants are still down around his knees. Both Bella and Rosie are standing up, looking down at him. As he hurriedly tries to pull up his pants to cover his nakedness, Bella laughs at him. But then she says, "Nuthin to worry about kid, we're all family here." Then, she gets busy stuffing the bedding into her big plastic bag.

Rosie continues to stare at him, and that makes Jobe uncomfortable. What does that look mean? Is she thinking about what her mother did to him last night? He quickly turns away, but it's too late: he knows his face is already turning red. He tries to think of a Biblical quote about no need to be embarrassed, but with her looking at him like that, he can't think of a single one.

Bella brings his attention back by jerking at the blanket that's under him. "Hey, snap outta it, kid. We got things to do."

"We do?" Jobe jumps up and looks at the sky. "The sun is barely coming up."

"Yeah, we do. Like for starters, gettin' me a drink. I can't think straight when I'm straight." She looks at Jobe like she's waiting for him to say something. She punches his shoulder, fairly hard. "Get it? Can't think straight straight?"

Jobe isn't sure what she means, but he nods and smiles anyhow.

That seems to satisfy Bella. She says, "And then we better be gettin' us somethin' to eat. I bet you're hungry, ain't ya?"

Jobe realizes he *is* hungry. Very hungry. It's a feeling he knows well, but her mention of getting some food makes the hollow feeling inside his stomach even more intense than usual.

"Well? Speak up, Jobey boy."

"Yes, I am hungry."

"Well then, times a wastin'. Let's get a move on."

She gathers up her stuff and heads for the edge of the park at a fast walk. Rosie falls in behind her, looking at the ground as she goes.

Jobe follows, wondering where Bella is leading them.

Bella winds a path through the still-sleeping men. Some of them are covered only with thin blankets, and others have no blankets at all, only newspapers and cardboard. Jobe can't imagine how they get through the cold nights like that. He wonders if they've somehow gotten used to being cold.

When they get closer to the edge of the park, Jobe's hunger reminds him of the dried-up apple and the two very-ripe bananas he has in the pockets of his sweatshirt. With everything that's been happening, he forgot all about them. Should he tell Bella about the fruit? It would be selfish to keep it all to himself. The Bible says *Whoever is generous will be repaid by the Lord.* On the other hand, he went out and found the fruit all by himself. He didn't sit and wait for somebody to bring it to him, and the Bible says *If anyone is not willing to work, let him not eat.*

But maybe Bella has some money and is planning to buy him something to eat. He decides to give her the bananas; they're already so ripe and squashed they won't last long anyhow.

He hurries up next to Bella just as they arrive at the wide street. "Uh, Bella, I've got a couple of bananas. I mean if you're real hungry."

"No thanks, kid. Can't eat on an empty stomach, if you get my drift."

Jobe doesn't get her drift, but he takes out the two bananas anyhow. He holds the best looking one out to Rosie.

It didn't look like she had been paying any attention, so Jobe is a bit surprised when Rosie quickly grabs the banana. She immediately peels it and doesn't look at him as she wolfs down the entire thing in a couple of quick bites. She drops the peel on the sidewalk and turns to watch the cars go by.

Jobe can see that she was very hungry, so he holds the other banana out to her. She grabs it out of his hand and eats it just as fast as she ate the first one, and again, she drops the banana peel on the sidewalk.

Jobe thinks about picking the banana peel up and putting it into the nearby trash can, but decides against it; the girl's mother saw her drop the peels, and she didn't complain, so who is he to go against a mother's way of doing things?

He wonders if he should give Rosie the apple. He takes it out and looks at it. It's so dried up, it might not be all that good to eat, but the Bible says *Share what you have, for such sacrifices are pleasing to God.* Jobe holds the apple out to Rosie.

She glances at it and turns away.

Jobe realizes she's right: even though he had to climb way up to the top of that tree to get it, the apple *is* in pretty bad shape. He takes it to the trash can and drops it in. Now he has nothing to eat at all, and that makes him feel even more hungry.

Bella leads them across the wide street, and Jobe hurries to get up along side her. "Uh, where are we going, Bella?"

"Main street. Only place anybody'll likely be around this time of day. Damn few at that, but maybe we'll get lucky."

Jobe is not sure what getting lucky means to Bella, and he's not even sure why he's following her. He's still thinking about what she did to him in the night, a thing that has never before happened to him in his whole life, and he's not sure how he's supposed to think about it. He's still worried that it might have been the work of the Devil. But he knows the Lord must have had a purpose in leading him to these two people, and even though the day is only beginning, he has already gotten a chance to give the girl the fruit he found. God would approve of that. The girl seemed very hungry, and she really is very, very thin. Who knows how long it had been since she'd had anything to eat. Maybe the Lord brought him to the Mormon's temple gate last night so that he might be of help to this poor girl.

He decides to follow along. After all, he's got nowhere else to go, and he has to trust that God is still guiding him.

Several blocks later, they come to a street that has taller buildings all along it. Here, Bella stops and lays out her things next to a building's directory sign. The sign says the building has offices for lawyers, investment advisors, and tax preparers.

Bella takes out her paper cup and her cardboard begging sign. Then, she sits down on her folded-up blanket and waits.

Rosie sits down next to her and goes right back to staring off into space.

Jobe doesn't know what to do with himself, so he just stands next to them. Bella seems so patient, satisfied to just sit there and wait. Does that type of begging actually work, just sitting and waiting? Maybe a lot of people feel sorry for Rosie and put money into Bella's paper cup.

A man in a suit arrives and goes into the building without even looking at Bella and her daughter. Didn't that man see Bella's sign? Does he have no compassion for a poor retarded girl? The Bible says *Be kind to one another, tenderhearted, forgiving one another.* Jobe knows that if he had any money, he'd give it to Bella to help Rosie, so why won't these men in suits give her anything? They probably have a lot of money in their pockets.

Jobe glances at the sign in front of the building again. It says there are lawyer offices in there. Maybe that man was a lawyer. The Bible doesn't have very nice things to say about lawyers. It says *Woe to you lawyers! For you load people with burdens hard to bear, and you yourselves do not touch the burdens with one of your fingers.*

Another man in a suit arrives and hurries into the building without giving Bella any money. Jobe begins to wonder why Bella would pick this spot when none of the men seem at all interested in giving her any money.

The next man to arrive at the building is a short man in a dark suit that seems too big for him. He too tries to enter the building, but without really planning it, Jobe steps in front of him and points toward Rosie.

The man seems startled by Jobe's action, maybe even a little afraid.

That look of anxiety on the man's face makes Jobe realize he's a lot taller than the little man. In fact, looking down at the man's nervous face gives Jobe a feeling of power he's never known before. He doesn't even mind that he seems to be making the man nervous. After all, why shouldn't these men give up some of their money if it will help a poor little girl? Jobe points at Rosie. "Come on, mister. You can spare a buck or two for the little girl. Just look at her."

The man glances at Rosie, but seems unsure of what to do.

Jobe is also not sure what he should do next. But then, it comes to him: he remembers what Mother used to do in situations like this when she was trying to get money from men. She'd use the Bible against them. She called it "wrapping them around her little finger."

Jobe shakes his Bible at the man and says, "Remember what the Bible says, Do not set your hopes on the uncertainty of worldly riches, but be rich in good works."

It works! The man takes out his wallet and hands him a twenty-dollar bill. Jobe hands the bill down to Bella before doing a little bow to the man. "The girl's mother thanks you. The poor little girl thanks you. And Jesus thanks you too." Jobe points toward the door to the building. "You may go now."

The nervous little man hurries inside, holding onto his wallet with both hands.

After the man is gone, Jobe looks down and sees that Bella is holding the bill up and is looking closely at it as if she can't quite believe it's real.

She laughs and waves the bill at Jobe. "By God, kid, that was somethin' else. Twenty bucks. How'd you do that?"

Jobe feels proud, but he just shrugs. He looks toward Rosie to see if she approves, and although she isn't looking directly at him, there's something about the look on her face that makes Jobe pretty sure she saw what he did, and maybe she liked it.

Bella notices another man coming up the sidewalk. She winks at Jobe. "Here comes another suit. See if ya can do that again."

Jobe decides that he will try it again, if not for Bella, at least for Rosie.

When the next man tries to enter the building, Jobe blocks his way. "Can you spare a little for this child, brother?"

This man, who is about as tall as Jobe, says "I'm not your brother. Get out of my way."

Jobe doesn't move. He smiles and replies, "But we are all brothers in the eyes of the Lord, my brother."

The man gets a disgusted look on his face, but he doesn't try to force his way past Jobe. He says, "Oh, for Christ's sake. This is all I need this morning. How much do you want to just leave me alone?"

Jobe holds his Bible up in the air, as if he's pointing it up to Heaven. "It's entirely up to you, sir. As our Lord said, '*When you give to the needy, do not let your left hand know what your right hand is doing. Your Father sees all and will reward you.*'"

The man takes out his wallet and hands Jobe a five-dollar bill. He tries to push past Jobe, but Jobe again moves to block him. "Five dollars? This little girl needs special treatment. Do you have any idea of how expensive that can be?"

The man snatches the five-dollar bill out of Jobe's hand and replaces it with a twenty-dollar bill. "That satisfy you now?"

Jobe smiles at the man. "Our task in this world is not to satisfy each other but to satisfy God, the Lord of us all. He's sees your generosity and will remember you in Heaven."

The man mumbles, "That'll be the day," and hurries inside the building.

Jobe hands the bill to Bella and waits for his due congratulations from her.

But as soon as Bella stuffs the money into her pocket, she gets to her feet and starts gathering up her things.

Rosie is also up, and this time she's looking at Jobe with what might be taken for a tiny bit of a smile. Under Rosie's gaze, Jobe feels embarrassed. Did she think he was showing off for her benefit? Well, maybe he was, but didn't she like him getting money for her treatment?

Bella grabs Jobe's arm and leads him down the street. She leans close and whispers, "Don't know how you did that, kid, but I'm not one to look no gift horse in the mouth. We'd better get the hell out of here 'fore they call the cops. Hey, we got forty bucks now, right here in my pocket. You know what that means? It means we can blow this Goddam town and go somewhere where it's warmer. What you thinka that, kid?"

Jobe is not quite sure what she means about blowing this town. Does she want him to leave Salt Lake City? He's never been outside of Salt Lake City, not once in his entire life. And why would she think he'd want to go along with her?

Bella is walking fast and mumbling to herself. "Goddam stupid town anyhow. Coldern shit. Don't know why we ever decided to come here in the first place."

Jobe slows and says, "You know, Bella, I'd rather you didn't take the Lord's name in vain."

Bella keeps on walking, but she does turn to look at him. "So, all that Lord will bless you stuff is for real, is it? Not some kind of con? You really are a real live Goddam Bible thumper, ain't ya?"

Jobe stops abruptly. "I'm sorry, Bella. I just can't abide that kind of language. My mother told me you can tell who to associate with by the depth of their belief. Maybe I'd better find my own way and go—"

Bella comes back to take his arm. She's smiling like she heard something funny. "Now don't get all het up, Jobe. Ya know, I've taken a liken to you. And my Rosie here has also taken a liken to ya. Ain't that right, Rosie?"

She pushes Rosie up against Jobe, and Rosie doesn't resist. She just stands there, her chest right up against him.

Jobe isn't sure what he's supposed to do. With the feel of Rosie's little body pressed up against him, he's sure his face is turning red again. He wants to think of Rosie as a young girl that is mentally damaged in some way and needs God's help, but part of his mind keeps on wanting to think of her in another way, as a pretty girl that's maybe almost his same age.

"See there?" says Bella. "See how much she likes ya. You can't go wanderin' off by your lonesome now. What would poor little Rosie do without ya?"

Jobe can't think of how to answer her. The only thing he knows for sure is that he likes the feel of warm little Rosie pressing up against him. Maybe he should go along with these two, at least for a little while longer. After all, if God led him to them, then He must have a purpose in it.

"Okay then," says Bella, "it's settled. I'll watch my language and the three of us'll stick together. Like a little family, eh?"

She pulls Rosie to her side and grabs Jobe's arm to put him on her other side. "Okay, here we go, guys. Off to see the wizard. You stick with me, boy, and you'll see some things. I guarantee you'll get everything you want. Won't he, Rosie?"

Rosie doesn't reply. She just looks straight ahead, but Jobe is sure that for a moment he detected a slight look of concern on the girl's face.

After making a stop at the Utah State Liquor Store for a bottle, Bella leads Rosie and Jobe to a gas station that has a lot of big trucks in it. She buys two candy bars from a machine and hands one to Rosie and the other one to Jobe. She tells Jobe to keep an eye on Rosie while she goes to try to get them a ride.

Jobe sits next to Rosie on the curb while they munch on their candy bars. Rosie is still not talking, so Jobe just sits next to her and watches Bella go from truck to truck, climbing up and talking to each of the drivers.

Jobe says, "I wonder what she's telling those truck drivers."

Rosie doesn't answer; she just stares straight ahead, taking very tiny bites from her candy bar.

By now, Jobe doesn't expect Rosie to respond to his questions, but he does wonder what the girl sees with all that staring. And he wonders what she thinks about in her silence. He decides to ask her. "I wonder what you think about all the time, Rosie. Do you think about what you're seeing? Or maybe you think about why God made you and me the way we are. I think about that a lot. My mother talked to me all the time about that. She said she didn't know why God had created her and sometimes she said she wished He hadn't. I was never sure why she would say something like that. Do you think about God, Rosie?"

Rosie doesn't answer, but she does turn to look at Jobe. But the look only lasts for a second before she turns away.

"Well, Rosie, I guess that means you don't. Mother thought about God a lot. She didn't think God had been kind to her. She thought that was why people didn't like her. And sometimes she compared herself to other people. Like those old pictures she had. Pictures of people. She kept them in a special box that had lots of words she'd written on the outside of it, and she'd pasted red and blue stars all over the outside of it too. It was her special box, tied shut tight with a pink ribbon. She had colorful magic cards in that box with pictures of the Devil with horns coming out of the top of his head and pictures of skeletons holding swords. She looked at those magic cards sometimes, mumbling to herself. But mostly, she looked at those old pictures of people. Sometimes at night, she'd get those pictures out and talk right out loud to them. One night, she held up a picture of an old woman and told me God had made her different from the people in her pictures, and she didn't know why. I was never sure what she meant by that. But you know what I think, Rosie? I think God made us all different for some reason of His own. I don't know what that reason is, but He must have had one. Maybe if I could have got to go to school more, I could have found out. Did you ever get to go to school, Rosie? I only got to go to school one time, but it wasn't for very long. It was when I was little. One day, the teacher started taking about something called evolution. She said us humans were evolved from monkeys. When I got home from school that day, I told Mother about it. She said it wasn't true, and it was unGodly to even think thoughts like that. She hit me a bunch of times for even talking about such a thing, and after that, she wouldn't let me go to any school anymore. She said she'd teach me herself at home. That's when she started making me memorize every word in the Bible." Jobe shows Rosie his Bible. "See here, Rosie? This is that very Bible. It was my mother's Bible. I know everything in it. Did you ever get to read the Bible, Rosie?"

Rosie is still looking straight ahead, but this time, Jobe is sure he saw her eyes narrow, just for a moment. Jobe is not sure if that thing she did with her eyes means she *did* get to read the Bible or she didn't? Jobe wonders if Rosie can even read. He's about to ask her that question when he sees Bella heading toward them.

She's followed by a big fat trucker who suddenly stops and uses his chewed-up cigar to point at Jobe. "Hey, what's this? You didn't say there was a boy too."

Bella grabs the guy's arm and grins at him. "Well, you didn't ask. But hey, you don't expect me to leave my boy behind, do ya? He won't get in the way. He's quiet as a mouse. Aren't ya, Jobe?"

Jobe doesn't want to mess up Bella's chance to get a ride, so he just shrugs. He wonders if he's supposed to get up and shake hands with the trucker, but Bella is whispering something to the man, so Jobe stays where he is and waits to see what's going to happen.

Bella still has ahold of the trucker's arm, and she's still grinning at him. "Hey now, you said you wanted to get a look at the girl." She points at Rosie. "So, here she is. Whatta ya think? Pretty cute, eh?"

The trucker puts his cigar back into his mouth, and then he moves it to the side. "Yeah, not bad. Not bad at all. So I get you and the girl too?"

"You bet," says Bella. "Me now, and the girl soon as we get there. Is it a deal?"

The truck driver seems a bit unsure, but Bella starts tickling his side, and he laughs as he pushes her hands away. "All right. All right."

"Well," says Bella, "let's get to it then. I'm hot as a three-dollar pistol."

As Bella and the trucker head back toward the man's big truck, Bella looks back at Jobe. She puts her finger to her lips and points at Rosie.

Jobe assumes that means he's supposed to keep quiet and continue to watch over Rosie. Jobe is happy to do that. He watches Bella and the trucker go to the man's truck and climb up inside. Then, there is nothing to do but sit there and continue to tell Rosie about things. He's not sure how much she understands, but he likes talking to her. He tells her about how once when he was still a little boy, a mean man made him and Mother stay in a little tiny room in the back of his dirty car-repair garage. "Maybe I shouldn't tell you this, Rosie, but me and Mother had to use a big white bucket as our toilet. And there wasn't anything for me to do in that place, except once in a while the man would go out somewhere and lock us in. So while Mother slept, I'd go look at all the tools that man had. He had a lot of different tools that were in a big red metal box that had lots of drawers in it. When the man came back, he'd take Mother away to lie on a dirty mattress he had in another part of his shop. I didn't like him doing what he did to Mother." Jobe looks around to be sure nobody is close enough to hear him. "Now listen, Rosie. I'm going to tell you something I've never told anybody. It's about this one night when I could hear that the man was hurting Mother, so I snuck in to where they were on that mattress. He didn't have any clothes on and Mother didn't either, and he was on top of her.

I whacked him on the back of his head with a big wrench, and that made him start crawling around on the floor holding his head and yelling real loud. Mother jumped up and slapped my face. I didn't know why she was so mad at me. I was only trying to help her not get hurt. I thought she'd thank me for hitting the man who was hurting her, but instead she was really mad at me. She said we had to run away quick and hide in another part of town, So that's what we did."

Rosie slightly turns her head toward Jobe and narrows her eyes again.

Jobe is starting to think that thing she does with her eyes means something special, like she's wanting to say something to him. But Jobe isn't sure what it is she wants to say, and Rosie won't talk, so there's no way for him to find out.

Because of that little bit of a response with her eyes, Jobe decides maybe Rosie likes his stories. He decides to tell her about the basement place he and Mother had to live in even though there were black widow spiders that hid under the noisy furnace. "Well, Rosie, those spiders were real scary because me and Mother were sleeping on a mattress that was right on the floor. Those spiders would come out at night and sometimes they would crawl on us. One night one of those black spiders bit my foot, and it swelled up real bad."

Jobe looks at Rosie for a long time to try to decide if she has been listening to him. He's not sure, so he decides to try again to get some kind of response from her. "Do you know about spiders, Rosie?"

Rosie gets a funny look on her face, and Jobe thinks that probably means that at least she's listening, so he goes on. "I'll tell you something, Rosie. I know a lot about spiders. Me and Mother lived in a lot of places that had spiders. And other kinds of bugs. A lot of bugs. When I was little, I used to make corrals out of some Popsicle sticks I'd found. I'd herd in a bunch of daddy longlegs spiders and other kinds of bugs into my corrals and play like they were cows and horses and other kinds of animals. Sometimes, I'd get a lot of them penned in all together, and I wouldn't let them get out."

Rosie doesn't react, so Jobe assumes she either doesn't know about spiders or doesn't care. Or maybe he's talked too much. He stops talking and just stays sitting there on the curb with Rosie until finally, the door of the truck opens, and Bella leans out to wave them over.

Jobe stands up, but Rosie doesn't seem to want to go. She just sits there, looking up at him.

Jobe doesn't understand why she's looking at him like that. "Come on, Rosie. Your mother is calling you." He takes her hand and helps her stand up. He waits until all the big trucks have gone by before he leads her across the wide gas station driveway. When they get there, Bella reaches down to help Rosie up into the tall truck. She then reaches down to help Jobe up, but he holds back. He's not sure why she wants him to get into the truck. It's like she just expects him to go along without even asking him if he wants to. And why would she want him to go along with her and Rosie anyhow? Is it because of what she did to him last night, the same thing she probably did to that trucker just now? It seems to Jobe that maybe she does that kind of thing all the time in order to get her way.

But as Bella impatiently reaches for Jobe's hand and tells him to hurry up, he actually *is* thinking about going along with them. He's now becoming even more sure that God led him to these two people for some reason. It might be because of some kind of special lesson he's supposed to learn. Besides, he likes talking to Rosie and taking care of her. Maybe taking care of Rosie is the reason God put him into this situation. And Jobe is really worried about Rosie because of what the trucker said, something about getting to have the girl too. If the trucker means he wants to do *that* to Rosie, then Jobe should definitely go along to make sure it doesn't happen. Maybe he's being charged by the Lord to protect this poor girl who maybe has something wrong with how things work inside of her head. After all, the Bible says *We who are strong have an obligation to bear with the failings of the weak, and not to please ourselves.*

He decides he'd better go along with them, at least for a little while. He lets Bella help him climb up into the truck.

The trucker, behind the wheel, moves his cigar to the other side of his mouth and gestures with his thumb. "In the back."

Bella pushes both Rosie and Jobe behind the front seats and through a curtain.

To Jobe's surprise, it's like a little room back there, and there's a mattress.

From up front, he hears Bella say, "Fire this rig up, buddy. Saint George, here we come."

Chrissy 4

Well, my secret dairy, today is the big day, my thirteenth birthday. It means I'm now a teenager, almost as old as a lot of the mothers here.

After breakfast, my real mother and my two not real mothers spent all morning at the kitchen table going over the shopping list. My real mom seemed to think it was a waste of time to go over the list again, but my other two mothers kept on jabbering away about what groceries they were gonna get and fretting that something might have got left off the list and how they'd be blamed if that happened. Mom tried to convince them that they hadn't left anything off because anything that anybody could possibly want must have been included because they'd already gone over the list three times.

Their non-stop arguing about groceries and cleaning supplies and paper products was so boring I went outside to sit on the back porch to look at the desert and the nice red cliffs in the distance. I tried to imagine what it would be like to go up there and look around like the boys sometimes get to do. I know it's not very appropriate for me to resent that the boys get to do fun stuff like that and us girls don't ever get to do anything, but sometimes I just don't think it's fair. When I was littler, I asked Mom about that, but she just said that boys are girls are different. She said we girls have a different role in life than the men do because the men have the responsibility to take care of things out in the world, so it is up to us women to stay home and take care of the home and the children. I asked her if she had ever wanted to go out into the world do things herself, but she said it's better not even to think about things like that because it will only make you unhappy, and being unhappy was not productive. I didn't understand why "being productive" was the only important thing, but I didn't say that. But I do think about things like that. One of the main reasons I wanted to get myself a diary is so I can put down thoughts like that. Maybe that makes me bad. There has to be answers about what it means to have a life besides just being happy and being productive. If I can't talk about things like that out loud, at least I should be able to write them down and think about them. That's why I was still thinking about how to maybe get Mom alone so I could talk her into buying me a diary notebook for my birthday. It seems like a girl who has just become a teenager should get at least one present on her birthday, even if the

Prophet had gone and decreed that giving kids birthday presents and Christmas presents will only spoil them and teach them that they can get things in life without having to work for it. But if that's true, then why do boys sometimes get presents like sports equipment and new clothes? That's another thing I don't think is fair.

By the time I came back inside, my mom seemed really fed up with the constant worrying and constant complaining that Mother Vicki and Mother Laura were doing. It's the same thing every time. With so many kids to shop for, plus all the food to get, it always takes them so long to make up the shopping list, they never get on the road to town until it's afternoon. And then, once they get to Saint George, the shopping always has to be done quick in order to get back home before it gets dark because the Prophet won't allow anybody to be out of the community after dark. I knew that meant if I was going to even try to somehow get myself a real diary, I'd have to slip away from them and find a way to get it quick.

But then, I don't know why I keep on thinking about that. I know it's impossible because I don't have any money. That thought depresses me even more. It's not fair that the Prophet passed his stupid rule that girls are not allowed to have any money of their own. He didn't even bother to say why he made up such a rule, but his brother told us in school that it was to protect us from ungodly temptations. I bet what he was really doing is making sure us girls didn't get to have any life of our own until we're old enough to get married. No wonder all the girls in this community want to get married right away as soon as they're able to have babies.

Jobe 5

In the darkness of the little room-like space, listening to the hum of the truck engine and feeling the rhythm of the truck tires on the pavement below, Jobe clings tight to his Bible and tries to think if this is the right thing to be doing. He likes being close to Rosie, protecting her, but he's never been out of Salt Lake City before, and he can't quite believe how fast things are changing in his life. He hopes God knows what He is doing by leading him in such a startling new direction.

He lies back and puts his Bible under his head as a pillow, hoping the words inside the Holy Book will come through into his head and guide him.

It's warm in the tight space, and the sound of the truck's big wheels is making him feel a little sleepy. But he's not about to go to sleep, not with Rosie lying so close to him. She's so close in the confined space, he can hardly avoid touching her, so close he can feel the warmth of her thin little body.

For a long time, he lies very still listening to Rosie's breathing. From the sound of it, he's pretty sure she's gone to sleep.

He relaxes a bit and thinks about everything that's happened in the last two days. First, Mother died, and then he met a strange women and her strange daughter, and then there was that thing that happened with Bella last night in the homeless park. And now, here he is, going away from Salt Lake City in a big truck, apparently heading for someplace called Saint George where it's supposed to be warmer.

He stares up into the darkness and wonders what it will be like to be out of Salt Lake City. What will the world look like in an entirely new place? Will there still be snow-topped mountains nearby? He wouldn't like a place that didn't have mountains. He always liked looking up at those big mountains, and ever since he was little, he wanted to go and see what it was like up there. Many times, he asked Mother to take him up there, but she said you had to have a car to get there, and besides, there was nothing to see but a bunch of rich people who skied on top of the snow didn't care about anybody but themselves.

And if he leaves Salt Lake City and goes to another place, Jobe worries that he might not be able to find good places to go watch people and think about what their lives might be like. As the big truck rumbles on, he can almost feel Salt Lake City trying to pull him back. Maybe he should crawl up into the front and demand to be let out. They haven't been going for all that long. He could probably get somebody in a car to give him a ride back to Salt Lake City.

From up front, Jobe hears a lot of squawking words, like there's some kind of radio up there. People seem to be talking on the radio, but there's so much static, Jobe can't understand what they're talking about. And he can hear Bella and the truck driver talking too, but with the noise of the truck, he can't tell for sure what they're talking about. But then he hears Bella complain real loud, "Hey buddy, don't Bogart my bottle." The trucker says something, then it gets quieter except for whispers and laughter.

Jobe suspects maybe they're doing unGodly things up there. He thinks about peeking through the curtain to see, but decides against it. Whatever they're doing, he knows he shouldn't see it. As the Bible says, *If you were blind, you would have no guilt; but now that you say, 'We see,' your guilt remains*.

Jobe puts his fingers into his ears, thinking he should not be associating with such people. He again thinks he should tell them to stop and let him out. They'd have to let him go, wouldn't they? That trucker didn't want him along in the first place.

But before he can do anything, he feels Rosie move closer to him. He holds his breath as she presses her little body tight up against him. Does she want him to hug her? Or does she want something else?

He holds real still, and her rhythmic breathing tells him she's still fast asleep. She's just snuggling. That makes her seem more like a child, and it makes Jobe ashamed of what he'd been thinking. He turns toward her and gently puts his hand on her side, but only in a protective way. In response, she puts her arm around him. That kind of excites Jobe, but he's pretty sure she's still asleep.

Rosie going to sleep so quickly means she trusts him, and that gives Jobe an odd feeling, like something he's never felt before: for the first time in his whole life, there's somebody who seems to really need him. It means he definitely *should not* get out of this truck and go back to Salt Lake City because that would leave poor Rosie alone without anybody to protect her from that bad trucker who probably wants to do bad things to her.

Jobe now understands that the death of his mother truly *was* a sign from God: God was telling him that his time of being taken care of was over, and his time of taking care of others was about to begin. It explains why God led him to that Mormon Temple gate to meet Bella and Rosie.

He lies very still, not wanting to wake Rosie up. Lying still in such a warm place, and listening to Rosie's quiet breathing, is making Jobe feel sleepy. And peaceful, for the first time since he came home to find Mother's dead body. God sent him out into the world and brought him together with this strange girl. He should just accept God's wisdom and allow Him to lead him. Like Mother always said, God works in strange ways.

Jobe is roughly awakened by Bella shaking his shoulder. "What the hell are you two doing all bunched up together back here? I won't have you doing anything behind my back. You hear me?"

As he tries to get himself fully awake, Jobe realizes the truck has stopped. From up front, he hears the trucker's voice: "What's goin' on? Were they screwin' back there?"

Jobe sits up. "No! Wait. We were asleep. That's all."

Bella grabs Rosie's arm and pulls her out of the truck. They walk a short distance away.

Jobe starts to follow them, but then he realizes he doesn't have his Bible. He can't go without his Bible. He ducks back into the little room, but it's so dark, he can't see it anywhere. He frantically feels around for it, and finally he feels his hand touch the hardness of the Bible's cover. He grabs it and quickly climbs down out of the truck. He blinks in the bright sunlight. They seem to have arrived in an entirely different kind of town, a place with no tall buildings, and it's a lot warmer than it was in Salt Lake. They're in a gas station, and there are big trucks all over the place. More big trucks are parked out behind the gas station, all lined up next to each other.

Jobe runs to join Bella and Rosie, and he's surprised to see how angry Bella is. She's shaking her finger in Rosie's face and yelling at her. "I won't have this, young lady. We've talked about this before."

Jobe looks back and sees that the trucker is leaning out of his truck. He shouts at them: "Hey, what's goin' on?"

Bella waves her hand at him. "Give us a minute. I've gotta straighten somethin' out between these two."

Jobe sees that the trucker is climbing down from his truck. He whispers to Bella, "He's coming."

Bella forces the big plastic bag of blankets into Jobe's arms. Then, she grabs his arm and Rosie's arm and urgently whispers, "Run!"

Jobe begins to run, even though he doesn't know why. The three of them run across the wide gas station driveway and out to the busy street.

From behind them, Jobe hears the trucker yell, "Hey, where you goin'? Give me that girl, God damn it! We had a deal."

Jobe keeps on running next to Bella, but when he looks back, he sees Rosie has stopped. She seems bewildered. Jobe runs back and grabs her hand. "Come on, Rosie. You don't want that bad trucker to get you."

Rosie looks back at the fast approaching trucker and seems to understand. She allows Jobe to pull her along, and he's happy to see that she's a pretty good runner.

Jobe keeps on running and looking back, and then he sees that the trucker has stopped. The big fat man is all red-faced, and he's leaning forward with his hands on his knees.

Somehow, the three of them manage to get across the wide street without getting hit by one of the fast-moving cars. Jobe is sure the trucker will never catch them now, but Bella makes them keep on running until they see a store and a parking lot ahead. The big sign on the front of the store tells Jobe it's a Walmart store. It looks almost exactly like the one Jobe has walked past back in Salt Lake City.

Bella takes the bag of blankets away from Jobe and stuffs it behind some bushes. Then she pulls Jobe and Rosie inside the store and keeps them moving until she finally lets them stop in an aisle that's mostly school supplies and things like pencils and notebooks. She shakes her finger at Jobe. "I want to know what you two were doing in the back of that truck, and I want to know it right now!"

Jobe holds out both of his hands. "We weren't doing anything, Bella. We were both asleep. Honest."

Bella glances at Rosie who seems to be looking at some hanging clear packages that have colored pens inside.

Bella turns her attention back to Jobe. "Well, okay then. But I'm warning you, you gotta stay out of Rosie's pants. It's a rule. Got it?"

Jobe shrugs.

"No, Jobe, I want you to say it out loud. Say you won't do anything like that to my Rosie. Not even if I'm not around."

Jobe shrugs again. "Sure, but when are you planning to not be around?"

"Well, ya never know. But if for some reason I'm not around for a while, I want you to take care of Rosie. She likes you. I can tell it. And she'd probably go along with anything you want, but you have to trust me, she wouldn't know what she was doin'. So don't do it. Understand?"

Jobe nods, but he's not so sure Rosie wouldn't know what she was doing. She never talks, but sometimes she has a look that says she knows about things.

Bella seems like she's about to say something else, but just then a group of three women and a young girl with red hair come into the aisle, way down at the far end. Bella turns to look at them. The women and the girl are all dressed strangely in bright-colored long dresses that are tight around the collar. All four of them seem to have long hair, but it's braided together tight at the back of their heads. Jobe wonders why they're all dressed alike. Are they members of some kind of look-alike group?

The women are pushing two large carts that are stacked high with food and clothes and all kinds of other things. The girl is moving slowly away from them, looking at things on the store shelves.

Bella grabs Jobe's arm and pulls him close. "Hey, check out that girl. Looks a lot like my little Rosie, doesn't she?"

Jobe doesn't think the girl looks anything like Rosie. She probably a little younger than Rosie, and Rosie has dark eyes and short dark hair. This girl has blue eyes and fair skin, and her red hair stands out against the light blue color of her long dress.

Jobe watches the girl as she wanders down the aisle, coming closer. She's looking at everything that's on the shelves, and her eyes are alive with curiosity as she checks out one thing after another.

Still holding onto Jobe's arm, Bella nods toward the girl. "She's cute, isn't she? You like her?"

Jobe isn't sure what Bella means about whether he should like the strangely-dressed girl. She is really pretty, in an innocent young girl kind of way, but why is Bella so interested in the girl, and why does she want him to like her?

The girl stops to look at an array of notebooks, and Jobe is surprised when Rosie steps forward; she seems to be watching the girl closely.

Bella tells Jobe to stay put and keep an eye on Rosie. She slips up next to the girl and seems to be looking at the same rack of notebooks the girl is interested in. Bella pulls one off the shelf and says something to the girl. Jobe is pretty sure Bella is not interested in notebooks, so he wonders what she's up to.

The girl says something to Bella and reaches out to take a smaller notebook off the shelf. Bella takes the notebook from the girl and looks it over. Then, she turn to point at Jobe and Rosie. She takes the girl by the arm and brings her over.

Still holding onto the girl's arm, Bella says, "This is my daughter Rosie. And my boy Jobe."

The girl smiles shyly and puts out her hand toward Rosie.

Rosie surprises Jobe again by actually reaching out to take the girl's hand. She's looking right at the girl's face and doesn't seem to want to let go of her hand.

Bella laughs and reaches out to separate their hands. "See there, Rosie likes you, and let me tell you, she doesn't like most people." Keeping ahold of the girl's hand, she grabs Jobe's hand and puts their two hands together. "And this is my boy Jobe. Jobe, this nice girl tells me her name is Chrissy."

The girl seems shy, and her handshake is very delicate.

Jobe smiles at the girl and pumps her hand. He says, "Glad to meet you, Chrissy," and for some reason, he finds himself doing a little bow. Then, he's embarrassed that he did that, and he's afraid that his face might be turning red

Bella shows Jobe the small notebook. "Chrissy here wants this notebook because today is her birthday. But she doesn't have any money. What say we buy it for her?"

Jobe shrugs and says, "Sure," but he has no idea why Bella would want to buy this strangely-dressed girl a notebook.

Bella turns back to Chrissy. "Come with us. We'd be glad to buy the notebook for ya."

Chrissy looks back toward the older women at the far end of the aisle. "Well, actually, I'd better stay with my mom."

Jobe can see that the three women are studying a piece of paper, and they seem to be arguing about something. They don't seem to have even noticed that Chrissy has wandered off.

"Okay," says Bella, holding up the notebook. "But are they gonna give you the money to buy this here nice notebook?"

The girl shrugs and looks down at the floor. "I guess not."

"Thought so," says Bella. "No problem. Tell you what. I'll buy the notebook for ya and wait for you outside. That way, you can get it and nobody'll be the wiser. Okay?"

Chrissy looks nervously back toward the women.

Jobe wonders why the girl can't just ask her mother to buy her the notebook. Is there something wrong with having a notebook?

Chrissy says, "Well, okay. But could you not talk to me outside. I mean not . . . right away. I mean—"

"Sure," says Bella. "If you don't want to be seen gettin' the notebook, we'll wait for ya in our car. Out in the parking lot. Come and find us."

Chrissy again glances back at the women who are now busy taking things off of the shelf and putting them into one of the shopping carts. She leans toward Bella and whispers, "Okay. I'll find you. She turns to Rosie and Jobe and smiles. "Nice to meet you, Rosie. Nice to meet you too, Jobe."

As the girl hurries back toward the three women, Jobe sees that Rosie is watching her go. Jobe wonders if Rosie is thinking she just met a new friend, but now she's losing her. It makes Jobe wonder if Rosie has ever once had a young friend in her whole life.

He's still trying to imagine what might be going on inside of Rosie's head, when Bella hurriedly pulls him and Rosie out of that aisle. She leans close to Rosie and whispers, "Don't you worry, sweetie, I'll get her back for ya."

Jobe isn't sure what that means, but it worries him. Does she mean she'll make that red-haired girl want to be Rosie's friend? How can she do that? And what did Bella mean when she said she'd meet the girl at their car? Bella doesn't have a car, so what car was she talking about?

Bella guides them into a section of embarrassing women's underthings and stops to hand the notebook to Jobe. "Here, Jobe. Hide this under your shirt."

Jobe takes the notebook, but he says, "Why don't we just pay for it? You have that money we made in Salt Lake."

Bella scoffs. "Don't ever pay for nuthin' you don't hafta, boy. This store is one of the biggest outfits in the world. They won't miss it. Now let's go find us some food."

Jobe looks at Rosie to see if she's noticing any of this, but she seems to be more interested in the store's ceiling lights way above.

Jobe does as he is told and stuffs the notebook down inside the front of his shirt.

Bella leads them to the grocery area and hurriedly grabs a loaf of bread, a package of hot dogs, and a big bottle of water.

After paying for the food, Bella herds Jobe and Rosie out to the parking lot. She retrieves her plastic bag full of blankets, and then she leads the way through the rows of cars. When they finally get to the last row of cars, Bella slows down and starts looking inside of every car they pass.

Jobe catches up to her. "What are you looking for, Bella?"

"Pay attention and learn, boy. See how far we are from the store's entrance? No lazy customer is ever gonna park this far away. These hafta be employee cars."

Jobe, says, "So?"

Bella ignores him and keeps on looking inside the cars.

When she comes to an old four-door sedan with faded silver paint, she says, "This one'll do. People with cars this old don't bother to lock 'em. They probably won't even be sorry to see this old wreck go." She opens the car's door.

Jobe now understands what she's planning to do. "Are you going to steal it?"

"Borrow it is all. Rosie, you get in the back seat. Jobe, you keep a watch out."

All Jobe can do is watch helplessly as Rosie obediently gets into the back seat of the car. She closes the car door and sits quietly, staring straight ahead. Jobe wonders if she's seen Bella do this kind of thing before.

Bella tosses in the plastic bag full of blankets and the food, and then she crawls under the car's steering wheel.

Jobe watches, fascinated, as Bella begins pulling out wires from under the car's dash. Should he be going along with this? Jobe tries to remember what the Bible says about stealing, but he can't think of any direct advice except, *If a man shall steal an ox, or a sheep, he shall restore five oxen for an ox, and four sheep for a sheep*. He's not sure if that Bible verse applies in this situation. He's pretty sure if Bella steals the car, she wouldn't want him telling her the Bible says she'll have to buy the owner five cars later on. Or maybe only four, since it's not such a good car.

Apparently, Bella finds the wires she's looking for because she takes out a pocket knife and begins to cut into them.

Jobe leans into the car to see what she's doing. "Where did you learn to do that, Bella?"

Bella doesn't look up. "I know a lot of things, boy. Watch and learn. Watch and learn."

Jobe decides against telling her what the Bible says about stealing. Instead, he'll do what she said, watch and learn. Like the Bible says, *Let the wise hear and increase in learning and obtain guidance.*

But part of him is very worried about what Bella is up to. It might be something bad, maybe something to do with what she said to that girl about having a car. Still, Bella said she was only going to borrow the car, so maybe he should just wait and see.

In almost no time, the car's engine starts. Bella sits up in the driver's seat and tells Jobe to hurry up and get in.

Jobe gets into the front seat next to Bella.

As Bella pulls out of the parking space, she says, "Give the notebook to Rosie."

Jobe pulls the stolen notebook out from inside his shirt and hands it to Rosie who grabs it and holds onto it with both hands.

Bella drives the car up near the entrance to the store and backs into a parking space. She keeps the car running and doesn't say a word as she intently watches the people that are coming out of the store.

Jobe spots the three women and the girl coming out of the store's front door. He points. "There they are."

Bella says, "I see 'em. Now you watch what the girl does."

The girl stops to tie her shoe, and the women go on without her, pushing the two heavily-laden shopping carts through the first rows of cars.

As soon as the two women are out of sight, Bella jams the car in gear and pulls up next to the girl. She rolls down her window and says, "Hi, Chrissy. Rosie has your notebook. She uses her thumb to point over her shoulder at Rosie.

Rosie holds up the notebook and then does something that completely surprises Jobe: she swings open the car's back door.

When Chrissy hesitates, Bella turns to Jobe. "Jobe, don't be so impolite. Go around and help Chrissy get her new notebook.

Jobe isn't sure what he's supposed to do, but he does as he is told and goes around to stand next to Chrissy.

Bella says, "What's the matter, Chrissy? Don't you want your notebook? Let Rosie show you the inside of it. It's a nice one."

Rosie smiles, still holding out the notebook, but she's sitting so far on the other side of the back seat, Chrissy can't quite reach it.

Bella says, "Come on, girl. Take your notebook. I gotta get goin'."

Chrissy leans into the car, and Rosie shocks Jobe by grabbing Chrissy's hand and pulling her in.

Bella says, "Jobe, why don't you get in the back there with the girls. You kids can look over the notebook together."

Jobe gets in next to Chrissy, but he's still wondering what Bella is up to.

Rosie hands the notebook to Chrissy who clutches it to her breast.

Bella takes off so fast, it causes the back door to slam shut.

Chrissy lets out a little squeak and reaches across Jobe for the door handle. But Rosie puts her arms around the girl and pulls her back, hugging her tightly.

Chrissy looks surprised, but she doesn't seem to be very scared. She shyly says, "I'm sorry, Mrs. Bella, but I have to go back. We're going out for ice cream, and then we have to head for home before it gets dark."

Bella glances back over her shoulder. "Ice cream? Yeah. That's exactly where we're goin'."

Chrissy is looking out the back window. "Well, won't my mother be wondering . . . I mean . . . where I've gone?"

"She knows, Chrissy. We're supposed to meet up with her at the ice cream place."

Chrissy says, "We are? You know my mother?"

"Sure do. We'll be at that ice cream place in nuthin' flat. Just relax and look at your nice new notebook."

Jobe isn't sure he likes where this is going, but he doesn't mind sitting next to Chrissy. She seems like a very nice girl. Maybe God has assigned him to protect her, just like he's supposed to protect Rosie. It's all starting to make sense why God led him into this situation; it must be yet another lesson he needs to learn in order to be a grown-up man.

The car picks up speed as they leave the parking lot, and Chrissy shyly touches Jobe's arm. "Are you sure my mother knows we're supposed to meet up at the ice cream store?"

Jobe has half a mind to order Bella to stop the car right this minute and take this poor girl back to her mother, but something about the way Chrissy is touching his arm excites him. He has never once in his whole life been this close to any girl, and now, in only one day, he's been in the back of a big truck in the dark hugging with one young girl, and then this even prettier new girl is sitting very close to him, touching his arm in a very nice way. He fights down the unGodly kinds of feelings he's having, and tries hard to change it to a feeling of brotherly protection, the same kind of feeling he has for Rosie. After all, this girl might really need his protection: there's no telling what Bella has in mind for her.

He tries to think it through: is Bella trying to get this girl to be a playmate for Rosie? Rosie is still hugging this new girl like she's afraid she's going to get away. Getting a friend for Rosie might make sense: Rosie must get very lonely traveling around all the time with only her mother and those homeless people Jobe saw back at the homeless park in Salt Lake City. But it doesn't seem fair to make this girl be Rosie's playmate without even asking her permission. Jobe tries to decide what he should do. He wishes Mother was still alive so he could ask her. Maybe she would say to just trust in God's wisdom. He decides the only thing he can do is try to make the girl feel more secure. He takes her hand and shows her his Bible. "Be strong and courageous. Do not fear or be in dread for it is the Lord your God who goes with you."

Chrissy stares at him. "Is that from the Bible?"

Jobe says, "Yes it is." He holds up his Bible. "This Bible was my mother's. It always has the right answer."

"But what do . . . those words . . . mean?"

Jobe smiles at her and continues to hold her hand. "It means you have nothing to fear. God is with you. And I am with you too. I won't let anything bad happen to you."

From up front, Jobe hears Bella chuckle. "You listen to Jobe, sweetie. We don't mean you no harm. We just want ya to go for a little ride with us. Wouldn't you like that? See some new places?"

Chrissy looks confused. "I thought you said we were going to get ice cream."

"Time enough for ice cream later," says Bella. "First, I want to show you somethin'."

Jobe feels Chrissy's hand tighten. She's staring at him as if she's asking a question. Jobe likes the warm feel of her hand, and he's now almost happy that Bella decided to take the girl along with them. He has a feeling that he and Chrissy might get along really well. He wouldn't mind having some time to get to know her better. Of course, then they'll have to take her back to her mother, and then everything will be fine. Chrissy will have had a great adventure to tell her friends about, and there will be no harm done. It will be a learning experience for her, and a learning experience for him too. After all, as the Bible says, *An intelligent heart acquires knowledge.*

As Bella drives fast down the street, she looks back at them over her shoulder. "Hey you kids, why aren't you looking at Chrissy's new notebook?"

Rosie reaches for the notebook, but Chrissy clutches it even tighter against her chest.

Jobe is impressed that the girl is being so brave. Even though she's not crying or anything, she looks really scared. Jobe knows that when he's scared, he depends on God to help him be less scared. He leans close to Chrissy and whispers, "Don't worry. I won't let anything hurt you. Remember, the Lord is faithful. He will establish you and guard you."

Chrissy stares into his eyes for a long minute, and then she seems to make some sort of decision: she grabs his arm and puts her head against his shoulder. As they speed out of town, she holds tight to Jobe's arm. Jobe thinks she might be crying now, but only a little and very softly. He gently strokes her nice red hair and whispers, "It's all right. Don't be afraid. I'll always be with you. I promise."

But even as he says those words to comfort Chrissy, Jobe is now very sure Bella is not going to take this girl back to her mother, at least not right away. She's driving farther and farther away from that town, and it's getting dark. Jobe is still not sure what he should do about this situation. He knows God has a plan for him, and he knows God wouldn't have made these things happen if they were wrong, but he wonders what part he's supposed to play. He's pretty sure his new role must have something to do with protecting Rosie, and now maybe it also means he's supposed to protect this new girl too. But what does *protecting* mean? Does it mean he should just make sure this new girl doesn't get hurt? But couldn't it also mean he should try to make her happy? The problem is, Jobe isn't sure what would make a nice young girl like Chrissy happy. He's never been around any girls, except for Mother, and she was almost never happy. Now that he thinks about it, even though Chrissy seems like a pleasant enough girl, he has never once seen her smile—not when she was back in that store, not when she was walking out of that store with those older women, and not once since she got into this car. Is she an unhappy person? Has she had an unhappy life? If so, maybe God's plan is for him to make her happier. He's not sure how to do that, but he's willing to try.

For now, he'll just keep his tight hold onto her hand and make sure nothing bad happens to her. He likes the feel of her little hand in his, and he likes very much the feel of her leaning against his shoulder. Even after Bella started driving, she didn't move away from him. In fact, she hasn't hardly moved at all since they drove out of that town. He wonders if maybe she's fallen asleep. He very quietly whispers into her ear, "Are you asleep?"

She shakes her head.

So, now he knows Chrissy is awake, just not moving. He decides he should also keep very still. If he doesn't move at all, maybe she'll continue to stay where she is, leaning close against him. That would be the best thing. He wants her to feel safe.

As they go on and on, driving fast in the dark night, it begins to get colder. He whispers to Chrissy, "Are you cold?"

Again, she shakes her head. She doesn't seem to want to look at him. Jobe wonders why that is. She looked at him that one time right after Bella started driving, but since then, she's only been looking down and not moving hardly at all. She seems to have stopped crying, so Jobe hopes that means she's not as scared as she was before. He decides not to say anything more to her unless she asks him something. He'll just hold very still and wait for the Lord to tell him what the right thing to do is.

After a while, it feels like Bella has driven off the highway onto a bumpy dirt road. She drives for a long ways on the dirt road before she stops the car.

Jobe looks out the window and sees half of a moon in the sky. It's sitting low over what seems to be a mountain, or maybe it's just a big hill that's close by. From the dim light of that half moon, Jobe can tell they're in a place where there are hardly any plants. Wherever they are, it sure is a very different place from Salt Lake City.

Bella turns off the car and looks back at Jobe.

Even though it's pretty dark, there's enough light to see that for some reason Bella is smiling. Jobe wonders why she's all smiley like that. Maybe she's happy to see that Rosie is still hugging Chrissy.

Bella tosses a blanket back to Jobe, and then she lies down up there on the front seat. Jobe assumes that means Bella is planning to go to sleep now, and she must want everybody else to go to sleep too. He carefully spreads the blanket over Rosie and Chrissy, keeping only a small corner of it for himself.

Chrissy hasn't moved, so maybe that means she hasn't yet noticed that they've stopped. He holds his breath and listens. From the sound of their breathing, it seems like both of the girls have gone to sleep.

Jobe is not sure he can sleep, not with Chrissy leaning so close against him. Since he's awake anyhow, he tries to think through all the things that have been happening to him. How did he end up in a car parked out in the middle of nowhere with these three people? After Mother died, God sent him out into the world to learn new things. And it's true that he is learning new things, but what does it all mean? If only Mother was still here to ask why God has put him on this path. But maybe she wouldn't know either. In the past, whenever he asked Mother what God's plan for him was, she just said God acts in mysterious ways. She told him to remember the Bible verse that says *The heart of man plans his way, but the Lord establishes his steps.* Maybe that means he should just go along with what is happening and let the Lord guide his steps. After all, so far, this situation isn't really so bad: he's sitting in the back seat of a car with the prettiest girl he's ever seen, and she's leaning right up against him. If this is God's plan for him, he should have faith that everything will turn out all right. For now, the best thing to do is to just be very still and stay awake while everybody else sleeps. For the whole night long, while they're all sleeping, he'll be the wide-awake protector, praying and thinking only pure thoughts. He presses his Bible close to his chest and takes comfort from the feel of it. He'll spend the night praying. If he does it right, God will soon reveal His plan.

Chrissy 5

Dear secret diary. It's night now, and I have something really really important to tell you about what happened to me today. But if I'm going to remember everything that happened and get it all down in the right order, I'd better start at the beginning.

When we finally got to town, Mom pulled into the big Walmart store's parking lot and said we'd got such a late start today that we would have to do all the shopping first and then see how much time we had left to go for the ice cream.

She probably thought I'd be real disappointed if I didn't get ice cream, but I wasn't thinking about that at all. I was thinking that a big store like Walmart would probably have all kinds of notebooks, and if I could find even a little tiny notebook, it would still work as my diary. I decided that if I found one, I'd grab it and try to get Mom to buy if for me as my birthday present instead of ice cream. After all, once a girl turns into a teenager, she should be able to write down the important things that start to happen to her in her life. And she should be able to write them down in a real diary notebook and not just in a made-up mental diary like this.

Once we got inside the big Walmart story, I did find the aisle where they had a bunch of different kinds of notebooks. But then something happened. I was looking at them when this big woman who was dressed sort of like a man came up to me and started talking to me about the notebooks. I showed her the one I liked the best, and after I told her it was my birthday, she congratulated me and said she would like to buy me a present. That surprised me. I didn't know why a complete stranger would want to buy me a present, even if it was my birthday. She asked my name and I told her, and then she said her name was Bella. She said because it was my birthday, I should meet her kids. She introduced them to me. Her daughter is named Rosie, and she has the strangest way of looking at you, like she can see right through you and see what's deep inside of you. I've never met anybody like her before, and I'm still not too sure what to make of her. I think she's maybe a little older than me, but I'm not sure about that because she stays completely silent. Bella's son is named Jobe. He's older than me, but not too old. He shook my hand and bowed to me. I thought that was funny, but I didn't say anything because he seemed a little embarrassed that he'd done that. He's actually kind of shy for a boy, and I kind of like that.

Mrs. Bella asked me if I still wanted the little notebook, but I told her I didn't have any money, and I didn't think my mother would want to buy it for me. She said she'd buy it and wait for me in her car to give it to me.

And sure enough, when I came out of the store, she was there in her car, and Rosie was in the back seat with my new notebook. I just wanted to take the notebook and thank Mrs. Bella for it, but Rosie wanted me to get into the back seat of their car to look at it.

That's when the really scary thing happened. Bella just drove away with me in the back seat. She said we were going to meet my mother at the ice cream place. I know we've been taught to believe whatever an adult tells us, but I wasn't sure how she knew my mother and when she might have talked to her about taking me to get ice cream.

But she didn't drive to the ice cream place. Instead, she drove right out of town with me in the back seat between Jobe and Rosie. That's when I started getting real scared. They seemed like nice people, especially Rosie and Jobe, but I didn't understand why they were taking me away with them.

Jobe held my hand and told me not to be scared because he'd protect me and make sure nothing bad ever happened to me. Jobe always has his Bible with him and he knows a lot about what's in it so that made me feel a little better. But he's a boy and I'm a girl so I'm not sure I should have been holding onto him so tight when Bella drove us out of town, but I had to because I was so scared. Rosie was on the other side of me, and she was hugging me too, and that made me a little less scared.

It was really dark and probably really late at night when Mrs. Bella finally stopped driving. She went to sleep lying down in the front seat of the car, and me and Jobe and Rosie were all hugged together under a blanket in the back seat.

After a while, it seemed like everybody was asleep. I started wondering if I could sneak out without waking them up. But I was stuck between Jobe and Rosie, and even if I could get out without waking them up, which way would I go? From looking out the window, it looks like we're out in the middle of the desert. There was a half moon out there high in the sky, and I know that kind of moon will sort of be toward the south, but which way did we go out of Saint George? I sure wish I would have paid closer attention.

Like I said, I thought everybody was asleep, but when I looked at Jobe, he looked back at me. He was awake the whole time! How could he sit so still for so long and not move at all? And he was smiling at me! I hope that means he's a nice person, even if his mother isn't. Maybe when it gets to be morning, I can talk to him and convince him to make his mother take me back home.

I closed my eyes and pretended to be asleep, but I wasn't really sleeping. I was thinking about how to get away. And that got me to thinking about what will happen to me when I get back home. Will the Prophet be mad at me for getting into a car with strangers? In his sermons, he always says we're not even supposed to talk to strangers. The prophet told us that if a car drives into our town that we don't know, we're all supposed to run inside of our houses and hide and not answer the door. So what would he think of a girl who made a secret plan to meet a strange women at her car just to get a real diary for my birthday that I wasn't supposed to have in the first place? Will I get banished like Carl did?

Actually, that wouldn't be the worst thing that could happen to me, at least not if they'd let me go live with my brother. But I'd miss my Mom and my little sister a lot because I know the Prophet would never allow them to come visit me. But if I do get banished, at least I won't have to get married off to some old man who I don't even know.

Jobe 6

Something wakes Jobe up. It's still dark, but he's disappointed in himself because he wasn't able to do what he said he was going to do, stay awake all night praying and being the wide-awake protector.

But then he realizes Chrissy is no longer leaning against him. Did she move to the other side of the car to hug with Rosie? He peers through the darkness and sees that Rosie is lying down on the car seat. She seems to be fast asleep. Chrissy is not there. But how could she have gotten out of the car without waking him up? Was he that sleepy?

It's really cold, and that means it will be a lot colder outside. So why would she want to get out of the car?

Jobe tries to be logical. Maybe she had to pee. After all, Bella never did stop driving after they left that town, and when she stopped the car. she just expected everybody to go straight to sleep.

Jobe grabs his Bible and quietly slips out of the car. He's very careful to close the door without making any noise at all. He looks around. Where could she have gone? If she's gone to pee, he should give her some privacy, but he has to make sure she doesn't get lost in the darkness.

He wanders around looking for her, but there aren't really any places she could hide to do her peeing, only short weeds and prickly cactus plants. He looks in the direction they drove in on. Could she be trying to follow the dirt road back to the highway? But it's too cold, and all she's wearing is that blue dress. Bella drove a long ways away from that highway. Would Chrissy really try to walk that far? Maybe he should look for her footprints.

He starts down the road, leaning forward, trying to make out any footprints. But the road is kind of rocky, and it's so dark, he can't find anything that looks like a footprint. He stops and looks around. Is there anywhere else see could have gone? No, only flat dirt as far as he can see. He decides the only thing to do is keep following the road.

As he walks, he notices that the sky ahead is getting a little bit lighter. It must mean the sun is going to come up soon. That could be even worse for Chrissy: after the sun comes up, she could be lost in the heat of the day with no water. He hurries on, hoping he's right and this is the direction she's going.

And then he spots something that could be a footprint. He gets down on his hands and knees to look closer at it. Sure enough, it is a footprint in the dust, a small one, like a girl's. It has to be Chrissy's. It means she really is trying to run away. She's trying to walk all the way out to the highway.

Jobe breaks into a run. He has to catch her, has to save her, maybe from dying when the sun comes up.

Soon, he sees her ahead. She's not running; in fact, she might be limping a little. Did she hurt herself? Even though she's limping, she's still moving fairly fast What a brave girl she is. To try this, all by herself, out in the middle of nowhere. He runs to catch up with her, but she hears him coming and starts to run. He calls to her: "Don't run, Chrissy. I won't hurt you. I want to help you."

She stops running, but she keeps on walking.

Jobe catches up to her and walks beside her. "I don't think this is going to work, Chrissy. It's too far back out to the highway. It's going to get hot when the sun comes up, and we don't have any water. And besides, Bella will soon see we've gone. She'll just get in the car and catch up to us."

Chrissy turns to him. She has tears in her eyes. "You said you were going to help me, Jobe. But you didn't make her stop. You didn't make her take me back to that store where you met me. You said you were going to help me, and you didn't."

She's right. He might have been able to convince Bella to stop and take her back. But he didn't, and now he wonders why. Did he like having her next to him so much he just let Bella just keep on driving?

"Well? Why don't you say something? Why didn't you make your mother take me back?"

Jobe reaches out to her, but she pulls back. "I'm sorry, Chrissy. You're right. I don't know why Bella wanted you to come with us. I should have stopped her. But she's not my mother. I don't even know why I went along with her. Maybe because I felt so sorry for Rosie."

Chrissy stops walking. "She's not your mother?"

Jobe looks in the direction he thinks might be where Salt Lake City is. "No, my mother died. Just . . . recently. And I didn't have any place to go, so I went along with Bella and Rosie. Now I'm sorry I did that. I'll make Bella take you back home, and then I'll go back to Salt Lake City where I belong."

"Is that where you're from? Salt Lake City?"

"Yes. I was born there, even thought my mother didn't want me to be born, and I've never been anywhere else. Until now, I mean."

"She didn't want you to be born?"

"Well, not at first, and then she did. Anyhow, after I was born, we only lived in Salt Lake City. Nowhere else."

Chrissy looks the same direction he's looking. I've never been anywhere either. Is Salt Lake City nice?"

Jobe shrugs. "I guess so. I like it better that this desert anyhow. There's nothing out here. No big mountains with snow on top of them. They have real big mountains there, on both sides of the city."

For a while, they both just stand there, not saying anything. Jobe finally says, "I wish we *could* walk back to town, Chrissy. But I think it's too far. And like I said, Bella will see we're gone, and she'll come with the car."

Chrissy looks at the ground. "I guess so."

"Let's go back now, and I'll tell her we have to take you home. Okay?"

"You will? You promise?"

"Yes, I promise. I'll tell her this has gone far enough. I'll tell her you've had enough of an adventure, and it's time for her to take you home."

"Okay, if you promise. Let's head back."

"Can you walk okay?"

"I think maybe I got a blister. These shoes aren't very good for walking."

"If you want to get on my back, I'll carry you."

Chrissy seems embarrassed by that. She shakes her head. "No, it's all right. I can make it."

As they walk slowly back to where the car is, Chrissy wants to know more about Salt Lake City, so Jobe tells her about growing up there, about how hot it gets in the summer and how it gets cold in the winter and how it snows a lot, and it's nicer when it snows.

Chrissy tells him she's lived in the same little town her whole life. She says it's like a special kind of community. She says it gets cold sometimes, but it hardly ever snows.

As the sun comes up, Jobe is feeling good. Even though Bella did a bad thing by taking Chrissy away from her mother, it gave him the opportunity to make a new friend. And she's a girl. He's never had any kind of friend before, let alone a girl. He's sorry she has to go back home now, but he hopes maybe he might be able to visit Chrissy sometime in the future.

By the time they get back, Bella and Rosie are awake and standing next to the car.

Rosie runs to Chrissy and grabs her hand.

Bella has her hands on her hips. "Okay, you two. Where the hell have you been?"

Jobe points back down the road with his thumb. "We couldn't sleep, Bella. That's all. We went for a little walk."

"A walk, eh? I bet. You think I don't know what you've been up to. Sneakin' off to get it on without us hearing ya."

Jobe steps forward and holds out both of his hands. "No, Bella. Honest. We weren't doing anything. We just talked."

"Well, it's good that you're gettin' to know each other. Not that I mind what you and her do, but from now on I want to know where the two of you are. At all times, get it?"

"I need to talk to you about that, Bella. Chrissy is tired of this adventure. She wants to back home now."

Bella laughs. "She does, does she?"

"Yes. And I agree with her. We should take her back right away."

Bella shrugs. "Well then, I guess that's what we'd better do. But for right now, I want her and Rosie to get to know each other a bit more. Then we'll go. Hey, aren't you hungry, Jobe? And what about you, Chrissy? Aren't you hungry?"

Chrissy just looks down at the ground.

"Well, I bet you are. And I bet you're cold too. The sun is comin' up, but it's still damn cold. What say we send Jobe here off to find some dry wood? We'll have a nice fire and get somethin' to eat, okay?"

Jobe realizes she's right. It really is cold. He's mostly used to being cold, and he has his sweatshirt with its hood, but all Chrissy has on is her blue dress. She must be getting really cold. He hurries away to find some wood for a fire.

When he comes back with an armload of wood, he sees that Chrissy and Rosie are walking around together, holding hands. He wonders if Chrissy will miss Rosie when she goes back home.

He's pretty sure Rosie is going to miss Chrissy. She's always either hugging her or holding onto her hand.

Bella gets a fire going and calls to the girls to come sit by it.

Rosie plops down in the dirt in front of the fire, and Chrissy, after a moment's hesitation, straightens her dress and sits down next to her.

Jobe doesn't know what to do with himself, so he just stands on the other side of the fire by himself.

Bella hands each of them an uncooked hot dog wrapped in a piece of white bread. "Well, isn't this cozy. A nice little family out camping in the desert." She winks at Chrissy. "So, Chrissy, isn't this fun? Just think of all the adventures you're gonna get to tell all your little friends about when you get home."

Chrissy swallows her bite of hot dog and bread before she speaks. "I know you mean well, Mrs. Bella, but I really am ready to go back home now."

Bella holds up one hand. "It's just plain Bella, Chrissy. Bella the bell. That's me."

"Yes, Bella. But when am I going to get to—"

"Hey, what's the hurry?" says Bella. She's smiling as she points at Rosie. "Aren't you glad to have a new friend? I can tell Rosie really likes you."

"Yes, Mrs. Bella, but my mother will be really worried about where I went. I'm not sure what she'll do when—"

Bella gets a surprised look on her face. "What? You don't like Rosie?"

Chrissy turns to look at Rosie. "Oh, yes. Rosie is very nice. But still—"

"Well, if you don't like my little Rosie, then I guess I will have to take you back to town. But let me tell ya, Rosie is gonna be real unhappy about that."

Chrissy looks at Rosie who is staring at the ground. "Yes, I do feel bad for Rosie. Maybe we could all go back to my house and—"

"No, no," says Bella. "If you don't like Rosie, I understand." She shrugs and looks away. "My Rosie is kind of a unusual girl. I can see how you wouldn't like her. But let me tell ya, it's been a long time since she had a friend. A damn long time." She tosses another piece of wood into the fire and looks away.

Rosie scoots closer to Chrissy and leans her head against Chrissy's shoulder.

Chrissy puts her arm around Rosie. "It's not that, Mrs. Bella. I really do like Rosie. She's really nice and I don't mind being friends with her, but—"

Bella snaps her fingers and stands up. "Well, that settles it then. We'll stick together. Let's go. Everybody back in the car."

Jobe tries to kick some dirt onto the fire to put it out, but Bella yells at him to leave it and come sit in the front seat with her. She tells the girls to get in the back seat.

As soon everybody is in the car, Bella starts the car and they take off fast down the bumpy and dusty road. Jobe looks back at the girls and sees that Rosie still has both of her arms around Chrissy. Jobe is not sure if that means Rosie really, really likes her new friend, or if it means she's afraid of losing her. He turns to Bella. "So, we're taking her back now?"

"Sure we are. Didn't I say it was only gonna be for a little while? I was just trying to give her a few adventures first." She laughs, but Jobe doesn't know why.

When they get back out to the highway, Bella picks up speed and starts humming to herself.

Now that the sun is high in the sky, Jobe is enjoying the scenery. The desert is not very interesting, but there are some nice red cliffs in the distance. He wonders what it would be like to go up there.

He looks back, and notices Chrissy is also looking out the window at those red cliffs. He hopes she's enjoying her little trip, but he's glad Bella is taking Chrissy back to that town. He knows he'll be sorry to see Chrissy go, but he keeps on hoping that someday, somehow, he might get the chance to see her again.

They haven't been driving for very long when Bella turns off onto another dirt road.

Jobe points back in the direction they came from. "Aren't we going back to that town? I thought we were going to take Chrissy home."

"No problem," says Bella. "Soon. Just checking out this road."

Jobe looks back and sees that Chrissy is trying to sit up to see where they're going, but Rosie has got her all wrapped up in her arms and almost seems to be holding her down.

Chrissy soon gives up trying to see out the window and settles back with her eyes closed.

Rosie snuggles her nose into Chrissy's neck. Jobe can see that she's really happy to be with her new friend. But what's she going to do when it's time for Chrissy to go?

The dirt road ends at place where there are a bunch of skinny cows gathered around what looks like an old iron bathtub. It's full of water. There's a windmill that's slowly turning, and water squirts from a pipe into the bathtub. Jobe is interested in what the windmill and the iron tub are doing out here in the middle of the desert, but he's not about to get out of the car and check it out—who knows what those big cows might do to him.

But he doesn't get the chance to get out anyhow because Bella turns the car around and drives all the way back out to the highway. She resumes driving in the same direction as before. Now Jobe is not so sure Bella really is planning to take Chrissy back to that town. She's been driving on the highway for a long time, and they don't seem to be coming to any towns. He's about to say something about that when Bella turns off onto another dirt road. Where is she going now?

Bella drives for a long way on the dirt road before she finally stops. This time there are no cows and no windmill; there's nothing around except a big rocky hill.

Bella shuts off the car and stretches. "Well, this looks like a good a place as any. What say we spend the night here?"

Jobe can't believe she wants to spend another night out in the middle of nowhere. "But Bella, I thought we were supposed to be taking Chrissy back to her mother."

Bella shrugs. "Sure we are. One more adventure, and then it's back we go. It'll give the girls some time to get to know each other."

She turns back to the girls. "Last stop for today, girls. Everybody out. You girls go out and play or somethin'. Get to know each other." She points at Jobe. "Jobe, you know your job. Go find us some firewood."

"But Bella."

"No buts. It'll get cold out here tonight. Go find us some firewood and we'll have a nice fire to sit around."

Jobe gets out of the car and sees that Rosie and Chrissy are already out and heading for some nearby bushes, hand in hand. Rosie is the one doing the leading.

Bella says, "Leave 'em alone, Jobe. Girls need to be on their own sometimes. Get it?" She winks.

Jobe doesn't get it and he doesn't know why she winked, but he says, "Okay, Bella. But I have to ask you, how long are we going to stay out here?"

"Not long. You just get to lookin' for firewood. When it gets dark, it'll turn cold here in the desert, just like last night."

Jobe does as he is told. If gathering firewood is his only job, then he'll try to do it well. Normally, he'd look for signs and wait for God to tell him what to do, but for some reason, God hasn't been talking to him lately. But he still has his little Bible, and it still talks to him. This time, it says *Commit your work to the Lord, and your plans will be established.* That must mean God wants him to do a good job of finding firewood, so that is exactly what he will do.

As he gathers firewood, Jobe tries to keep an eye on the girls. They're sitting on the ground, somewhat hidden behind a spiky desert plant that looks like a bunch of green spears stuck into the ground. They seem to be playing some kind of game that involves taking turns scratching things in the dirt with sticks—pictures, it looks like. Jobe is amazed to see that Rosie actually seems to be participating in the drawing game. Apparently, Chrissy has somehow drawn Rosie out of whatever was going on inside of her head. Maybe that's why Bella wanted to keep Chrissy with Rosie instead of taking her back to her mother like she promised to do. Maybe she thinks Chrissy can help with whatever problem is going on inside of Rosie's head.

When Jobe comes back with a good-sized armload of wood, he sees that the girls are still in the same place, sitting cross-legged next to each other, bending forward to focus on the pictures they're drawing in the dirt. Jobe can't help but wonder what those pictures might be. Seeing them playing together like that, anybody might think they were sisters. Chrissy is prettier than Rosie, mostly because she has that nice red hair, and because her blue eyes always seem to be alive. Rosie is kind of nice-looking too, but she's a lot thinner than Chrissy, and she usually seems to be lost inside of her own head.

Soon Jobe has created a really big pile of firewood, and he doesn't know what to do with himself. He looks around for Bella and sees that she's sitting in the front seat of the car listening to the car's radio. Why is she doing that?

As Jobe approaches the car, Bella quickly turns off the radio and turns to him. "Whatta ya want? Didn't I tell ya to go get firewood?"

"I did, Bella. A great big pile. And don't you think the girls will be getting hungry? All they had was that one hot dog."

Bella frowns. "All right, all right. Let's get a fire going. Tell ya what, this time why don't we cook our hot dogs. Go find us some thin green sticks and we'll have us a weenie roast."

Jobe goes off to find some sticks, and by the time he gets back, Bella has a fire going and has the girls sitting next to it.

As Jobe approaches, Bella says, "There's our boy. And look, he's got some weenie-cookin' sticks. How about it girls, ready for a weenie roast?" She takes a stick from Jobe and pokes it through the middle of a hot dog. She hands it to Chrissy and tells her to get to roastin'.

Chrissy does as she is told and uses her stick to hold her hot dog above the fire.

Bella does the same thing with another stick and hands it to Rosie.

Rosie pulls the hot dog off of the stick and stuffs it into her mouth.

Seeing Rosie do that, Chrissy pulls her hot dog out of the fire and quickly eats it.

Bella shrugs and says, 'Well, you don't have to cook it if you don't want to, Chrissy. That's the rule with us. Here, you're free to eat your hot dog any way you want to. Up to you, but me an Jobe are gonna have fun roastin' our hot dogs. Right, Jobe?"

Jobe considers doing the same thing the girls did, but he has never tried cooking a hot dog over a fire, so he decides to try it. As the hot dog cooks, he remembers how Mother sometimes gave him money to go to the store to buy the cheapest hot dogs he could find. Usually, they didn't have a stove, so they had to eat them cold, like Chrissy and Rosie just did. But once, when they were living in a grumpy man's spare room, the man would let Mother use his stove to boil the hot dogs in a pan of water. Usually, Mother would forget about the hot dogs, so Jobe would eventually have to go turn off the stove. Those over-boiled hot dogs never tasked very good. He wonders if these hot dogs cooked over a wood fire will taste better.

Bella chuckles and also holds her hot dog over the fire. "Fun, eh Jobe? We're havin' fun, not like the spoil-sport girls, eh?" She bumps her hot dog on a stick against Jobe's.

As his hot dog cooks, Jobe watches Chrissy, wondering why she's starting to act more like Rosie. Both she and Rosie are silently staring into the fire, not paying any attention to what he and Bella are doing.

Bella warns Jobe that his hot dog is getting burned and hands him a piece of bread.

Jobe pulls his hot dog out of the fire and watches Bella to see how to eat it. She uses her piece of bread to pull the burned hot dog off of the stick and begins to eat it. Jobe copies her method and carefully takes a bite of the hot dog. To his surprise, it doesn't really taste much like hot dog—more like wood and fire.

After the hot dog roasting is over and done with, Bella leans back against her big plastic bag and points out the first few stars that are appearing in the sky. "Well now, isn't this nice. Camping out with good eats and a nice warm fire. What more could a girl want? Right, Chrissy? I bet you never got to do anything like this before did you?"

Chrissy doesn't respond; she's still staring at the fire.

"Didn't think so. Well, Chrissy, I hope you know how lucky you are ta have run into us. We do fun things like this all the time. You'll see."

Bella turns to Jobe. "We're gonna show our little Chrissy here how to have fun, aren't we Jobe? Years from now, she'll be tellin' everybody about the time she got to camp out and cook hot dogs over a nice fire."

She turns back to Chrissy. "We're gonna have so much fun, you'll never want to go back to being with people who dress in weird long dresses and who won't even buy a girl a nice little notebook when she needs it." She waits for Chrissy to respond, but when she doesn't, Bella adds, "And I bet I know just what you were planning to do with that notebook, don't I, Chrissy. You were gonna start a diary, right?"

Chrissy looks up at her. She seems to be surprised at Bella's words. That makes Jobe think that maybe Bella was right; maybe the reason Chrissy wanted that little notebook so bad was so she could start a diary. But why wouldn't those women want her to have a diary? One of those women in the weird dresses must have been her mother. Why wouldn't a mother let her daughter have a diary if she wanted one?

Bella nods. "Yeah, that's what I figured. Pretty mean of them, I think. Not to let a girl have a diary to keep all her girl secrets in. Well, with us here, we don't have those kinds of bad rules. Here, a girl gets to have whatever she wants. Guess what I got in my pocket, Chrissy? What would a girl need once she got herself a diary? Right. A pencil. And I got one, just for you." She pulls the stub of a pencil out of her pocket and holds it out to Chrissy.

For some reason that Jobe can't figure out, Chrissy looks at Rosie. It's almost like she's asking for Rosie's permission to take the pencil.

But Rosie is still staring into the fire, so Chrissy leans forward and grabs the little pencil out of Bella's hand. She stares at it, and then quietly says, "Thank you, Mrs. Bella."

"No need to thank me, Chrissy. Around here, a girl gets whatever she wants."

Chrissy jumps up and runs to the car. Soon, she's back with the notebook. She sits back down and shows the notebook to Rosie.

Jobe isn't sure, but he thinks he saw Rosie give the slightest nod of approval.

Chrissy opens the notebook to the first page and seems about to write something in it. But then she looks up at Bella and seems to change her mind. She closes the notebook and holds it close to her chest.

Bella chuckles and stands up. "Well, kids. It's gonna get a mite cold out here in the desert at night. What say we turn in. We got a big day tomorrow." She dumps the blankets out of her big plastic bag and hands two of them to Jobe. "Put down one of these here blankets and use the other one on top of you and Chrissy."

Chrissy seems startled. "Me and Jobe together? But Mrs. Bella, I don't think Jobe and I should—"

"Nuthin' to worry about, girl. Jobe'll take care of ya. He'll make sure no critters sneak in durin' the night and get ya. Me and Rosie'll be right over here on the other side of the fire. Nuthin' to worry about. It's fun to sleep out with friends. An adventure. One you'll never forget. Isn't that right, Jobe?"

Jobe isn't sure what kind of response Bella wants from him. Does she really want him to sleep under the same blanket as Chrissy? That would almost be like the two of them would be in a bed together.

But Bella doesn't wait for his response. She's already spreading out the other blanket a little ways away for herself and Rosie.

Jobe lies down on the blanket, and holds up the other blanket so Chrissy can get in.

But Chrissy won't get under the blanket with him. She just stays where she is, with her arms wrapped around her knees. To Joe, with the firelight dancing on her, Chrissy looks amazingly pretty. Her nice blue dress hides her figure, but he can tell she must look nice and slim under it. Jobe hopes her pretty dress isn't getting too dirty having to sit around all day in the dirt. But she hasn't once complained about that. Jobe is again impressed by what a brave girl she is.

The fire is dying down, and it's starting to get cold, so Jobe covers himself up with the blanket, hoping it will encourage Chrissy to also come under the blanket to get warm.

But she doesn't, and as the time passes, it gets colder and colder. Jobe is sure Chrissy must be getting really cold, but she still won't join him. She just sits there, her head down, not moving at all.

Jobe can't believe she's able to withstand the cold so well. He's getting a bit cold, and he's under a blanket. He's starting to think this pretty girl who seems fine and fragile is actually tougher than she looks. It reminds him of one of the Bible verses mother used to read to him whenever she thought he was acting weak: *Have I not commanded you? Be strong and courageous. Do not be frightened, and do not be dismayed, for the Lord your God is with you wherever you go.* He wonders if Chrissy knows about that verse from the Bible. Did her mother ever teach her things from the Bible?

Jobe knows he must be as strong as Chrissy is. He decides to stay awake all night and keep an eye on her. To protect her. Bella said there might be critters out here in the middle of the desert, so it's his duty to stay awake and keep watch. Even though he'd like it a lot better if she would come under the blanket with him, he won't force her. He will just lie still and be the patient protector.

But when the half of a moon rises in the sky, the same as it did the night before, Jobe can see Chrissy is shivering. He quickly sits up. "Chrissy, you're getting too cold. Please get under this blanket with me. I promise I won't even touch you. I mean, not unless you want me to. I mean to help you get warm."

She hesitates, but finally she moves onto the blanket. "You have to promise you won't touch me, Jobe. It wouldn't be . . . right."

Jobe smiles at her and holds up the blanket so she can get under it. "All I want to do is help you get warm."

She slides under the blanket with him, but immediately turns away and pulls her knees up to her chest.

Jobe tucks the blanket around her, and then he lies very still. He's excited to be so close to such a pretty girl, but he's determined to keep his promise. He won't touch her at all, unless she wants it. But he can tell that she's still shivering, so he whispers to her, "Chrissy, you're still too cold. Let me help you get warm."

She doesn't respond, so Jobe he moves a bit closer to her.

She immediately pulls away, almost going off of the blanket.

Jobe decides he'd better not try that again. He'll stay right where he is. After all, he is still very close to her, even if he isn't touching any part of her. Maybe even being this close will give her some of the warmth he feels for her. He searches his mind for a Bible verse for his situation, but he can't quite come up with the right one. The closest one he can think of is a verse from Luke: *Stay awake at all times, praying that you may have strength to escape all these things that are going to take place.*

If God put those words into his head, what things might happen if he didn't stay awake? Is God warning him that something bad is going to happen?

Chrissy 6

Dear secret diary. I need to catch you up on what has happened. I'm still not home. After Bella took me away in her car,she drove for a long time and then pulled off on a dirt road. It got dark and me and Jobe and Rosie had to sleep all night in the back seat. Early in the morning, I sneaked out of the car without waking anybody up, and I started off in the direction I thought would lead me back to the highway. But I didn't get far. Jobe is a fast runner and he caught up with me. He said it was too far to walk, and then he promised he'd get Bella to take me back home.

Then he told me something that really surprised me. He said Bella wasn't his mother. He said his mother had died and Bella took him along with them because he didn't have anywhere else to go.

As we walked back to where the car was, he told me about growing up in Salt Lake City. It sounds like a nice place and maybe I'd like to go there sometime. The important thing was that now I've got an ally to help me convince Bella to take me home.

After we got back to where the car was, Bella made a fire and then she gave each of us one hot dog to eat, that's all.

After that, we all got back in the car, and Jobe told Bella to take me back home.

But Bella didn't do that. Instead, she drove for a long time, first down one long dirt road and then another one until I guess she found a place she liked and we stopped there. It was way out in the desert, and from the long time we drove on that dirt road, I think we're a long ways from the highway again, too far to walk.

Bella told us to get out while she stayed in the car, so Rosie took my hand and led me a ways away from the car. We sat down on the ground behind some bushes, and after Jobe went off somewhere and we were alone, I told Rosie that I really did like her, but I wanted her to try to convince her mother to take me home.

Rosie leaned close to me and whispered, "No. You stay here."

I started to ask her why she wanted me to stay with her, but then I realized she had talked! I whispered to her that I didn't even know she *could* talk.

She said, "Nobody knows." She picked up a stick and wrote BETTER NO TALK in the dirt. Then she erased it and whispered, "No tell. Our secret."

Then she used her fingernail to pretend to cut both of our wrists, and then she put our wrists together and said, "Blood oath. No Tell."

I agreed not to tell anybody she could talk, and I can't because everyone knows a blood oath is sacred.

So now me and Rosie have a secret together that nobody else in the whole world knows about. She still doesn't talk too much and instead writes one or two word messages in the dirt with her stick. Sometimes she also draws pictures of stick people doing things. She does it to show me things that have happened to her in her life. I think she's showing me that her and Bella have traveled to a lot of different place.

I try to answer her in same way, by drawing words and pictures with my own stick to tell her about what it's like to live in the community I live in.

Then Rosie drew a person and used her stick to write two words in the dirt. NO TRUST.

I wrote in the dirt WHO? JOBE?

She wrote JOBE OK - NO TRUST BELLA.

I wrote NO TRUST BELLA? ISN'T SHE YOUR MOM?

She wrote NO.

Wow. That was some big news. Can it be true that Bella is not really her mother? It makes me wonder if one time Rosie got taken away in a car like Bella did to me. Except maybe it was a long time ago, maybe when Rosie was still a little baby.

Anyhow, even though I miss my mom, at least now I have a nice friend. Rosie and me made a pact to always be true to each other forever and ever and not to trust anyone else, no matter what. We put our wrists together and made another blood oath on that too. I've never had a real friend before, but now I have one and I know we will always be friends.

Then I told Rosie I still wanted to go back home pretty soon. She said she'd find a way to get me free of Bella, because that's what she wanted to do too. That was another surprise. She said she'd figure out a way for both of us to get away, so because we are best friends I know she really will help me get away from Bella.

I really do believe Rosie will figure out a way to get us escaped from Bella because I think she's really smart, even if she doesn't like to talk to anybody but me. And when Rosie comes home with me after we escape, she will help me explain to my mother what happened and how it wasn't my fault that I went away.

I sure hope the people back home won't be mad at me for getting taken away. But I bet the Prophet will blame me. He's always warning us not to talk to strangers. He'll say this is what happens when you do. Maybe he'll even make an example of me in a church sermon to everybody, a sermon about how the outside world is evil and this is what happens if anybody makes contact with that evil. And then everybody will be really mad at me and blame me. I hope they give me a chance to explain that some outsiders, like Rosie and maybe Jobe, are not evil, even if they don't believe the same things we do. And when Rosie comes home with me, they'll see what a nice person she is and not evil at all.

Me and Rosie kept on talking about our lives and sharing pictures scratched in the dirt until Bella came and made us sit next to a fire she'd started. I decided to be like my new friend and not talk. We both just sat close together and looked at the fire until Bella gave us a hot dog on a stick. Rosie didn't want to cook her hot dog over the fire, so I didn't either.

After we ate our hot dogs, Bella did something nice to me. She gave me a pencil so I could start my real diary in my new notebook. But now I'm afraid to write anything in it because Bella might want to see what I wrote and I'm afraid to let her know the secrets me and Rosie have.

But then, my secret diary, I have to tell you another bad thing that happened. Bella wouldn't let me and Rosie stay together at night. Instead, she wanted me to sleep under a blanket with Jobe. I told her I couldn't do that because Jobe is a boy and I'm a girl and it just wouldn't be right. But Bella said I had to.

Jobe got under the blanket and he wanted me to get under it with him, but I stayed outside until I got real cold, and then Jobe said if I'd get under the blanket with him he promised not to touch me. I was so cold I had to do it, but I stayed as far away from him as I could.

I stayed perfectly still, but I was thinking that after everybody else went to sleep, this could be my chance to run away from them. But even under the blanket I was still cold, so that meant it would really be cold if I tried to walk all the way back to town, even if I did know the way which I don't. Besides, I'd sort of promised I'd stay with Rosie until she could find a way for us both to run away together, so I just stayed where I was and tried to get some sleep even though I was still really cold.

Jobe 7

Jobe wakes up with Bella pulling on his arm. He sits up and sees that it's just starting to get light. He rubs his eyes with the backs of his knuckles, trying to get himself fully awake.

Bella won't stop pulling on his arm. "Come one, Jobe. Get your ass in gear and go get some more firewood. It's too damn cold. She rubs her hands together. "It's stupid that it's so nice and warm in the daytime and then gets so cold at night."

Jobe does as he's told and goes to find some wood, but he keeps his eyes on Chrissy. She's sitting up with the blanket wrapped around herself. Poor girl. Jobe can tell she got really cold in the night. If only she would have let him wrap her up in his arms, he could have warmed her right up. Maybe tonight, if they stay here for another night, she'll realize that and let him hold her tight. That would be really nice, for both of them.

But then he shakes his head hard to make those kinds of thoughts go away. If she doesn't want him to touch her, then he should just accept that. Like it says in the Lord's Holy Book: *Flee youthful passions and pursue righteousness*. God is telling him such thoughts are only youthful passions and must not be pursued. He focuses on gathering wood and tries not to think about anything else.

When Jobe gets back with an armload of wood, Bella immediately starts a new fire and tosses all of the wood he brought onto it. Then she gathers them all around the roaring fire and passes out the usual hot dogs and bread.

Jobe notices that both the hot dog package and the bread package are now empty. Has Bella been eating without sharing?

They eat in silence until Bella says, "Well, it was a cold night, wasn't it? But it looks like it's gonna be a nice warm day." She turns toward Chrissy. "Isn't this fun? Now, how about you and Rosie go play. Me and Jobe got some things to do."

Rosie didn't seem to be paying any attention, but she immediately takes Chrissy's hand and leads her off to their favorite spot behind a bush.

Bella watches them go. "Now ain't that the sweetest thing you ever saw? Two cute girls, and best friends already." She turns to Jobe. "How was it sleepin' with her, Jobe? Pretty nice I bet. You get all the luck. Me, I had to sleep with Rosie, freezin' my ass off, while you get to have a go at a really cute gal."

Jobe wants to correct her about what happened during the night. He should tell her he never even touched Chrissy.

But Bella is already up and heading back toward the car.

Jobe decides this can't go on. He catches up with her. "Bella, what are we doing out here? I thought we were going to take Chrissy back to that town."

"Why? Don't you like her?"

"Well, yes, she's a nice girl, but she wants to go home now. It wasn't right to take her away with asking anybody's permission."

Bella laughs, and Jobe doesn't know why. "But Bella, we have to take her back. Why do you want her to stay with us anyhow?"

Bella waves him away. "Don't ask so many damn questions, Jobe. I'm working thinks out."

Jobe gives up on talking to her and heads back to the dying fire. He stands there and watches Rosie and Chrissy who've gone back to hiding behind the spiky bush to do their game of drawing things in the dirt with sticks. Sitting together in the dirt like that, the two girls are the picture of innocence, and that again makes Jobe feel ashamed of the kind of feelings he was having about Chrissy in the middle of the night. He resolves not to feel like that anymore. From this moment on, his role will be to protect these two innocent girls. He will be like their big brother. It says in the Bible that those who care for the weak will be blessed. Jobe promises himself that from this moment on, that's exactly what he'll do, protect them, and that is all. He will be strong and resist temptation, no matter what.

He wonders what he should do while he waits for Bella to reveal her plan? Bella is spending all her time in the car listening to the radio, and the girls seems to want to be left alone to play their drawing with sticks game.

He wanders around, looking at all the weird spiky and stickery kinds of plants they have in the desert, and that reminds him that he's been out in the desert for all this time and he's hardly noticed anything about it. Has all that's happened in the past few days somehow changed him so much he's losing track of things? Has what happened with Bella and the strong feelings he's been having about Chrissy muddled his brain so much he can't think about anything else? Everything in his life has changed, and he's in a brand new place outside of Salt Lake City.

He needs to pay attention or he might miss the important signs and completely lose the thread of this new reality. That thought makes him worry that maybe he's already let some of it slip through his fingers. It's almost like since that night when he saw Bella and Rosie sitting in the cold outside of the Mormon's Temple, reality changed, and he just went along with it, like he was out on some kind of big ocean and got drifted away from the shore without even noticing. What could have happened to make him forget to notice things? Sometimes when Mother was entertaining a man friend, she'd let him out of his closet and tell him to get lost. Happy to be out of the closet for a change, he'd wander around Salt Lake City, just looking at people, wondering what their lives were like. It must have been because he had nothing else to do all day, but it did make him notice things. Now, so many things are happening in this new life, it's like he doesn't have time to notice anything else, or time to think about what it all means.

He remembers the lonely feeling he had that night after Mother died. It was like nobody in the whole world knew him. In fact, seeing people talking to each other, he got the bad feeling that he might be the only person in the world that nobody knew. And now, that's all changed and he hardly noticed it happening. Here he is, traveling around with three other people, and one of them is a really nice, really pretty girl who seems to like him. Jobe can hardly believe everything could have changed so fast. He should think about that. He should think about change and why things changed so quickly after he met Bella and Rosie. It seems like he was still the same person he was up until that first night when Bella did that thing to him. After that, things started to move too fast to keep track of. First, he got some money from some men in suits, and then he got to ride inside the back of a big truck with Rosie hugging him. It was all new. He'd never once in his life been in a big truck, and he'd never once had a girl hug him. And then Bella stole a car, and since then he's been riding around in that car with her and Rosie and Chrissy.

So many things changing, and so fast. Up until now, he'd never once even been in a car, except for the time that man friend of Mother's took him in his car clear out to the edge of Salt Lake City and dumped him out on the side of the road. It took all day and half of the night to walk back to the trailer. Mother was mad at that man for doing that, but the man said the kid "bothered him." He said Jobe was always staring at him and if she didn't want "something bad to happen to the kid," she should get rid of him. But luckily, Mother didn't do what that man wanted. Instead, she got rid of that bad man.

Jobe looks up and realizes he's walked a long ways from the car. How did that happen without him noticing it? Maybe he shouldn't get caught in thinking about past things like that. Mother always said it's better not to get caught worrying about the past. She said we should just live for today, and to hell with the past. And today, for Jobe, his life is Chrissy and Rosie and Bella. He should be happy to be having a new reality. He should accept it and learn from it. Besides, he now has a purpose in life, to protect Chrissy.

That thought gives Jobe a scary feeling. What if Bella decides to take Chrissy away? She could put Rosie and Chrissy in the car and just drive away. He'd be left with nothing, just like that night Mother died

He runs as fast as he can back to the car, and he's happy to see that Bella is still there. And the girls are still in their play place, drawing pictures in the dirt with their sticks. For some reason, seeing them all still right where they were before he went walking, makes him feel more secure. It's like everything is just the way it should be. Maybe it's like what Bella said before, that they really are his family now. What a strange thing, to just be drifting along lost on a big ocean and end up in a brand new family. God must have felt sorry for him after he took Mother up to sit by his side. Jobe silently thanks the Lord for being so kind to him.

But even if they are all a family now, he knows he still shouldn't trust Bella. She stole that car and she took Chrissy away without asking permission. Why did she decide to do that? Before, she was just traveling around with Rosie, a mother and her daughter alone. But then, Bella wanted him to come along with them. Was it only because he got those men to give them some money? Or was it because of what she did to him in the night? Maybe she really does like him. And maybe she understood that he was the type of person who would help protect her daughter. And then, she decided to bring Chrissy along with them. Why did she do that? Was it because of him? Or was it because she wanted Rosie to have a friend, like she said?

He turns to watch the girls drawing their pictures in the dirt. How did Bella know the two girls would get along with each other so well?

Jobe gives up trying to figure it all out. Too much has happened in too short a time. It must just be God's way of making things happen, and like Mother always said, no person can know what God's plan is.

But what is God's plan for him? And what is Bella's plan? She's got them just sitting out here in the middle of a desert while she listens to the car radio. Why? He doubts that Bella knows how to pray to God, at least not like he does, so why could God be getting inside of Bella's head to make a plan for him? Maybe he should try to find out if Bella has any plan at all. He goes to the car and taps on the window.

Bella quickly turns off the radio and rolls down the window. "Yeah, whatta ya want, Jobe?"

"What I want to know, Bella, is what is the plan?"

"The plan? What're you talkin' about?"

"I mean, how long are we just going to sit out here? We're not doing anything, and it looks like the food is all gone. Aren't the girls going to get real hungry? I mean, why are we just being out here?"

Bella stares at him, frowning. Then, she begins to roll the window up again.

But Jobe decides he can't continue to let her ignore him and not tell him what the plan is. He grabs the top of the window before she can get it all the way up. "Listen, Bella, I don't get any of this. Why did we take Chrissy away like that? I mean, I like her. Actually, I like her a lot, and Rosie seems to like having her here too. But isn't it about time we took her back?"

Bella abruptly opens the car door, pushing Jobe back. She gets out and puts her face real close to his face. "Okay, mister smart guy. You think we should go back to that town? I was just listenin' to the radio, and guess what I heard? They're lookin' for ya."

Jobe isn't sure he heard her right. "Me? I mean, who is looking for me?"

"The cops. It said so on the radio. It said the police are all out lookin' for a little red-haired girl that went missing outside of the local Walmart store. The cops looked at the store's surveillance video outside the front of that store, and it showed a boy shoving a girl into the back seat of a car."

"Did they mean me? I didn't shove her."

"Of course they meant you. And now it's you they're lookin' for. They got cops out all over hell lookin' for ya. And other people are lookin' for you too. Regular people besides the cops. Everybody's lookin', and it's you they're lookin' for."

"But, Bella, that's not fair. You are the one that took her away."

"Yeah, but that's not the way people think about it. Listenin' to the radio, I can tell all they can think about is a pretty little red-haired girl being grabbed by some evil guy who wants to take her away to do who knows what to her."

For the first time since they left Salt Lake City, Jobe feels like this is all getting too real. He's just been kind of floating along with Bella because he didn't really have any other place to go, and maybe because of what she did to him under the quilt that first night. But now look at the trouble she's got him into. He grabs onto Bella's arm with both hands. "Bella, we have to take her back. Right now!"

Bella pries his hands off of her arm. "Sure, we will. But we hafta do it the right way or else those cops'll catch ya and toss you right inta their jail. They'll call it kidnappin'. Know what that means? It means they'd lock you up and throw away the key. You'd never see the light of day again."

Jobe looks into her eyes and sees something new and unexpected: she's actually happy about this turn of events. It's like this whole thing is a fun new game to her.

She pats his arm. "Tell, you what, Jobe. Don't worry about it. I'll find a way to get you out of this. I'll go into town to scope out the situation. Besides, like you said, we need food. And water and other stuff. I'll go in and scout out the situation and get us some supplies." She points toward Chrissy and Rosie. "You stay here and protect the girls. I'll go to town and be back here in a flash."

Jobe looks at the two girls. They look so innocent sitting there in the dirt, leaning close to each other as they play their game. He realizes Bella is right: he should stay and protect them. It's what God would want him to do.

He turns back to Bella. "All right, I'll stay here and look after them. But you have to promise to get back here quick. And then, if it's safe, we can take Chrissy back to town tonight after it gets dark."

"Will do," says Bella. She calls to the girls. "Listen, girls. I got to run into town to get us some food. You stay here and do whatever Jobe tells you."

Chrissy looks at Bella, and seems about to stand up, but Rosie grabs her hand so she can't get up.

Jobe watches Bella drive away. The car kicks up a column of dust as it goes, and for some reason, the sight of the car going away so fast makes Jobe feel kind of lost. If Bella is telling the truth about cops looking for him, will he ever get the chance to explain that it was all Bella's idea and not his? Maybe they wouldn't believe him. Then what would he do? They might put him in jail, just like Bella said.

He watches the car until it's out of sight, and then he turns to look at the two girls. They've gone back to scratching their pictures in the dirt, their heads close together. Jobe is glad to see they're getting along so well, but what if Bella can't find a way to take Chrissy back to that town? What should he do then? He realizes he doesn't even know where they are. He turns to look at the big hill that's nearby. Maybe if he hikes up there, he might be able to see where they are. It's not a really tall hill, not like the snow-topped mountains back in Salt Lake City, but it might be nice up there on top of even this little mountain. Peaceful. And closer to God maybe.

He goes to the girls to tell them. They're still in their play spot behind the spiky desert plant, still drawing their odd things in the dirt.

As he approaches, the girls quickly scratch out their drawings. It's like they don't want him to see whatever it was they were drawing. Jobe figures it must be some kind of girl thing.

"Girls," he says, "I'm going for a short hike. You stay here."

Chrissy jumps up and grabs his hand. "No, Jobe. Don't leave us here alone. Please."

He smiles and pats her hand to reassure her. "Don't worry, Chrissy. I'll be right back." He points toward the hill. "I'm just going to get a little higher up. To look around."

Jobe is surprised to see Rosie reach up to grab Chrissy's arm to pull her back down. It's like Rosie doesn't want Chrissy to leave her side, not even for a minute. It must mean Rosie is afraid to be alone now that her mother has driven away in the car. That makes Jobe decide he'd better not go too far. If the girls are nervous just because he's going for a little walk, it means they now understand that he's there to protect them. And if Chrissy gets real scared, she might start thinking she could walk back to town like she did that last time. That would be really bad because even though he's not sure how far they came, he's pretty sure it's way too far to walk. He decides not to go too far up the hill, just high enough to try to see where they are. And he should keep the girls in sight at all times.

When he gets to the base of the big hill, Jobe looks back, and he's glad to see that Chrissy and Rosie have gone back to scratching in the dirt with their sticks.

As he heads up the hill, Jobe checks out the desert plants, wondering if any of them are edible. There isn't much to choose from, a lot of cactus and a bunch of other types of spiky plants. That must have been God's plan, giving these desert plants a way to cling to life out here in these harsh conditions, and making them so prickly and so spiky none of the desert critters will try to eat them.

That thought makes Jobe begin to wonder what kinds of critters there are out in a desert place like this. Snakes, probably, and all kinds of bad bugs and stinging creatures too maybe. He tells himself he'd better be careful not to step on anything that moves. And what about bigger wild animals? Can animals live out in this kind of desert place? There must be some kinds of animals that could live in such a place. He looks up toward the top of the big hill. Are some animals hiding up there? Are they watching him right now? What will they do if he gets too close their hiding place? He stops. Maybe he shouldn't be going off this far by himself. But then he tells himself he's just imaging things. The desert floor is so dry and sandy, if there were animals, he would have seen their tracks. That's logical. Mother always said to be logical. Animals have to have water, don't they? There's no water around here anywhere, so maybe there aren't any animals. That's logical too. He keeps on going up even though it's getting steeper and the ground is getting a lot more rocky.

He stops to look back down at the girls. They're still in the same place, still playing their scratching in the dirt game. But then he wonders if maybe it's more than a game. Rosie doesn't talk, but maybe she can communicate with Chrissy using pictures. That might mean Rosie really is starting to come back out into the world, at least enough to communicate with Chrissy. If he gets a chance, he should try to see what kind of pictures they're drawing. And maybe he should try again to talk to Rosie, try to find out what kind of person she is inside all that silence. That thought makes Jobe wonder if there's something secret hiding inside of Rosie. What makes her not talk and just stare straight ahead most all of the time? Bella said Rosie was autistic, whatever that is. Maybe autistic means she doesn't know how to talk, but it could also mean she just doesn't want to.

He looks out across the valley below, holding his Bible up to shades his eyes from the hot afternoon sun. He can clearly see the dirt road they came in on as it snakes out across the desert. But eventually, that road goes behind a distant hill and disappears from sight. He can't see any other roads. If for some reason, he and the girls had to walk out of here, it would be a very long walk. And Bella didn't leave them much water. Did she do that on purpose to make sure they didn't try to walk out? If they tried it without water, would all three of them die?

As the sun sinks lower down in the sky, Jobe stays where he is to keep an eye on that dirt road. At any minute, he should see the cloud of dust that will indicate Bella is coming back in the car.

But when the sun seems like it's about ready to go down behind a hill in the distance, he decides he'd better hurry back down. If Bella doesn't come back soon and he's not down there to protect the girls, they'll get worried. Without Bella there, Jobe knows it will be his job to reassure them.

But what if Bella doesn't ever come back? What if the cops grabbed her? Maybe Bella wouldn't admit anything. That would mean nobody would know they were stuck out here in the desert with no food and no water. How long a person can go without food and water? Probably not very long. If Bella doesn't come back, they could die. Maybe someday somebody, a hiker or somebody like that, will come along and find their three skeletons.

But then, Jobe pushes that thought away; there's no way a mother would abandon her daughter, not even a bad mother like Bella.

By the time Jobe gets back down from his hike up the big hill, it's almost dark and he's starting to think Bella is not coming back anytime soon.

At the campsite, Chrissy and Rosie are standing up waiting for him. Right away, he understands why they're both looking at him like that: they're waiting for him to tell them what to do. In his whole life, nobody has ever expected him to tell them what to do. He wants to be the man and take care of them, but with no food left and not much water, what can he do?

He decides the main thing he can do is reassure them. Even though he's only a few years older than them, he has to act like the adult and make some decisions. He tries to think what his first decision should be. Well, first off, it's getting cold. There's still some firewood left. He should make a fire. That way, they could all stay warm, and maybe Chrissy would like to sit around the fire next to him and talk. Maybe with Bella gone, he can get her to tell him more about herself. "Well, girls," he says, "it feels like it's going to get cold pretty quick tonight, so I think I'll make us a fire. Let's go over to the fire place."

They do as he said, and that makes Jobe feel good. The two girls sit down close together and stare into where the fire is going to be.

But then, Jobe realizes he doesn't have any matches. Did Bella take the matches with her? He looks in the direction the car went when Bella drove away. Why didn't he think ahead and ask her to leave the matches? That makes him realize he's never been much of a think-ahead kind of person. Mother mostly kept him locked in his nice little closet while she took care of things. Then she went and died without teaching him anything about how to be in charge. Why didn't she think about that before she died?

What is he going to tell the girls? That he forget to ask Bella for the matches? Darn. His first task at being the responsible adult, and he doesn't do it right. He has no food for the girls, and he can't even keep them warm.

But it's all Bella's fault, not his. She said she'd be back soon, so there was no need for her to leave the matches.

The girls are still sitting quietly waiting for him to tell them what to do. But what can he do without any matches?

Jobe decides there is only one answer, the same answer as always: he has to ask God.

He tells the girls to just stay where they are while he walks a little ways away and waits for guidance. He goes behind a clump of low bushes and looks up to Heaven. He knows better than to ask God a specific question, but he needs some kind of guidance about how to be a man and be the one in charge.

And then, as if God himself has spoken, Jobe remembers a line from the Bible: *If two lie together, they can keep warm.*

Is that really in the Bible? It doesn't matter if it is or not, it provides the solution.

Jobe walks back to where the girls are waiting. "Girls, I've changed my mind. There's no use wasting the firewood. We might as well just go to sleep." He points at Bella's big plastic bag. "Chrissy, you spread out one of the blankets. We'll put the other blanket and the quilt over us. That way, we'll all be warm and cozy."

Chrissy seems about to do what he said, but then Jobe sees what might have been a slight shake of Rosie's head, and Chrissy stops.

"But Jobe," says Chrissy, "now that Bella is gone, don't you think it would be better if Rosie and I slept together. You know, seeing as how you are a boy and we are girls and . . . well, you know."

Jobe is absolutely sure he doesn't want that to happen. Sleeping next to Chrissy last night was one of the very best things that ever has happened to him in his whole life, and he doesn't want that to change now that he's the one in charge. Beside, sleeping under the same blanket with Chrissy *and* Rosie, might be ever better. He shakes his head in a way he hopes looks very firm. "But Chrissy, don't you remember how cold you got last night? And it feels to me like it's going to be even colder tonight. No, we'd all better sleep together. It's the only way we're going to stay warm."

It looks like Chrissy isn't sure what to do. She looks at Rosie who immediately goes to get Bella's big plastic bag. Chrissy helps Rosie take out a blanket, and as soon as they have it spread out on the ground, Rosie plops down on it and Chrissy joins her there.

Jobe happily goes to get another blanket, and he carefully spreads it over the two girls. Then he does the same thing with the heavier quilt. He slides under it next to Chrissy, being careful not to touch her.

Lying very still and looking up at the first few stars to appear in the sky, Jobe feels happy that the girls went along with his plan to sleep all together. It shows they respect his authority. After all, he the male, and he is older than them. The Bible says that's important. It says the males should be in charge and the females should be submissive to them. It says *Do not permit a woman to teach or to assume authority over a man. She must be quiet.* Jobe remembers how one time Mother got mad at him for him telling her she shouldn't let those men always be bossing her around. She hit him and made him memorize the part in the Bible where is says God formed Adam first, and then made Eve out of a little bit of Adam. She said that proves women have to do what the man says. That got Jobe to thinking, and he asked Mother if maybe that meant he could give her advice sometimes, because, after all, he was a male too. Mother bopped him on top of his head with her hairbrush and told him that with a mother it's different—a mother is supposed to tell a child what to do, never the other way around.

Jobe sits up a little bit and looks at the two girls. They're hugged together over at the far edge of the blanket. Jobe lies back down and pulls the blankets up to his chin. He doesn't think it's fair that Chrissy and Rosie get to hug together so close to get warm, while he, the male in charge, has to lie all by himself? Carefully, he inches closer to Chrissy's back. He feels like putting his arms around her and pulling her close to himself, but he decides against it. It would be nice to feel her body against his, but maybe it's better to let her sleep. Besides, he's so close to her now that he can feel her warmth, so actually, that should be enough, if it really is warmth he's concerned about.

But shouldn't the man in charge get more than that? Maybe he'd better ask God about that.

He stares up at all the stars and waits for a message from God. And then, almost like a voice speaking to him inside of his head, he remembers something from the Bible: *There is great gain in godliness with contentment, for we brought nothing into the world, and we cannot take anything out of the world. But if we have food and clothing and warmth, with these we will be content.*

It means he should just be content with what he has. It's almost like he's in a bed with two pretty girls, and he's so close to Chrissy, he's almost touching her. If he might fall asleep and end up hugging her, well, it would be just for warmth and nothing else. He lies still imagining that. It's almost as if he can feel her nice little body curling up against him. He'll just wait and see what happens in the night.

Chrissy 7

Dear secret diary. I'm still right where I was yesterday, out in the middle of some kind of flat desert. But I don't feel so scared and lonely anymore because now I have my new friend Rosie to talk to, and we have a secret plan to get away. Jobe said he'd convince Bella to take me back home, and he tried, but I'm starting to think he's not going to be able to convince her of anything. She keeps on saying she's going to take me home, but then she never does.

Another thing - I've finally started my real on paper diary. But I'm not writing my secret thoughts in it. Instead I'm drawing pictures of what I'm seeing. I'm not a very good drawer, but I've tried to draw a lot of pictures of Rosie. At first, my pictures didn't look very much like her, but I'm getting better at it. I've drawn a few pictures of Jobe too, but I haven't been drawing any pictures of Bella because I'm afraid she might see them and not like it.

As a sort of diary, I've also been drawing pictures of all the different kinds of plants that grow around here and of the places I've been over the past few days. I started out by drawing a picture of a big building with the name WALMART on the front of it. And then I drew a picture of Bella's car, and picture of a highway along with a sort of a map, even though I'm not exactly sure where we went. Maybe we went south from Saint George, but I could be wrong about that.

I'm finding that I really like drawing pictures, and Rosie likes my pictures too, especially the ones I draw of her. I also drew a picture of a house to show Rosie the kind of house I live in, and I drew a bunch of little stick figures all around the house, some of them with dresses on, to show her that I have loads and loads of brothers and sisters. I told her some of them are by different moms, but only one father. I even told her about the man we call the Prophet from God, and then, for some reason, I got started telling her the one thing I've never told anybody, about how the Prophet made me come into his office and made me take off all my clothes and sit on his lap while he touched me in places down between my legs that he shouldn't have.

Rosie looked mad when she heard that, and she scratched the words "BAD MAN" in the dirt.

That got me to wondering if it was really possible that the Prophet could be a bad man. How could a man chosen by God to be our leader be bad? I whispered that question to Rosie, and she just scratched two words in the dirt, NO GOD.

I've been thinking about what that meant. Does it mean Rosie doesn't believe there is a God up there in heaven who watches over us? Or maybe she was just saying she didn't think the Prophet really is a messenger from God. Bella and Jobe might think Rosie is dumb, but I don't think so. I think she's actually really smart in her own way.

The next thing that happened was that Bella said she was going to town to get us more food and water. I started to get up to tell her I wanted to go along with her, but Rosie grabbed my wrist and looked at me real urgent. She shook her head and whispered that she wanted me to stay with her until we both could go away together. I hesitated, but then I sat back down and didn't let out a peep. It will be really great if we could get away from Bella, and then maybe Rosie could come home with me. We have so many kids in my family, one more won't make hardly any difference at all, and we could go on being best friends.

After Bella drove away, Jobe went walking off somewhere. I got worried that maybe he was going to leave us too, but Rosie said there wasn't any need to be worried, that we could take care of our ourselves. She said it was even better with Jobe gone so we could talk out loud like normal human beings.

I asked her if maybe it was time to tell Bella and Jobe that she could talk, but she said no. She said she might talk to Jobe someday, but she'd never talk to Bella after what she did to her.

I asked what Bella did, but Rosie didn't want to say. It was the first time she wasn't willing to tell me something, and it made me feel bad that she was keeping secrets from me. I asked her what about the blood oath we'd made to be best friends forever and to tell each other everything. She got some tears in her eyes and hugged me and said she was sorry. Then she told me the reason she didn't want to talk to anybody before she met me was because of some bad things Bella had made her do when she was little.

I wanted to know what it was. What bad things?

She said it was bad things that some men liked to do with little girls. She said I didn't need to know about all that, but I should take it from her that it wasn't very nice. Not nice at all. She said Bella made her do those things in order to get money from the men. She said at first it wasn't so bad because all she had to do was lie still and think about other things inside of her head while the men laid on top of her and did things to her. But one night, she said a big smelly fat guy was on top of her and he went on for a long time and it was hurting her, so she started to cry and when he scolded her and put his hand over her mouth to try to make her stop crying, and she couldn't breathe so she bit his hand and started screaming and kept on screaming until Bella came running in with a knife and chased the man away. After that, she refused to let the men do things to her anymore, and she decided from then on not to talk either, not even to Bella. She just stayed inside of her own head most of the time and tried not to think about anything at all. She said I was the first person she had ever talked to since that day. She said it was having me as a friend that made her want to think about things again, and maybe try to learn how to be happy sometimes too. I hugged her and we both cried for a while, and it made me really proud that for the first time in my life, I had actually done something to help another person.

After a while, it got dark and Bella still hadn't come back from town. Jobe said it was going to get cold and we should all get under the blankets to stay warm. Rosie thought that would be okay, so that's what we did. It's night now and me and Rosie are hugging together under the blanket in order to stay warm. Jobe is under the blanket with us, but so far he's keeping his promise not to touch me. I like this arrangement much better because now Rosie gets to sleep with me instead of with Bella. If Jobe tries anything, she'll be here to protect me.

Jobe 8

Jobe wakes up in the night feeling cold. He turns over and accidentally touches Chrissy with his knees. He stops and holds his breath, Did she feel that? Is she going to wake up and be mad.

He's feeling irritated that the two girls get to hug together all night while he, the male who is in charge, has to be all by himself. It would be nice to be hugging together with Chrissy under the blanket. She's so pretty, and she probably has a really pretty body under that weird long blue dress that she won't take off, not even for sleeping. He tries to imagine what she would look like without that blue dress on. That thought gives him a funny feeling down in his boy part, and he reaches down inside his pants to touch it. But then he quickly pulls his hand away. Why is he having such unGodly thoughts? Mother would have punished him for having such thoughts. He must not allow lust to creep into his heart lest the Devil catch him in His web. Like it says in the Bible, even Jesus got tempted by the Devil when he got led into the Spirit of the Wilderness, but he didn't get fooled by the voice of the Devil. Instead, he heard the words of God.

Jobe will be like that and not listen to the words of the Devil. He will not allow himself to be tempted. He's supposed to be the protector of these girls, and nothing else. He's about seventeen years old, almost completely grown up, so now that Bella is gone, he should quit thinking bad thoughts and be the responsible adult.

But he wonders again what will happen if Bella doesn't come back? Can he really take care of Chrissy and Rosie all by himself?

Jobe turns onto his back and looks up at the unbelievably amazing amount of stars that are up there in the dark desert sky. Heaven is somewhere up in those stars. Is that where Mother is now? And what happened to her body after her soul flew off to Heaven? Did they take her away to bury her in that big cemetery that he once walked by? That cemetery was up there in the hills where the rich people live. But maybe it was only for Mormon people. Rich Mormon people. He tries to remember if he ever saw another cemetery anywhere in Salt Lake City, but can't remember seeing any.

Jobe wakes up. He thinks maybe he heard something. He sits up. It sounds like maybe it's a car approaching. Is it Bella coming back?

He pushes aside the blanket and stands up. The sun is just coming up over the red cliffs in the distant. He waits, his hands in his pockets because of the early morning chill, watching the dirt road for any sign of a car coming.

Both of the girls crawl out from under the blanket and come to stand next to him. Nobody says anything until Chrissy points and says, "There."

Sure enough, she's right. There's a cloud of dust coming closer. It has to mean a car is coming on the dirt road.

Jobe can't see the car clearly yet, and for a moment, he worries that it might not be Bella's car. What if it's the police? If it is, would it mean that Bella told the police where she left us?

When the car gets closer, Jobe recognizes it: it's the same old faded gray car that Bella stole from that Walmart parking lot.

Bella pulls up and stops, allowing the following cloud off dust to finally catch up. It rains down around them and Jobe holds his breath to try to keep from breathing it in.

Bella hops out of the car and waves to them.

She seems cheerful, and Jobe wonders why. Did something happen in town? Is it good news? Maybe the police have given up and stopped looking for him.

Bella reaches into the back seat and takes out a couple of plastic bags that say "Albertsons" on them. It means Bella didn't go back to that Walmart store; instead, she went to another grocery store. Those bags must contain food.

The two girls quickly come forward, and Bella is still smiling as she hands out a hot dog and a slice of white bread to everybody. Then she says she needs to talk to Jobe. She gives the girls a bag of potato chips to take to their play spot over behind the spiky plant. She tells them to take a blanket to put around themselves to stay warm.

Bella winks at Jobe and pulls him around behind the car. Jobe isn't sure why she winked at him like that. Does she have some kind of secret?

Bella opens the car's trunk and takes out an old beat-up automobile license plate. She hands it to Jobe. "Here, hold this while I get the tools to put it on."

Jobe takes the license plate, wondering what Bella is up to now.

Bella takes a new-looking screwdriver and a pair of pliers out of the trunk and squats down and begins to remove the car's rear plate.

Jobe asks, "What happened in town? What did you find out?"

"Not good, says Bella without looking at him. Turns out the girl's last name is Barlow. Christine Barlow. She's from a polygamist community near Saint George."

"A polygamist community? What's a polygamist?"

"You don't know about them? It's some kind of weird religion. A bunch of old-time religious nuts that hide out in their own little town out in the middle of nowhere. The men get it set up to have more than one wife and they make their wives dress up in those weird clothes. Long dresses, like old time pioneers. But who the girl is isn't what's important. The important thing is everybody's out lookin' for her. They've brought in a lot more cops too, some of them from as far away as Salt Lake. Even some of the regular people who live in Saint George are all out lookin' for the girl, all of 'em out beatin' the bushes up in the hills."

Jobe squats down next to her and touches her arm to get her attention. "We've got to take her back to that Walmart store, Bella. Right now!"

Bella shakes her head. "No way. Too late for that now. They've got roadblocks all over the place. Goin' through 'em scared the shit outta me. Thought they might recognize this car, or have the license plate number writ down. But they didn't. Like I figured, they're looking for you, not me. They lookin' for a male. But that's why I didn't come back last night. Had to stay in town and look for new license plates after it got dark. Swiped these plates off an old car up on blocks. Arizona plates." She turns to look at Jobe. "Guess why I wanted Arizona plates?"

Jobe can see what she's up to. "You think we should go to Arizona."

"Right you are, Jobey old boy. We got to head south. Gotta get outta this area, and fast."

"But what about Chrissy? If we can't take her back to that town, couldn't we take her home."

"Too dangerous. We'll take her with us. Just for a while. She seems happy enough hangin' out with Rosie, doesn't she?"

"Well, yes, but—"

"Well, that settles it then. Let's get a few things taken care of and hit the road before they start lookin' out this far from that town."

Jobe stays next to Bella, watching her change the car's plates. It scares him to think the police are looking for him. He tries to imagine a whole bunch of police setting up roadblocks to try to catch him. Maybe Bella is right about it being too dangerous to take Chrissy back right now. He has to admit he wouldn't be unhappy if Chrissy was going to have to stay with them for a little while longer. He really does like sleeping next to her, being her protector. And besides, she doesn't seem to mind being here where she can play with Rosie. Of course, he knows they'll have to take Chrissy back to her family sooner or later. As soon as the excitement of her disappearance dies down back there in town and they quit looking for her.

Bella finishes changing the car's license plates and calls the girls over.

Chrissy and Rosie come, and they stand close together, holding hands.

Bella says, "Come over here, Chrissy."

Chrissy holds back, still clinging to Rosie's hand.

Bella laughs. "Come on, girl. I'm not gonna hurt ya. I've got a special surprise for you." She reaches into the trunk of the car and pulls out a plastic bag. She holds it up. "Guess what's in here."

Chrissy still wants to hold back, but Rosie pushes her forward.

Bella takes a colorful box out of the bag and shows it to Chrissy.

Jobe can see what it says on the box: "Permanent hair color - Medium Brown." He immediately understands what Bella is going to do: she's going to change Chrissy's hair color from red to brown.

Bella grins at Chrissy. "We're going to do somethin' fun, Chrissy. Somethin' different. You'll like it."

Chrissy pulls back and looks at the ground, "I don't want to, Bella. I . . . I really like my red hair."

"But it will be fun, Chrissy. You can become a completely different person. Wouldn't you like to try being a different person, just for a little while?"

Chrissy shakes her head, still looking down at the ground.

Jobe says, "Well, if she doesn't want to, Bella. I mean—"

Bella holds up one hand. "We don't have any choice, Jobe. Stay out of this."

She turns back to Chrissy and takes ahold of both of her shoulders. "Listen to me, Chrissy. Somethin's happened. I only wanted you to come with us for a while so my Rosie would have a friend. She was getting real sad. And you must have noticed how thin she is. She wouldn't eat or nothin'. But now she's happy 'cause you're here with her. And she's eatin' again. You can see that for yourself. She needs you. But the people back in town wouldn't understand that. They thought we weren't going to let you go back home ever, so they called the cops. It's too bad, but now we have to wait until things calm down before you can go back home. Do you understand?"

Chrissy doesn't respond. She still won't look at Bella.

"The problem is, Chrissy, we're all in trouble now. Even Rosie here could be in trouble. I know it's my fault. I just wanted a friend for Rosie because I was so worried about her, but now I've gone and got Jobe and Rosie in trouble too. If they catch us before we can return you to your home, do you know what'll happen? They'll lock Jobe up in jail. And do you have any idea what they'll do to Rosie? They'll lock her away in one of those terrible old institutions. Forever. She'll die in there, Chrissy. I know it, and you know it."

Bella brings Rosie over and pushes the two girls together.

Chrissy puts her head down on Rosie's shoulder and begins to cry. Rosie strokes Chrissy's hair. That tells Jobe that maybe Bella is right: Rosie must really need to have Chrissy with her. She's always touching her and hugging her and holding onto her hand.

Then, Rosie seems to whisper something in Chrissy's ear. It could have been the word, "Please," but more likely, because Rosie doesn't talk, it must have just been a non-word pleading whisper of some kind. Whatever it was, it seems to have made Chrissy change her mind. She stands still, allowing Bella to do whatever she wants to her hair.

Bella uses a new-looking pair of scissors to quickly cut off most of Chrissy's hair.

Jobe can't take his eyes off of all that nice red hair falling and falling through the air to end up just lying there in the dirt. As soon as Bella puts a white towel around Chrissy's shoulders and starts dying her hair, Jobe quickly hurries to pick up as much of Chrissy's red hair as he can. He stuffs it into his pocket.

He notices Rosie looking at him with a strange sort of smile on her face. Jobe is pretty sure his face is turning red, but he doesn't care. He'll hold onto Chrissy's nice red hair to remind him forever of what Chrissy looked like the first time he saw her in that Walmart store.

As soon as Bella is finished dying Chrissy's hair, she tells Chrissy to take off her clothes. Chrissy doesn't want to do that in front of Jobe, so Bella leads her behind the car and tells Jobe to look away.

Jobe does turn away, but he can't help peeking, just for a moment, and after Chrissy's nice blue dress falls to the ground, Jobe gets a glimpse of Chrissy wearing only underwear. He turns away again, but that one quick glimpse showed him that Chrissy is even more beautiful than he had been imagining. That blue dress had been hiding her nice thin body.

Bella leads Chrissy back out from behind the car, and Jobe can't believe his eyes: Bella has turned Chrissy into a boy! She's got Chrissy dressed up in baggy brown pants and a mostly-brown plaid shirt. With her short brown hair, Chrissy could easily be mistaken for a cute boy. That must be what Bella is trying to do, make it so nobody will recognize Chrissy.

Chrissy runs to Rosie and cries on her shoulder. Rosie puts her arms around her and seems to be whispering something into her ear. Is Rosie talking to her? He's never heard Rosie say a word, but she does seems to be able to communicate with Chrissy in some way.

Bella leads Jobe away. "Give 'em a little time, Jobe. Chrissy'll come around. Rosie'll bring her around. You wait and see. What Rosie wants, Rosie gets. Then, after I get a few things taken care of, we'll hit the road. I know a place down in Arizona where we can hide out until all this blows over."

"And then we'll take Chrissy back to her home?" says Jobe. "You promise?"

"Sure we will," says Bella patting him on the shoulder. "Sure we will."

Bella tells the girls to walk around in the sun until Chrissy's dyed hair dries. Then, she gets into the car to listen to the radio.

Jobe doesn't know what to do with himself, so he wanders around, picking up pretty pebbles. Some of them are sort of pinkish, and a bunch of them are either pure white or pure black. Jobe has never seen so many different kinds of rocks.

He looks back at their campsite. The two girls are walking around together, and to Jobe, it again looks like they're having a conversation. But Rosie can't talk. It means for sure they've figured out some way of communicating with each other.

And Bella is still in the car. Why does she like to sit in the car listening to the radio all the time? He decides he'd better stay a little closer to make sure Bella doesn't try to drive away again.

Suddenly, Bella jumps out of the car and yells at the girls to come.

Jobe says, "What's wrong? Did something happen?"

"They just arrested somebody for Chrissy's kidnapping."

Jobe can't believe it. Would the police actually make that kind of mistake? "Who was it? Who did they arrest?"

"Some homeless guy. The cops grabbed him when he tried to pick up the ransom money."

"Ransom money? What's ransom money? But wait, that's good, isn't it? If they arrested somebody else, they won't be looking for us."

Bella looks both angry and worried. "No, it's not good, Jobe. Not good at all."

"Why not?"

She looks past Jobe and yells at the girls to hurry up and get in the car.

Rosie comes, leading Chrissy by the hand.

Jobe says, "I don't understand, Bella. Why is it bad that they arrested somebody?"

Bella grabs the front of Jobe's sweatshirt and jerks him close. "Shut your face, Jobe, and get the girls into the car. We got to go. Right now!"

Rosie jumps into the back seat of the car and pulls Chrissy in with her.

As soon as Jobe is in the front seat, Bella starts the car and takes off fast.

As they roar down the long dirt road, Jobe is trying to figure out why Bella got so upset that some homeless guy got arrested trying to pick up some ransom money. And why won't Bella talk about it? Did she have something to do with it?

When Bella gets them back out to the highway, she speeds up. Jobe is pretty sure she must be heading for Arizona, and he knows it's a waste of time to try to talk her out it. Besides, maybe going to a new place is better. Bella promised Chrissy some fun adventures, and it hasn't been much of an adventure to just be sitting out in the desert all the time with nothing to do. Jobe knows he's never been to Arizona, because he's never been out of Salt Lake City. Maybe Chrissy has never been to Arizona either.

Bella drives for a long time, but the sun is still fairly high in the sky when she turns off the highway onto another dirt road, this one even bumpier than the last one. Although there are some hills in the distance, to Jobe, it looks like they're still in a desert kind of place, and there are even more cactus plants than there were in the last place.

After driving for quite a while on the bumpy road, Bella makes a sharp turn and drives the car right into some tall bushes.

Jobe doesn't understand why she's using the car to smash right through the bushes, flattening them like she doesn't even care. He turns to look at the girls in the back seat, and they're hugged together. They look scared. Jobe wishes he could reassure them, but who knows what Bella is up to.

When Bella finally stops, they're completely surrounded by bushes. Jobe now understands why she drove into those bushes so fast: she must be trying to hide the car from anybody who might drive past on that bumpy dirt road.

Bella turns off the car and says, "Well, here we are kids. This is my secret spot. You're gonna like it. Come on, follow me."

She gets out of the car and leads them through the bushes.

After a short walk, they come out of the bushes, and Jobe is surprised to see a little stream flowing by. How can there be flowing water out here in this kind of dry desert place?

Bella takes Chrissy's arm and points at the stream. "Well, Chrissy, what ya think of my secret place? I discovered this place a long time ago, back when I was on the lam. Even though this is Arizona desert, this little stream runs nice and clean this time of year. In the springtime, the water comes down from the mountains. From snow meltin' up there I think. The water disappears into the sand not far from here, and far as I know, nobody else even knows it's here."

Chrissy looks at the water, but she doesn't say anything, and Rosie seems to hardly notice the water. She's looking off toward some tall mountains that rise like dark gray shadows in the distance.

"Hey," says Bella, "now that we got water, how about we all take a bath and wash out our clothes? We're all probably gettin' a bit stinky, eh?" She pulls Chrissy toward the water. "Come on. It'll be fun."

Chrissy pulls her arm loose and goes back to Rosie. She takes Rosie's hand, and they both just stand there, looking down at the ground.

Jobe wonders why Bella is so insistent that they should all take a bath in the river. Does she mean for them to take all their clothes off? Jobe knows he wouldn't mind seeing Chrissy and Rosie naked, but it doesn't look like Bella is going to be able to convince them to do it.

But Bella won't take no for an answer. She goes to the girls and herds them to the river.

Jobe follows, and when they all get to the stream, he discovers it's mostly only a few inches deep, even out in the middle.

Bella doesn't hesitate. She strips off all of her clothes and wades right in. She begins to rinse out her clothes, not even trying to hide her nakedness. Jobe thinks she doesn't look half bad without her old gray jacket and shirt on, but she's fatter than he first thought, and her boobs hang down in front.

For the first time, Jobe realizes that she might be about as old as his own mother. But Mother was much thinner. Whenever Mother asked him to come and scrub her back when she was in the bathtub, he could feel her bones right through the washcloth. That memory again makes him wonder what the authorities did with her body. He feels a little pang of guilt about not being able to take care of Mother's body, and he again wonders if when this is all over, he should go back to Salt Lake City and try to find out where they buried her.

Bella finds a deeper place in the water, up against a big boulder. She sinks down up to her chest and yells: "Get in here, Jobe. It feels great."

Jobe feels like he probably does need to get clean. He can't even remember the last time he had a bath. Besides, it's warm, and it might be fun to get wet, especially if everybody else is willing to take all of their clothes off too. If he takes his clothes off first, maybe Chrissy and Rosie will do it too.

He makes sure his Bible is safely placed on top of a flat rock, and then he takes off his clothes. He wades into the water rinses them ou. Then he drapes them over some big rocks to dry and goes to settle into the deeper water next to Bella. He leans back against the warm boulder and watches Chrissy and Rosie to see what they are going to do.

Chrissy seems sort of embarrassed, and Jobe knows it must be because she saw him naked as he went into the water. He wonders if she's ever seen a naked boy before. Probably not. And he also assumes no male has ever seen her naked either.

That thought gives him a stir of excitement, but he tries to push it away. After all, Mother always said the human body had been created by God, so there was no reason to hide it away all the time. He hopes Chrissy believes that too, and he keeps his eyes on her. If she's going to take her clothes off, he doesn't want to miss a single second of it.

Bella chuckles. Is she laughing at him?

Bella yells, "Hurry up and get undressed, girls. Jobe can't wait to see you without your clothes on. Can you, Jobe?"

Jobe shrugs. "They don't have to if they don't want to."

Bella laughs again. "But they do have to. They need to be clean for where we're goin' next. And besides, we're all the same in God's eyes, right?"

Jobe mumbles, "I guess so."

Bella yells at the girls again. "Come on now. Get in the water or I'll have to come over there and make you do it. Rosie, help your new friend undress. You two need to get in this water and wash yourself up. Wash your clothes and then wash yourselves up too, especially between your legs." She edges closer to Jobe and nudges him with her elbow. "Isn't that right, Jobe?"

Jobe just keeps his eyes on Rosie and Chrissy. Will they do it?

Bella yells at Rosie to get a move on, and that seems to wake her up. She quickly removes all of her clothes, even her underwear.

Jobe is shocked to see how very thin she is. Without her clothes on, she looks almost as thin as Mother was. And she has enough dark hair down there between her legs to make Jobe suspect she may be older than he thought.

Rosie then turns to Chrissy and begins to unbutton her shirt.

Jobe holds his breath.

Chrissy pushes Rosie's hand away and glances toward Jobe.

But then, Rosie puts her face up close to Chrissy's ear. Did she say something to Chrissy? Whatever if was that went on between them, it makes Chrissy start to remove her own clothes. When she gets everything off except her white underwear, she follows Rosie who is already wading out into the middle of the stream.

"Uh uh," calls Bella. "Take everything off. I want you clean as a whistle before we go to where we're goin'."

Rosie nods to Chrissy, and that one little nod seems to be all it takes to get Chrissy to agree. She takes off her bra and panties, dips them into the water several times, and then hangs them on a bush. Then she quickly wades back out into the middle of the steam to join Rosie who is busy rinsing out her clothes.

Jobe notices that Chrissy also has a bit of fine red hair down there between her legs, but not near as much as Rosie. It must mean she's not as old as Rosie. But she does have breasts, sort of. They are just starting to get rounded looking. But even if her breasts are not very big, to Jobe, they are perfect. In fact, she's perfect in every way.

Rosie finishes rinsing out her clothes and hangs them on a bush to dry.

Then she comes back and splashes Chrissy with water. Chrissy does the same thing back to her, and that starts them both kicking and throwing water at each other, laughing and squealing.

Jobe can't take his eyes off of Chrissy. She's even more beautiful without any clothes on. He realizes that long blue dress she was wearing when they first picked her up had all but completely disguised her figure, and even that glimpse he got of her in her underwear when she was changing her clothes wasn't enough to fully reveal how really perfect her body is.

Jobe is still focusing on Chrissy's beauty when he feels Bella reach down under the water to grab onto his private boy part.

He pushes her hand away. "Quit that, Bella."

But she grabs right back on again and whispers into his ear, "She's really fine, isn't she? I hope you know I got her just for you."

Jobe tries to ignore what she's doing to him down under the water; he only wants to keep his eyes on Chrissy and Rosie as they frolic together over in the shallow water.

But soon Bella is moving her hand faster and whispering in his ear. "You like this don't you, Jobe?"

Jobe tries to keep his focus on Chrissy. He only wants to think about how beautiful and precious she is, but what Bella is doing under the water is making it hard not to think about how nice it is to get to sleep next to Chrissy at night, and how nice it would be if he could sleep closer to her, and maybe even touch her when they're under the blanket together. What if she'd be willing to take off her clothes when they're in bed together? What would that be like?

"Now, Jobe, I want you to remember something," whispers Bella. "I got Chrissy just for you. And it was me that made her sleep with you. It means you're only supposed to be doing her, not Rosie. Got it?"

Jobe can only nod. He can feel something very strong happening to him down there under the water as he watches Chrissy playing naked out there with Rosie. There's something magical about how she looks with the water glistening on her skin as it runs off of her cute little breasts and trickles down between her legs.

All of a sudden, the same thing happens to him as happens when he's alone in bed and using his own hand to do this.

Bella seems to know what happened: she gradually slows the movement of her hand and then stops. She whispers, "You liked that, didn't you, Jobe?"

Jobe doesn't dare move, but he has to admit it was a very powerful feeling to have someone else do that to him instead of having to do it himself. And it was especially nice to have it happen when he was watching Chrissy play in the water, completely naked.

"You can have anything you want, Jobe. You just keep on doing Chrissy, and do me from time to time too. Other than that, you got no rules. Except one: you hafta keep that thing of yours outta Rosie. You got that?"

Jobe nods. Bella must think he did something to Chrissy that night when they were camped out in that other place. He has to admit he thought about it, but even though they were together under the same blanket back then, they were both still wearing clothes. Even if Chrissy didn't have any clothes on, like now, he isn't sure he'd dare try anything, at least not without her permission.

But now, it's like Bella is giving him permission. She's saying it would be okay to do whatever he wants to Chrissy at night under the blanket. But Jobe knows it wouldn't be right, not unless Chrissy wanted to do it too. That gets Jobe wondering if maybe Chrissy *would* like him to do something to her. The best thing would be to just ask her. He decides that the next time they're under a blanket together at night, he'll ask her. If that's what she wants, then it's okay with him too. It wouldn't be a sin against God if they both agree to do it.

He hears Bella chuckle again and he feels her squeeze his private boy part. "Ah ha, that got ya going again, didn't it? We'll come on, let's go for a little walk together upstream and get it on." She stands up and reaches for his hand.

Jobe hesitates, glancing back toward the girls. It's Chrissy he wants, not Bella, but he has to admit that what Bella did to him under the water with her hand really felt good, especially because she did it while he was looking at Chrissy's beautiful naked body. He looks back at Bella. Her naked body is not near as nice as Chrissy's, but it's not really all that bad, so, why shouldn't he go with her? He's a young guy, and isn't a young guy supposed to learn what it's like doing it with girls, even if the girl is a lot older than he is?

He allows Bella to help him to his feet, and she leads him out of the water toward some thick bushes.

He looks back at the girls, but they're so busy playing, they don't even seem to notice him leaving with Bella.

But then Jobe hesitates. What he's about to do with Bella really might be a sin. That night in the homeless park, he only *allowed* Bella to do something to him. He didn't know what she was going to do and he didn't actually participate except to just lie there and let it happen. But now, following Bella off into the bushes specifically to do the same thing again, seems somehow different.

"Come on, boy. Quit dawdlin'. I'm ready for ya. Now!" She pulls him along even faster.

Jobe allows himself to be led deeper into the bushes, but he has doubts. Why is he even going along with this? Is the memory of what they did under the blanket that night in the park so strong he can't resist doing it again? He has to admit, he hasn't forgotten how good that felt, but the question remains, would doing it again be right? Doing it once was a learning experience, but doing it again might be an actual sin. He wishes Mother was still alive to guide him.

But then, he remembers something from the Bible: *No temptation has overtaken you that is not common to man. God is faithful, and he will not let you be tempted beyond your ability, but with the temptation he will also provide the way of escape, that you may be able to endure it.* Jobe is not exactly sure what that means, but it seems to have something to do with learning. It says God won't let him be tempted beyond his ability, and maybe it also says he should endure it and learn from it. So that's what he will do; he won't seek it, he will only endure it and learn from the experience.

Bella finds a little patch of sand surrounded by bushes. She flops down on it and pulls him down on top of herself.

Jobe waits for God to tell him what to do. Surely God won't let him be tempted beyond his ability to resist.

"Well, are ya gonna do me or not?"

Jobe thinks he has a pretty good idea of what he's supposed to do, but being the one on top seems somehow different. Maybe he shouldn't be doing this at all.

Bella says, "Oh, for Christ's sake," and she pushes him over onto his back. She hops on top of him and does the moving part, moving very fast.

Jobe now has to decide what enduring means. God's words said he should be able to endure it, but does that mean he should do the same thing he did that night in the homeless park, just lie still and let her do it all. If he doesn't really participate in any way except to lie still, it can't be a sin. God took Mother away for a reason. It had to be to put him on a path of learning. This must be a necessary part of that learning. After all, Mother did a lot of this kind of thing with the men she was with, and she still had God on her side. Jobe wasn't very old the first time he peeked into Mother's bedroom to find out what she was doing with those men. Mother was the one on the bottom, letting the men do this kind of thing to her. And now Jobe is also on the bottom, letting the same thing happen to him. Jobe is not sure what that means, but he's pretty sure it's something a seventeen-year-old boy needs to learn about. It has to be part of what it means to be out in the world, part of what it means to be a man. He lies very still and lets Bella do whatever she wants. He should try to feel exactly what is going on down there and learn from it. It feels very good, but as long as he doesn't move very much, it means he's not participating—he's only learning.

And just like before, as soon as the usual thing happens, Bella rolls off of him and stands up. She seems mad at him, but she doesn't say anything. She just heads back to the stream.

Jobe follows, and when they get, Jobe can see that the girls are dressed and have gone back to playing their game of sitting in the dirt drawing pictures with sticks.

Bella nods at them. "Looks like the girls have had enough of the water. I guess we'd better get 'em somethin' to eat." She starts to put her clothes on and Jobe does the same, hurrying to get completely dressed before the girls might turn and see them still naked.

After they are dressed and Jobe has retrieved his Bible, Bella calls to the girls to come sit around a circle of rocks. Jobe wonders who made the circle of rocks. They seem to have been arranged that way a long time ago.

When Bella hands out the same old hot dogs and plain white bread, Jobe is about to ask why hot dogs are the only thing Bella ever gets for them to eat, but the girls don't seem to mind, so he decides to keep his mouth shut.

By the time the eating part is over, the sun has already gone down. But it's still warm. Jobe wonders why it is so much warmer in Arizona than it was back in Salt Lake City. Maybe it's because it's all desert here, and there are no snow-capped mountains.

Bella stretches her legs out in front of herself and yawns. "Well, Chrissy, isn't this a neat place? Like I said before, I don't think anybody but me knows about it."

Jobe notices that Chrissy seems interested in what Bella is saying, but Rosie has gone back to staring off into the distance like she used to.

Bella doesn't seem to care if anybody is listening or not. She goes on: "Nobody that is, 'cept the wild burros. Ever seen a wild burro, Chrissy?"

Chrissy shakes her head.

"Well, a long time ago, this was a big gold mining area. Prospectors all over the place. But when the gold ran out, those old prospectors just let their burros go, figurin' they'd have to make it on their own or else just go somewhere and die. Well, guess what happened, Chrissy? Those burros did just fine out here, thank you. They can eat anything, even cactus. Wait until it starts to get dark. They'll come sneakin' in here to get themselves a drink. I bet you'd like to see that, wouldn't you, Chrissy?"

Chrissy smiles and nods.

"Well, they'll probably show up tonight. But now, we'd better all get some sleep. Big day tomorrow. Tomorrow, we go to the big city. You're gonna like it there, Chrissy. Lots of fun things to do there."

Chrissy surprises Jobe by telling Bella she wants to sleep with Rosie. But Bella won't allow it. She says she has to sleep with Jobe in case any bad critters come in the night. That way, Jobe will be there to protect her.

Under the blanket with Chrissy, Jobe can't seem to go to sleep no matter how hard he tries. He can't stop thinking about how nice Chrissy looked playing naked in the water.

And he can't stop thinking about what it felt like letting Bella do that thing to him with her hand under the water. And he especially can't stop thinking about how Bella she said it would be okay if he and Chrissy did whatever they wanted to at night when they are under the blanket.

And as the night goes on and Chrissy is right there next to him, Jobe can't stop wondering if maybe Chrissy would like doing that kind of thing as much as Bella seems to like it. Maybe all girls really do want boys to do that kind of thing to them, just like Bella does.

He turns toward Chrissy and lets his hand rest lightly on top of her hip. She doesn't move, even though Jobe is almost sure she woke up, so he snuggles up close to her and lets his arm go around the front of her stomach. He whispers, "Wasn't that fun to be naked in the water today?"

Chrissy doesn't answer, but now he's sure she really is awake. And she isn't pushing his arm away, so he pulls her even closer, feeling his boy part inside of his pants push up against her bottom. "Maybe we should take our clothes off again like that. Would you like that?"

Chrissy grabs his wrist and pushes his arm away. Then she moves away from him, almost out from under the blanket.

That tells Jobe Chrissy doesn't want to do anything like that with him. Maybe all girls are not like Bella; maybe some girls don't want it as much as boys do.

He turns away from Chrissy and lies very still until he's sure she's gone back to sleep. Than he carefully reaches down and begins to stroke his own boy part. Things are happening down there, and it's beginning to feel very good.

But then he stops. Why is he doing that? Is Bella turning him into the same kind of person as she is? Even worse, she might be trying to turn him into the kind of men that came to visit Mother. Jobe never liked those men, and now he feels ashamed that he might have been tempted to become like them. He's pretty sure Chrissy likes him, but that doesn't mean she wants him to do that kind of thing to her. She's too pure and innocent for that. But she does seem to want him to be the man in her life. At least she wants him to protect her. She didn't seem to mind when he put his hand on her hip, but then he went too far, and now he's spoiled his chance to even do that. It makes him want to cry. He grabs his Bible and holds it tight against his chest. He has to push the bad thoughts away, once and for all. Such thoughts might very well be the work of the Devil. The Devil could be using Bella to lure him into sin. God sent him out into the world to learn about life, not to become the kind of person who can be driven by lust. As it says in the Bible, *Abstain from fleshly lusts, which war against the soul.* How could he have forgotten the many warnings Mother gave him about lust? He especially remembers one thing she would often quote from the Bible: *You can fall into temptation and a snare, and into many foolish and hurtful lusts, which drown men in destruction and perdition.*

Jobe knows he has to stop the Devil from luring him onto sin. He has to drive the Devil out, and he knows exactly how to do that. You do it with pain. Mother said the Devil is afraid of pain, and she often gave him pain to make sure the Devil didn't get into him.

He flips over onto his back and begins to pinch the bottom parts of his ears, just like he did that night back in that homeless park in Salt Lake City. He pinches them even harder this time, doing it so hard he can barely keep himself from crying out. But Jobe knows it's the good kind of hurting because he's doing it exactly like Mother would do if she was here. Whenever she realized he'd been having bad thoughts while he was locked in his nice safe closet, she'd drag him out and hurt him. He squeezes his ears harder and harder, accepting the pain, wanting it. He keeps on making his ears hurt until finally it comes, the kind of pain that keeps you from feeling anything else, the kind of pain that keeps you from thinking about anything else. His fingers must have somehow become as strong as Mother's, as if his hands had become her hands, as if she's right there with him right now, hurting him in order to help him, hurting him to drive the Devil out of him.

As the pain becomes part of him, Jobe feels much calmer. The pain has given him back his self control.

He stops pinching his ears and looks up at the zillions of stars in the sky. He will focus on those stars up there in Heaven and not even think about touching Chrissy, and he will not touch himself. He will stay awake and pray all night and focus on only being Chrissy's protector.

As the night goes on, he lies awake, listening to the gentle wind whisper through the bushes.

But then he hears a splashing sound. Something is out in water. He quickly sits up, and then Chrissy sits up too.

"What's the matter?" she asks.

"There's something out there," he whispers. "In the water. Something big."

Chrissy grabs his arm. "An animal?"

Jobe put his arm around her, focusing on being her protector and nothing else. "I don't know what it is. It seems big."

Chrissy clings to him, and Jobe likes that very much. She may not want him to hold her when they're under the blanket, but she understands that if they are in danger, he's the man and it's his job to protect her.

As he listens to the splashing sounds, Jobe decides it might be more than one of whatever is out there in the water. He clings to Chrissy, trying to be the brave man, the protector, but unsure of what he'll do if it is a really is a group of dangerous animals.

Chrissy whispers, "Do something, Jobe. I'm scared."

Yes, Jobe knows she's right: he should do something. Even though this is his first time out of the city, and he has no idea of what kind of dangerous animals might live out here in the desert, it's his responsibility as the male to be brave and do something. He whispers, "Bella. Are you awake?"

Bella's voice comes out of the darkness. "Whatta ya want now? We're tryin' to get some sleep over here."

"There's something out there, Bella. In the water. Wild animals. Big ones, I think."

Bella laughs. "Aw, it's nuthin. Didn't I tell ya they'd come? It's them wild burros. They come in the night to get a drink. Yell at 'em. They'll go away."

"Yell at them? But what if they charge at us?"

Bella laughs again. Then she yells real loud, "Hey, you burros! Git the hell out of here!"

There is the sound of pounding hoofs running away. Jobe is surprised at how many of them there were.

Bella says, "Now get to sleep. All of you. We got a big day tomorrow."

Jobe lies back down, and he's glad when Chrissy lies back down closer to him, and she has her hand on his arm. He doesn't move a muscle, afraid she might move away.

But she doesn't, and after a while, he can tell by her steady breathing that she's gone back to sleep. Good. He'll stay awake for the rest of the night to make sure no more wild animals come. From the slight lightening of the sky behind the big hills in the distance, it looks like it's almost morning anyhow. Until the sun comes up, he will lie very still and be her protector.

It isn't long before he hears Bella up and moving around. Apparently, she can't sleep either.

She comes to Jobe and shakes his shoulder. "Come with me, Jobe. I had a sexy dream, and I'm hotter than a Saturday night bar bitch."

"But, Bella. It's not even light yet."

"Don't matter. When I'm ready, I'm ready. Let's go."

Jobe feels Chrissy stir. "What's going on? Are we getting up?"

"Just me and Jobe," says Bella. "Go back to sleep. Me and Jobe are gonna go have a pow-wow."

Jobe grabs his Bible and follows Bella as she leads him back into the thick bushes. He assumes she's heading for that same sandy spot she took him to before. But this time, Jobe is not sure he wants to do that kind of thing with Bella anymore. He holds his Bible close to his chest to give him the strength to resist her.

When Bella reaches that same place as the day before, she flops down on her back and pulls her pants down. "Git to it, boy. That damn dream got me so ready, I couldn't get back to sleep. So let me have it."

Jobe looks down at her girl part. He's never looked at it this close before, and although it is interesting to see what that part looks like on a grownup woman, it doesn't seem very pretty, not near as pretty as that part of Chrissy looked when she was out there in the little stream with the sunshine making the water sparkle as it ran down between *her* legs.

Jobe decides he doesn't want to do it with Bella anymore. It's time to tell her. "Bella, I don't think I should be doing this."

She sits up. "What the hell? Here I give you free reign at my body and you turn me down? Who do you think ya are, some Goddam movie star? I may be a few years older than you, but you're not such a great prize either, kid."

Jobe sits down next to her. "I'm sorry, Bella. But I've been lying awake all night thinking and praying. I don't want to turn into the kind of person who gets capture by lust." He holds out his Bible to show her. "It says in here that those who live according to the flesh get their minds set on the things of the flesh."

Bella jerks her pants up. "So you're back to the Bible quoting crap again. I should have known you'd go back to that sooner or later, never letting that damn Bible out of your hands and all."

"I'm just saying—"

"What you're sayin' is that I'm like what you just said. That I—how'd you say it?—I've only got my mind on things of the flesh. Well, what about all I done for you? What about me takin' you out of that damn cold Salt Lake City where you were stuck with no home to go to and nobody to take care of ya? And didn't I take care of ya? Didn't I let ya share me and Rosie's blankets? Didn't I let you do anything you wanted to me that first night?"

"But, Bella, it was you that—"

"And what about me givin' you a great adventure like every young man should learn about? What about that?"

Jobe realizes she's right about the learning part: she has been helping him go to new places and learn new things, like God wanted him to. "I'm sorry, Bella. it's just that—"

"And what about me gettin' Chrissy for you? Huh? What about that?"

"Well, yes, I do like sleeping with her and—"

"Ha! I bet that's what this is all about. You're getting your rocks off doin' it to cute little Chrissy, so now you don't need my good old body anymore. Well, maybe I don't need you no more either. Did ya ever think about that? The three of us can do just fine without you taggin' along. Maybe I should leave you out here and move on without ya. How'd you like that, eh?"

Jobe reaches out and touches Bella's arm. "No, Bella, it's not like you said. It's not about Chrissy. It's just that I've been thinking about what I'm doing. I mean, what we're doing. I really do like Chrissy, and I think she likes me too. But taking her away from her mother like that just wasn't right. Her mother must be really worried. I think it's time we should take her back."

Bella stares at him. "So, now you're even gettin' tired of Chrissy. I don't get it. A young guy like you. Ya oughta be happy to get whatever pussy you can get your hands on."

"No, I—"

"Fine, do 'er or don't do 'er, but we can't take her back to Utah. Not yet anyhow. Like I told ya, that place is crawlin' with cops. And let me remind ya, it's you they're lookin' for, not me."

"Well, maybe you could just drop me and her off somewhere. In a town or something. I'll find a way to get her back home."

Bella shakes her head. "Not a chance. Let you two just walk away? After all I done for ya? Just let you walk away with her so you can get what you want from her and leave me hangin'? No way, buster. And what about my Rosie? Did you ever bother to stop to think about her for even a single second? What would Rosie do if she lost the only friend she's ever had? Haven't you noticed how Rosie is starting to come out of her shell? And she's eatin' again too. Gettin' healthy. Take Chrissy away from her? Not on your life, buster. I only care about my Rosie. You can go if you want to, but Chrissy stays with Rosie until I say so."

Jobe thinks about Bella's words. She's right about Rosie starting to come out of her shell, at least when she's with Chrissy. Maybe he is being selfish. Maybe he should let Rosie and Chrissy stay together. It means he can't leave. Who knows what Bella might do to Chrissy if he wasn't there to protect her. "Okay, Bella. I can see that Rosie and Chrissy have become best friends, and I guess that's good for Rosie. And I guess Chrissy likes having a friend too. But isn't there a way we can help keep them together and at least let Chrissy's mother know where she is?"

Bella stands up. "Don't you think I've been thinkin' about that? Just give me a little more time to work it out."

"Well, okay. As long as we really do find a way to get Chrissy back home before too long."

"Right. Right. Don't you worry about it, Jobe. I'll take care of it. Now, let's go back and get the girls fed. They're probably wondering where we ran off to for so long."

As they head back to the camp, Jobe makes up his mind. For now, he'll go along with Bella, but he'll pray and ask God to help him come up with his own plan to get away with Chrissy. He wants her to be happy, and if she's happy staying with Rosie, then that's fine. But sooner or later, she'll want to go back to her mother. When that time comes, he'll be ready to help her do it. Bella and Rosie were on their own before he met them, so they'll be just fine if they end up back on their own again.

Chrissy 8

So much happened today that I hardly know how to tell it all. When Bella came back from town early in the morning, she cut off most of my nice long red hair and dyed it brown. She said she had to do that because some police were looking for me. She said she had only meant to take me out for a ride in her car for a while so Rosie would have a friend, but now she says she can't take me back just yet because the police are looking for me and because if they find us Jobe will get in big trouble, and she said they'd lock Rosie up in a bad place that she'd never get out of. I wouldn't want that to happen, but I don't see why Rosie couldn't just come and stay with me at my house. We've got lots of room, and like I said before, one more kid wouldn't hardly make any difference at all.

Oh, and another thing, Bella made me take off my nice blue dress and put on a pair of brown pants and a brown shirt that was real itchy. I didn't want to do it right there in front of Jobe with only my underwear on, so Bella said I could go around to the other side of the car and Jobe wouldn't look. But I'm pretty sure Jobe did peek when I only had my underwear on.

After Bella cut off my hair and dyed it brown, me and Rosie went for a walk in the sun while my hair dried. Rosie said my new hair and my new clothes looked good on me. She kidded me and said I looked like a completely different person, like a cute boy. Maybe that's so, but I didn't like it that Bella did that to me, and I told Rosie that we had to get away from Bella so we could both go live together at my house. Rosie said she would like that, but we had to play along with Bella and wait for the right moment to make our getaway.

I said I wasn't so sure Bella would ever let us out of her sight long enough for us to get away, but Rosie said not to worry, she'd find a way. She said that now that I looked like a boy, nobody would be looking for a boy so after we got away we could go off together and have lots of great adventures. I thought maybe it would be good to have some adventures with Rosie, but I was still worried about what was going to happen when I got back home. The Prophet makes all the females in the community, even the mothers, keep their hair long, but always braided up at the back of our heads. And he says we all have to wear long dresses that cover up our arms and legs, even after we get married. When I get back home, what will he think about how short my hair is now? Will everybody hate me?

Rosie and me were still walking around talking when all of a sudden, Bella started yelling at us and made us get into the car in a big hurry. She drove away fast, but she wouldn't say where we were going even though Jobe kept on asking her.

I wondered what my new short hair looked like, but Bella had cut it off so short, I couldn't even pull enough of it down to see any of it. Finally, after we got out to a highway, I was able to sit up and look in the car's rear view mirror. It was short and spiky, a lot like my Annie doll's hair, except now it was brown, not red like Annie's. I was sad that my nice long red hair was gone, but it did make me look kind of more interesting. Like Rosie said, it almost made me look like a boy. I decided it also made me look more like the actual teenager I am now, less like a little girl. I don't think I mind that. And Rosie seems to like it a lot too. She keeps on touching my hair and whispering about how cute I look.

Bella drove for a long time, and I was getting real tired of just driving and driving with not much to see out the window. Finally, she turned off onto a bumpy dirt road that looked a lot like the desert place we were at before, but this place had more bushes and some rocky-looking hills not too far away.

She stopped the car in the middle of some bushes. It was right next to a little river, and Bella made us all take off our clothes so we could go into the river and get clean. I didn't want to take my clothes off, especially not with Jobe watching, but Rosie finally convinced me that there was nothing wrong with it, and it would be fun. She was right. We played in the river and got clean and splashed each other. It was about as much fun as anything I've ever done in my whole life. I kept on thinking that nobody in our community probably ever once got to take off their clothes and play in a river, not even the boys.

After that, Bella and Jobe went off into the bushes somewhere together, so Rosie and me got out of the water and dried off and put our clothes back on. A little ways away from the river, we found us a new secret spot behind some bushes and found some sticks so we could go back to drawing our pictures and words in the sand.

I told Rosie that playing in the river had been real fun, but it made me nervous that I had to take off my clothes in front of Jobe because he was a boy and I didn't think us girls were supposed to take off our clothes in front of boys. Rosie said we had to get clean, and it didn't matter if he looked at us. She said looking doesn't cause any harm, what matters is that I should never let him touch my breasts and especially I shouldn't ever let him ever touch down between my legs and do things to me like that bad prophet had done to me. She asked me if Jobe had ever tried to touch me in those places at night under the blanket.

I said no, but I said he does seem to like being close to me at night, but maybe it's only because he gets cold and wants us to be warm.

She said no, it's because he wants to do something bad. She explained that it was something all boys want to do to us girls, and she said I should never let any male do that to me no matter what. She reminded me again about the bad thing the prophet had done to me and the bad things Bella had made her do with men when she was little. She grabbed both of my hands and said I should never let any man do that to me, not even Jobe. She wanted me to promise, so I said I did promise. But she said no, just saying it wasn't enough. We should swear a blood oath on it. I started to put my wrist together with hers, but she said no, this time we had to do a real blood oath. She broke a big sticker off of a cactus and scratched both of our wrists until they started to bleed a little. Then we put our wrists together and swore what we said was the most important blood oath ever: we swore that we would always be best friends and that neither one of us would ever let a male do anything like that to either one of us, not ever.

Well, guess what? Tonight, under the blanket, Jobe did exactly what Rosie had warned me about. He put his arm around me and wanted me to take off my clothes. Luckily, when I pushed him away, he didn't try to do anything else. Then I think I heard him crying, so I think he was sorry he had tried to do that to me.

After that, some wild burros came down from the hills to get a drink from the little stream, and that scared me real bad. But Bella said they wouldn't hurt us, and she scared them away. Then, when it wasn't even light yet, she came took Jobe away somewhere.

Rosie came over real quick and got under the blanket with me and started hugging me. I told her about what Jobe tried to do to me during the night. She said she knew he might try something like that. He's a male and that's what all males want from us girls.

I told her I felt sorry for Jobe, and maybe all he wants to do is be closer to me. He seems so alone.

Rosie got irritated with me for saying that. She said if I ever let Jobe even touch me down there once, he'll want to do more. She said I should never allow him to even touch me because then he'll try to go farther and won't stop. Besides, she said, even if it would feel good, we don't need men at all.

I asked her if it really did feel good. I mean to do that kind of thing with a boy.

She said even if it does feel good at first, it always leads to other things that don't feel good at all. She said she'd show me that we don't need men to do the only part that feels good. She pulled down her pants and pointed to a spot down there between her own legs. She said that when a boy rubs his part against that spot, it's the only thing about it that feels good. Then she said she'd show me. She pulled down my pants and my panties, and then she used her fingers to rub on that spot, and she was right, it really did feel good, in a strange kind of way. It made me feel hot, and all of a sudden, I remembered that I'd had that same kind of hot feeling when the Prophet made me take off my clothes and sit on his lap while he rubbed on me. I think Rosie was rubbing on me in the same place he did. It made me feel hot and kind of dizzy that time too, but that time I was really scared and it hurt. This time, with Rosie doing it to me, I wasn't scared and it didn't hurt at all. Actually, it felt kind of good, so I let her keep doing it to me even though I was getting worried that maybe Jobe and Bella would come back and catch us. She said it would feel even better if we were doing it to each other at the same time. She pushed herself up against me and showed me where to put my fingers on her spot down there. I tried to do what she said, and at first I couldn't do it right, but then she held onto my hand and moved it to show me how to do it right. Then we were both doing it to each other at the same time, and it felt really good and I was only thinking about how it felt, until all of a sudden, something happened that made me sweat. I can't quite explain what it was, but it really did feel good.

After that she turned onto her back and kept on rubbing herself until after a while she made a moaning sound and stopped.

We were both lying there on our backs, both of us panting and sweating, still with our panties down around our ankles, and I knew I had just learned something important about being grown-up.

After that, Rosie started hugging me real tight and she was kissing me on my neck. She said, See there, I told you we didn't need boys.

I could see what she meant, but I couldn't help but wonder if this was the way other people did it. Back home, I never once saw girls sneak off to rub on each other. Or if they did, they kept it secret from me. I wondered if any of my mothers did that to each other. Maybe they did on the nights when Dad was in bed with one of his other wives.

Rosie whispered that when we got away from Bella and Jobe, we could do that to each other anytime we want to, and even though I wasn't sure it was a very normal thing to do, it really did feel good, so maybe, if we did get the chance to do it again, I think I would like that.

Jobe 9

When Jobe and Bella get back to camp, they find Rosie and Chrissy sleeping together under the same blanket. For some reason, that makes Bella mad. She yells at them: "Hey, what the hell are the two of you doing under that blanket together?"

Chrissy quickly sit up and seems about to say something, but then Rosie gets up and starts folding the blankets, so Chrissy gets up to help her.

Bella stands there watching them with her hands on her hips, and that makes Jobe wonder what she's so mad about. Why wouldn't she expect the girls to move under the same blanket after he and Bella were gone; even though the sun is starting to come up, it's still pretty cold.

Bella tells them to get a move on and get into the car. "No time to eat this morning, girls. We'll eat in the car. The sun's comin' up, and we're gonna head for a new place. A place you'll like. Chrissy, are ya ready for a new adventure?"

Chrissy looks at Rosie, and doesn't answer.

That makes Jobe wonder if she's going to start being more like Rosie. Maybe she'll even stop talking.

Jobe asks Bella what kind of adventure, but Bella won't say. She just piles them all into the car and passes out hot dogs and bread. They eat in silence as Bella drives on the bumpy dirt road back out to the highway.

Jobe says, "You said a new place, Bella. Is it in Arizona?"

Bella laughs out loud and smacks the steering wheel with her hand. "You bet it is. And I'm ready for it. Got me a hankering for the big city. Ever been to Phoenix, Jobey old boy?"

Jobe shakes his head. "No, Bella. In fact, this is the first time I've ever even been outside of Salt Lake City."

She glances at him. "No shit? Well, you're in for a real treat then, kid. Phoenix is a hell of a great place, and I know all the best spots. When it's still cold up north, it's the best place to be in the whole damn country. Warm. Even better, the whole town is loaded with suckers. Tourists from up north. Snowbirds they call 'em. Every damn one of 'em with bucks in their pockets." She glances at Rosie in the rear view mirror. "Isn't that right, Rosie? You like Phoenix, don't you?"

Rosie looks out the side window and doesn't respond.

But Chrissy scoots forward and touches Bella's shoulder. "Uh, Bella, it's nice of you to want to take me all the way to Phoenix, but it feels like it's getting a long ways away from my home and—"

"Now don't start that again, Chrissy. For now, until it's safe to go back there, I think the best thing for you is to get out and see somethin' of the world. Both you and Jobe need to know more about what's out here. You kids have been deprived, both of you, and I mean to do somethin' about that. Later, when things calm down back there, I'll take you right back home. And hey, just think of all the great stories you'll have to tell your little friends."

Chrissy seems about to argue with Bella, but Rosie reaches out to pull her back and shakes her head, no.

Jobe isn't sure what Rosie shaking her head like that meant. Did it mean she doesn't want Chrissy to ever leave her, or was she telling Chrissy not to talk to Bella? So much non-spoken communication goes on between Rosie and Chrissy, Jobe is beginning to think the two girls are starting to be able to read each other's minds.

Chrissy sits back, and Rosie leans her head against Chrissy's shoulder.

As they go along, Bella keeps on jabbering about all the fun they're gonna have in Phoenix. "We'll get us some serious money, Then we can really start to have fun."

Bella makes a quick stop for gas, and then she drives all the way to a big city. Jobe thinks this must be Phoenix, and he's amazed about how many houses there are. It looks like the whole desert is being taken over by houses, and they're mostly all alike.

When they get into the actual city part, Jobe can see that it's a lot like downtown Salt Lake City with some big buildings and lot of cars on the streets. He asks Bella where they're going.

Bella says she knows a good place, but first, she has to get something to soothe her dry throat. She stops at a liquor store, and soon comes back out with what looks like a bottle that's wrapped up inside of a paper bag. For a while, they sit still without driving while Bella drinks a lot out of the bottle without even taking it out of the paper bag.

Then she starts driving again, and Jobe can see that she's not doing it very well.

It reminds Jobe of the times Mother drank right out of a bottle like that, and then she couldn't even walk straight. "Bella, I don't think you should be trying to drive a car right now, especially not with so many other cars all around. And maybe you shouldn't be spending what little money we have on booze. What about going somewhere to get some good food for the girls? And not just hot dogs and plain white bread."

Bella turns to him and laughs out loud. "Well now, aren't you turnin' into the little papa." She takes another drink from the bottle and holds it out to Jobe. "Come on, Jobe. Get with the party. Have a drink."

"No. I don't want any. And you shouldn't be drinking it either while you're driving." Jobe knows the Devil is using Bella to try to tempt him. Mother drank booze sometimes, even though she was always getting mad at herself for doing it because she didn't think God would like it.

"Aw, hell, Jobe, cool your jets. All right, all right, we'll get the girls some good food."

"When?"

"Soon. Soon as we get some money."

"But what about that money we got in Salt Lake City?"

Bella frowns at him, and the car wanders very close to some parked cars.

Jobe has to reach over and grab the steering wheel to straighten the car out before it hits something.

Bella pushes his hand away, and keeps on trying to drive straight.

All Jobe can think about is that she's endangering the girls. He shakes his Bible at her. "Right here in this Good Book it says 'Wine is a mocker, strong drink a brawler, and whoever is led astray by it is not wise.'"

Bella suddenly pulls the car over to the curb and reaches out to grab the front of Jobe's sweatshirt. "All right, Jobe. I've had it with you. Knock that lecture shit off right now. First you wanna be the papa and take care of the girls, and now you wanna act like a Goddam husband or somethin'. I don't take that shit from no man. I had two husbands, and another two that pretended to be. Take it from me, they were all bastards. Thought they could tell me what to do and what not to do. Well, nobody tells me what to do. Not Bella the bell. And if you think you can, you can get the hell out of my car right this minute. You hear me?"

Jobe pushes her hand away. "Yes, I hear you, Bella. I hear you using bad words. And besides it's not even your car. You said you were only borrowing it, remember? Now here we are in a completely different city from there, and you're using bad words in front of the girls and even taking the Lord's name in vain. Besides, I'm not acting like a husband. I'm not even acting like a papa. I just want to make sure you don't crash this car and maybe hurt the girls."

Bella grins at him. "Well, by God. Ya do have some balls after all, don't ya? That's the first time I ever saw ya get mad. Didn't think you even had it in ya." She reaches out and punches his shoulder. "Ya know, I might make a man out of you yet." She glances into the back seat where the girls are hugging together, looking scared. "Or is it little Miss Chrissy you're tryin' to impress. That it?"

Jobe can see that Chrissy is looking at him in a funny way, and he's afraid that his face is turning red. "Let's just go get them some food, okay?"

Bella salutes him by snapping her hand up to her forehead. "Yes, sir, boss. Right away, boss? Whatever you say, boss."

She pulls the car back out into traffic, almost sideswiping a big white car that honks at them. Bella puts her arm out the window and shakes her middle finger at the driver of that car. She speeds down the street, mumbling to herself.

Jobe looks at the girls in the back seat and shrugs.

The two girls just look back at him, but Rosie, for some reason, has a little smile on her face. Jobe isn't sure he has ever seen her smile quite like that before. Does it mean she likes him standing up to Bella, or does it mean something else he doesn't understand? He turns back to keep an eye on Bella's driving, ready to grab the steering wheel again if necessary.

After a few blocks, Bella pulls into a parking place by a little store that has mostly glass on the front of it. She goes inside, and soon she's back with a large package of cookies and a small bag of potato chips. She tosses both of them into the back seat and says, "There you go, girls. Okay, lord and master, kiddies taken care of. Satisfied?"

Jobe doesn't answer, but he wishes she would have got something better for the girls to eat than cookies and chips.

Bella shrugs and pulls back out onto the street.

Jobe looks back and sees that Chrissy has opened both packages. She hands a cookie to Rosie, and Rosie is eating it. Jobe decides that maybe Bella knows better than he does about what young girls like to eat.

Bella jabs his shoulder with her finger. "Well, Papa Jobe? Ready to go make some money?"

"Me?"

Bella laughs. "Well, you're the money-getter aren't ya? What say we go try to scare up some bucks? I know a good place."

Jobe knows she wants him to try to get money out of people by quoting them words from the Bible, but he's not sure he wants to do that anymore, especially not if it's Bella ordering him to do it.

"What now?" says Bella. "Cat got your tongue?"

"No, a cat doesn't have ahold of my tongue, Bella. It's just that I'm not sure getting money by begging from people is the right thing to do. Why can't we—"

"Do what? You gonna get a job, Jobey? How you gonna do that with the cops out lookin' for ya?"

"No, it's just that—"

"Right. I thought so." She uses her thumb to indicate the girls in the back seat. "I got some food for the little darlings, didn't I? I got the only food they had in that store that I could afford. We blew almost all of the money already on food and gas. Now if you wanna continue to be the hero in their eyes, you'd better get busy and get us some more cash. Get it, Papa Jobe? Cash money? Ya don't want the little darlins to starve to death, do ya?"

Jobe understands what she's trying to do to him. She knows he wants to take care of the girls, wants to be their protector, so she's using that to get him to do whatever she wants. And he knows he's going to have to do it, but only to get food for the girls until he and Chrissy can figure out how to get away from Bella and be on their own. "All right," he says. "Where is this so called good place?"

Bella says, "You'll see. It's not far."

When they stop at a red light, Bella points at a man who is standing on the curb holding up a cardboard sign that says he's a veteran. "See that guy? That jerk'll be out there in the sun cookin' his ass off all day and maybe not get a dime. People in cars don't wanna stop. The place to be is on a busy sidewalk. For you to do your religion trick, we need to be where we can get people to stop. So you can talk 'em out of their bucks."

"It's not a religion trick, Bella. All I did back in Salt Lake City was ask those men to help Rosie. I told them God would reward them for their generosity."

"Right, right. That's the ticket, Jobe. Reward 'em for their generosity. That's a good one. Reward 'em in heaven. Amazing what the suckers will go for."

Before Jobe can protest her sarcastic attitude about the Lord's mysterious ways, she goes on: "And I know just the place for ya to give 'em their reward in heaven. Downtown. The financial district. Same kinda place as where we went in Salt Lake."

Jobe can see she's heading toward some tall buildings in the distance. He thinks about her words, and wonders if he really is doing the right thing telling people they will be rewarded in Heaven for giving money to help Rosie with doctor bills if the money is actually going to be used for food. After all, he too has been eating the hot dogs and bread Bella bought with the money he got from those men in Salt Lake. The Bible says the love of money is a root of evil. It says *The craving of money leads people to wander away from the faith and pierce themselves with many pangs.* Jobe searches inside of himself: is he being pierced by pangs? He knows he's being pierced by doubts. Does having a need for money differ from having a craving for money? He knows he doesn't crave the money; he only asked those men for money in order to help Rosie. But he suspects Bella really does crave money, and so far, none of the money he got has gone for any kind of medical treatment. He's not even sure if Rosie needs medical treatment. Is there medical treatment for girls who can't talk? Maybe it's only that she doesn't want to talk.

As Bella drives them closer to a part of town that has tall buildings, Jobe wonders if there is a way to get Bella to put away some of the money to help Rosie and not just end up spending it on food and booze. Before he met Bella, Jobe never had to decide such hard things. Mother told him what was right and what was wrong. She made him memorize the Bible, and she told him he could find the answer to any problem in the Bible. But now, he can't seem to think of any Bible verses to tell him what to do in this kind of situation.

As they drive along, Jobe looks out the window, thinking how different this Phoenix city is from Salt Lake City. There are trees all along the street, but they're not like the trees in Salt Lake City. These trees are very tall with thick rough trunks and no branches, only weird hanging down things that seem to be growing out of the center of the tops of the tall trunks. Jobe has never seen any trees like them before, if they really are trees. They sure don't have any leaves on them, so maybe that means they aren't really trees at all. And the sun is a lot brighter here that it was in Salt Lake. There's almost no shade anywhere, and the sun even reflects too bright off of buildings that seem to be made of glass.

It's all too much. He's feeling disoriented and so scared that he won't be able to move or even talk, like used to happen to him when he was little. This place is too different. His whole life is too different now. It's starting to make him have the kind of scary feeling he used to get when he was younger, the feeling that nothing is real. Back then, sometimes he couldn't control his thoughts, and that made him do crazy things. Mother would have to beat him until she got him "straightened out." Now, here it comes again, that same kind of feeling, a feeling that things are happening too fast and closing in on him. He hasn't felt this way in a long time, and the realization that Mother isn't here to help him get through it makes it even scarier. He's going to have to get himself straightened out by himself, but how? What would Mother tell him to do? Maybe she'd tell him to look for signs and omens. She always said that if you paid attention, God will provide signs to tell you what to do. That must be what he's been doing wrong; he's still forgetting to look for signs and omens, and that's why he can't tell what's going to happen next. The Bible says it so clear: *And there will be signs in sun and moon and stars, and on the earth distress of nations in perplexity because of the roaring of the sea and the waves, people fainting with fear and with foreboding of what is coming on the world.*

The Bible, as always, has told him what to do. He has to look for the signs. He realizes that when they were camped out in the desert, lots of things happened, and he never once saw them coming because he forgot to look for the signs. And now, here he is in a big city, a place he's never been before, and he hasn't even thought to try to spot the signs and omens. It's Bella's fault. She's got him thinking all wrong. He needs to start thinking right and look for the signs.

So, what are the signs? He can see that there are a lot more cars here than he ever saw in Salt Lake City. Is that a sign? And there are people here, lots of people, walking around. Why do more people walk around here than they did in Salt Lake City? Where are they all going? They drive past a store that sells watches and clocks. There's a great big clock attached to the front of the building. Is it trying to tell him to keep track of time? That could be one problem that makes him feel so unsure: he's been losing track of time. It seems like only yesterday when he met Bella and Rosie in front of the Mormon's big temple in Salt Lake City, and then they met Chrissy in that big Walmart store, and now here they are, all four of them still together, in a city that doesn't look anything like Salt Lake City. They pass a restaurant that has a glass front. Jobe can see people inside the restaurant. They are sitting at table, eating. Many times, back in Salt Lake City, Jobe stared through the window of a place like that, a place with tables and chairs inside and people sitting around those tables, eating and talking. Jobe has never once got to sit inside a place like that to eat food. Maybe if he gets Bella some money, she'll take him and the girls inside a place like that to get some good food. Or better yet, if he can get some money for himself, after he and Chrissy run away together, maybe they could find a way to eat in a restaurant like that.

He looks at Bella. She seems to be driving better. How did he ever end up with such a person as Bella? What were the signs that should have told him he'd end up in a whole new city like this with a bad person like her? He turns to look at Chrissy and Rosie who are still hugging together in the back seat. Should he have known he was going to end up in a car with them? Were there signs? Did he somehow miss all of them? It's too confusing. Back in Salt Lake City, before he met Bella, he never had to think about so many things all at once. Sometimes things changed, but Mother was there to tell him which things were omens and which things weren't. Back in Salt Lake City, before he met Bella, everything was pretty much the same every day. There was the trailer park and the railroad switching yards, and there was the downtown part of the city with the indoor shopping mall where you could go to watch people. Now all of that seems far away and long ago. But it wasn't all that long ago, was it? How long ago did he meet Bella and Rosie? He can't remember. Time has gotten all messed up.

Jobe realizes the car has stopped, and Bella is shaking his shoulder. "Hey, Jobe. Snap out of it. What's the matter with you?"

Jobe blinks his eyes to clear them and sees Bella staring at him. He looks back at the girls, and they're also staring at him. Did he fall asleep or something?

Bella punches his shoulder. "I said, are you ready to do your thing?" She points at the people walking on the sidewalk. "Just look at all those suckers, Jobe. Let's set up over there by that building. Ready?"

Jobe isn't sure he is ready. He isn't sure of anything anymore. He wishes he was back in Salt Lake City. He wishes Mother was still alive. If she was still alive, she'd tell him what he's supposed to do. Maybe he should find a way to get out of this situation as quick as he can and go back to Salt Lake City.

No, that's not right. He has to stay here and protect Chrissy. At least for a little while longer. Then the two of them will run away and be together. Then everything will be all right. He needs to keep going along until he can make that happen. He turns to Bella. "I'm ready. I guess."

After Bella parks the car on a side street, she leads the three of them to a place in front of the tall building, and sits down close to the entrance. She parks Rosie on one side of her and Chrissy on the other.

Jobe doesn't know where he's supposed to be, so he stands a little ways away, close to the building's entrance.

Bella puts out her sign, and Jobe sees that she's added the words, "GOD WILL BLESS YOU" under the words that ask for donations for her daughter's treatment. Jobe wonders when she did that.

People stream by, most of them in a hurry. Jobe suspects they're hurrying because the sun is so hot. Maybe they are all in such a hurry to get out of the sun, none of them will ever stop to give him any money.

When two men in suits stop to talk to each other by the building's entrance, Bella snaps her fingers at Jobe and nods toward them.

Jobe knows what she wants; she wants him to try to get money from the men. He approaches the two men. "Excuse me, men, could you spare a little money?" He points at Rosie. "It's to help that little girl over there. You see, she needs special treatment."

One of the men says, "Get lost, kid," and they go back to talking.

Jobe wasn't expecting that. Are people different in Phoenix than they were back in Salt Lake City? He tries not to be irritated at the man's attitude. Maybe the man just didn't understand. He grabs the man's elbow. "I was only asking because the kind of treatment she needs is very expensive."

The man jerks his arm away. "Hey, don't touch me, buddy. Didn't I tell you to get lost?"

Jobe smiles at the man and shows him his Bible. "This here Bible says it is good to give to the needy. It says your money will grow old, but you can provide yourself with a treasure in Heaven."

The man stares at Jobe. He's not taking out his wallet, so Jobe again grabs the man's arm and points toward Rosie. "But, can't you see? The poor little girl needs—"

The man pulls his arm loose and strikes out with the back of his hand, hitting Jobe in the side of the neck.

Jobe staggers backwards and puts his hand to his neck. He feels confused. He realizes he's never once been struck by anyone, except Mother, and that was only because he deserved it. This time there is no way he deserved to be hit; all he was doing was trying to help get money for Rosie. He decides the only thing to do is grab the man's arm again, and keep on grabbing it until the man finally understands that to strike a person who was only trying to help someone will make him look like a bad person in the eyes of the Lord. Like the Bible says, *Those who resist God, will incur judgment.*

He reaches out toward the man, but Bella is suddenly right there next to him and stops him. Keeping a tight grip on Jobe's arm, she smiles at the man. "Sorry, mister. My boy here only wanted to help my poor little Rosie. He's sorry he bothered you."

The man scowls at her. "Well, keep him on the leash, lady, before I have to teach him a lesson."

"He won't bother you anymore. Have a nice day."

She pulls Jobe away and whispers, "Damn it, Jobe. You can't be calling attention to us like that. You tryin' to get 'em to call the cops on us? Just do your Bible spouting thing, and if they won't cough up any bucks, just let 'em go on their way. This a game of percentages. Get it? The sidewalk is full of suckers. Some of 'em will give you money, but most won't. Just watch for the ones that will. Keep your eyes on me. I'll point out the suckers. I know about people. Listen to me and learn, Jobe. You'll get it eventually." She smooths down the front of Jobe's sweatshirt and pats him on the cheek. "Now make nice to the people and do your reward in heaven bit. That's what'll get the bucks out of some of 'em. Got it?"

Jobe shrugs and watches the two men walk into the building. Some part of him wants to chase after that man and teach that man that those who resist God will incur His judgment. Although God is good, He can also be a God of consuming fire. Mother often repeated those words, over and over again, while she was beating him to help him get rid of his bad thoughts.

But before he can decide what to do, Bella points. "Jobe, look what's coming." She's pointing at an elderly couple coming down the sidewalk toward them. I'll sit back down there with the girls while you snag those two."

When the old couple gets closer, Jobe steps in front of them and points at Bella's sign. "Excuse me, folks. Could you spare a little to help this woman's daughter? God welcomes into Heaven the person who gives generously to the needy."

The old man steps in front of the woman as if he thinks he needs to protect her. "Well, son, we don't actually like the idea of giving to the homeless. After all, there are services that will take care of you sort."

"Oh no, sir. We're not homeless. Not really. I'm, just trying to help that little girl there." He points at Rosie. She—"

The old woman pushes forward. "Oh, for heaven's sake, Paul. Give the boy some money. We're already late."

The man takes out his wallet and gives Jobe a five-dollar bill. Jobe suspects he could get more out of them, but he decides against it. He just thanks them and does a little bow.

The two old people go on down the street.

As Jobe hands the money to Bella, she winks and says, "That's the ticket, Jobe. You gotta pick your victims. Every one is different. You'll learn to spot the suckers. Watch and learn."

Jobe doesn't like to think of the people who give money for Rosie as victims or suckers. After all, the ones that are willing to give money for Rosie's treatment are the nice ones. He decides that at some point he needs to talk to Bella about her bad attitude when it comes to people. Like Mother always said, if people are bad it's only because they've turned their backs on God.

For the next few hours, Jobe stops people, and with each new person, he begins to learn how to deal with different kinds of people. He learns that some need to be begged, but others need to be cajoled. Sometimes, especially with men, he has to block their way and be insistent. But he has to be careful with that; some of them really don't like to have their way blocked. With those, you have to act submissive and tell them you are sorry to have bothered them.

Most people only give him pocket change, but some will give him dollar bills. Once in a while he gets a five dollar bill, or maybe even more. He always takes the money to Bella and then returns to his favorite spot where he can see down the sidewalk in both directions.

Suddenly, Bella stands up and pulls both of the girls to their feet. She grabs both of them by the hand and hurries away with them without saying anything to Jobe.

Jobe looks around to see what scared her. He's never seen her act scared before.

And then he see it: a blue and white police car is coming slowly down the street toward him. It looks like there are two policemen in the car. Are they looking for him? Did they get word all the way from Utah to be on the lookout for him?

Jobe quickly turns away and goes into the building. The building's wide hallway is empty except for a man and a woman who are waiting in front of an elevator. Jobe goes to join them.

But as the elevator doors open, he glances back and sees through the glass doors of the building's entrance that the police car is speeding away. Are they after Bella and the girls?

Jobe runs outside and sees that the police car has turned on its red lights. He hears the siren come on as the car speeds away. Maybe that means they got a call to go somewhere else. Good.

Jobe thinks about going to look for Bella and the girls, but then he realizes that sooner or later they'll have to come back to the car. That's logical. He goes to the car and gets into the passenger seat to wait.

Sure enough, Bella and the girls soon arrive. Chrissy has an ice cream cone, and she's sharing it with Rosie. That makes Jobe happy. He remembers that Bella promised to get Chrissy ice cream all the way back in that town in Utah. It's nice that Chrissy finally got something she was promised.

Bella gets the girls into the back seat and then joins Jobe in the front. "Well, that was exciting. I got worried that the tough guy asshole mighta called the cops on ya. But false alarm. Still, you gotta keep your eyes open, Jobe. You're the one standin' out on the sidewalk and we're gonna be sittin' down, so you got to be our lookout. You see any cops comin', in cars or walkin', you give me the sign, and we'll clear out. Got it?"

Jobe shrugs.

"Don't just shrug. You don't want to end up in jail, do ya? No. You don't. And me neither. So you got to keep an eye out. You got to be the lookout, right?"

"Okay, Bella."

She grins and punches his shoulder. "Good boy. Now, we did pretty good today, so what say we go get us some food and go camp out. I know a good place out north of here. It's a really big park up in the hills, but it's still like being out in the desert. I bet I'll still know some of the regular guys out there, and the cops don't usually roust anybody out, long as there's no trouble."

Bella drives to another little store that has a glass front on it just like the last little store did. She makes Jobe and the girls stay in the car while she goes into the store to get some food. She comes back with her usual package of hot dogs and plain white bread, but this time she also gets two package that have little yellow cakes in them. She gives the little cakes to the girls to share. At first Jobe wishes he would have got one of those little cakes too, but then he decides it means she's treating him the way he wants to be treated, as the man of the family, not a little kid who might like sweet yellow cakes.

Bella drives for quite a while and it looks like they're leaving the city and going back out into the desert again. But they aren't very far out of the city when Bella turns off the highway and pulls into a dirt parking lot that has a sign that says it's a trailhead. She tells them to get out of the car, and then she leads them up the marked trail. She makes Jobe carry the plastic bag with food in it while she carries the bigger plastic bag with the bundle of blankets in it.

Once they're over the top of the hill, Bella cuts off the trail and leads them down into a sandy valley.

It's starting to get dark, but Jobe can see that there are other people sleeping in the area. Jobe remembers the men who were sleeping all over the grass in that park back in Salt Lake City, and he wonders if this is that same kind of homeless place.

Bella leads them into a tight little ravine that's out of sight of the other people.

Bella lays out a blanket and Rosie flops down on it. Bella covers her with the thick quilt. Then she points to another flat place a short distance away and tosses the other two blankets to Jobe. "You two. Over there."

Jobe lays out the first blanket and waits for Chrissy to lie down on it. When she does, he gently covers her with the other blanket and slides in next to her. He's careful not to touch her, and he tries not to move as he waits for Chrissy to fall asleep. But she doesn't seem to be ready to sleep, so he moves closer to her and gently places his hand onto the top of her hip. She doesn't react, and that gives Jobe new hope that maybe she really does like him to do that. He whispers to her, "Can't you sleep?"

After a few moments, she whispers back. "I'm afraid, Jobe. I don't like to be in such a big city. I want to go home."

She turns toward him and puts her hand against his chest. In the dim light, Jobe can see there are tears in her eyes. Because of the wonderful feel of Chrissy's hand against his chest, Jobe can hardly breathe. For the first time, she's asking for his help, and he needs make her understand that he wants to help her, that he will help her. "I don't like that big city either, Chrissy. And I'm ready to get away from Bella. She doesn't care about us. All she cares about is money."

Chrissy takes ahold of his arm with both hands and says, "Back when we were in that desert place, you said you'd make Bella take me back home, but you didn't."

Jobe is worried that maybe she's mad at him now. But it wasn't his fault. He says, "I know. I'm sorry. But Bella keeps on saying we have to wait for things to calm down back up there in Utah."

Chrissy removes her hands from his arm. "But you said. You said you'd make her take me home."

"I'm sorry, Chrissy. I tried, but she wouldn't do it. But now I don't care what she says. We'll just run away by ourselves, and then I'll figure out a way to get you back home."

She puts her hand back on his chest. "And can you help Rosie get away too?"

Jobe isn't sure he heard her right. Why does she want Rosie to go with them? "Uh, you want Rosie to go too? Why can't we just go away by ourselves?"

"No, Rosie is my friend. She wants to get away too."

"She wants to get away from her mother?"

"Bella is not her mother. I think she stole Rosie just like she stole me. When Rosie was little, I mean."

Jobe is not sure he can believe the words Chrissy is saying. Bella isn't Rosie's mother? They seems so much like mother and daughter. They even look a lot a like, dark hair and dark eyes and everything. "Are you sure, Chrissy? They seem to belong together."

"Yes, I'm sure. Bella is not her mother."

Jobe tries to puzzle it out. Bella is trying to get special medical treatment for Rosie. Why would she do that if Rosie wasn't her daughter? It can't be true. But Chrissy thinks Rosie also wants to get away. "Uh, Chrissy, what makes you think Bella is not really Rosie's mother? I mean how did you . . . "

Chrissy shakes her head. "Rosie told me, and I believe her."

"But, Chrissy, how could she tell you? Rosie can't talk."

"Well, you just have to believe me, Jobe. Me and Rosie . . . well, we have ways of knowing what the other is thinking." She takes his hand and squeezes it between her hands. "Will you help us?"

It's hard for Jobe to even concentrate on what she's saying; he'd rather concentrate on the feeling of her warm hands holding his hand so firmly. Tonight, she seems willing to be close to him. That has to mean she likes him; maybe she likes him a lot. He mutters, "Sure. I mean, yes. Whatever you want, Chrissy."

"Okay," she says. "The next time Bella goes into a store, to get liquor or something, we'll take off. Just the three of us. Okay?"

"If that's what you want. Sure. Anything."

Chrissy turns away from him, but she does keep ahold of his hand, and she places it back on her hip. Then she pulls up her knees and seems ready to go to sleep.

Jobe tries to breathe normally, but he can't seem to stop himself from holding his breath. His hand is right on top of her hip, so close to that wonderful place between her legs that he saw that day she was bathing in that little river. All he'd have to do is move his hand just a little further forward and . . .

No. He has to stop thinking like that. She wants him to be her protection, and that's all.

But maybe if she wants to run away with him, maybe after that, she'd want more from him.

But why does she want Rosie to go along? Still, that might not be so bad. The three of them would probably end up sleeping under the same blanket and then—

Jobe quickly pushes that thought away. It's Chrissy he wants, not Rosie. Maybe he can figure out a way to talk Chrissy out of bringing Rosie along.

Chrissy moves, just a little, but then settles down and starts breathing in a way that indicates she's going to sleep. She hasn't tried to move his hand away. Maybe she likes it there. Maybe the feel of his hand on her hip reassures her. He again thinks about moving it forward, just a little, but decides against it. He doesn't want to spoil things.

Better to not take a chance. But what if he only touches her stomach. She probably wouldn't mind that. He slides a little bit closer to her and again holds his breath. She still seems to be sound asleep. He let's his hand move around to the front of her and gently touches her stomach. She still doesn't react. He very slowly moves his hand up until he feels something a little different. With a shock, he realizes he must be touching the bottom outline of her breast, her wonderful little breast that he got to see so clearly that day she was in the water. Hidden by the thick shirt Bella makes her wear, her fine little breasts are barely noticeable. If only she would agree to take off her clothes. No, maybe only her shirt. It's quite warm under the blanket. Maybe she'd like to have her shirt off, just to be a little cooler.

Suddenly, she moves and stops her steady breathing.

Jobe quickly pulls his hand away. He waits. She's not moving.

"Were you touching me?"

"Oh, sorry. I . . . I was asleep."

"I bet you weren't. You never sleep."

"I'm sorry. I just want to be . . . close to you."

"Is it the same as the other night. When you wanted me to take my clothes off?"

"No, I just . . . I mean, I would like that. Would you?"

Chrissy doesn't speak, and Jobe is afraid he said the wrong thing. He desperately tries to think what he can say to make her like him again. He wants to apologize for touching her, but that would tell her he did it intentionally.

Chrissy turns over to face him. "Can I ask you a question, Jobe?"

"Sure. Anything. And I'll always tell you the truth. I promise."

"Well, what I want to ask you about . . . it's something I heard. Are all boys like that? Do all boys always want girls to take off their clothes so they can do things to them?"

Jobe tries to think how to answer her. He did promise to tell the truth. Should be admit that he really would like to do to her what Bella did to him, even though he knows it wouldn't be right? He decides to tell her another kind of truth. "You know, Chrissy, to tell you the truth, I don't know much about what other boys are like. Or what they want. Seeing you out there in the water the other day . . . I mean with your clothes off, it's the first time I'd ever seen a girl naked. I mean I saw my mother naked all the time. She didn't like to wear clothes. So I knew pretty much what girls look like. But I'd never seen anything as beautiful as you. I guess that's why I want . . . I mean, I wanted to see you again with no clothes on."

Again, Chrissy is silent, and again, Jobe worries that he said the wrong thing, and now she'll never trust him.

But then she says, "I understand. I'd never seen a boy without clothes on either. Not any boy, even though I have a couple of brothers. We were taught to be very careful about that. We girls had our own bedroom and our own bathroom. It was a strict rule in the place I lived that nobody should ever be seen naked."

"Well, then I'm sorry Bella made you do that. It wasn't right, and I shouldn't have looked."

"It wasn't your fault, Jobe. Bella made you look. And I have a confession to make. I looked at you too. Just once. Like I said, I'd never seen a boy . . . like that. I mean with no clothes on. I guess I was curious."

Jobe quickly says, "I didn't mind you looking at me. I know my face turned red, but I didn't mind. Really."

"It's all right, but it was only because Bella made us all do it. But I don't think it would be right for us to see each other without clothes on like that anymore, would it?"

"No, not at all. You're right. I mean, yes, it wouldn't be right."

"Okay. Well, we'd better get to sleep now. You can put your arm around me if you want to, but don't touch me . . . you know, in my girl places."

"Oh, right. Of course not. I won't. I promise."

"And you also promise to help me and Rosie get away? As soon as you can?"

"Yes. Absolutely. I promise. As soon as we can."

"Okay then. Thank you, Jobe." Chrissy turns away from him, but she reaches back and takes his hand. She carefully places it on her hip, and then turns away.

Jobe doesn't dare move; the fact that she wants to be so close to him, and she's letting him touch her, means she really does like him, more than he even dared to think.

He lies still and thinks through what just happened. He and Chrissy had a real talk, and he found out more about her than he ever knew before. She said she didn't blame him for seeing her naked. Even more important, she admitted she looked at him when he was naked too. That fact must mean something important, but he doesn't dare to think about what. It's enough that she likes him. Maybe someday . . .

No, he doesn't want to even think about any possibilities like that. He'll just stay very close to her and protect her and soon they'll get their chance to get away together. It's too bad she wants to take Rosie along too, but maybe he can talk her out of that later.

Chrissy 9

This morning, Bella got us all back into her car and she started driving again. She said she was going to take us to a big city where we would have a lot of fun, but it worried me that we were getting farther and farther away from my home.

We stopped for gas out in the middle of nowhere, and Jobe and Bella got out. I told Rosie maybe we should take off, but Rosie said no, there was no place to go to out there. She said once we were in the big city with more people around, it would give us a better chance to get away to where they'd never find us.

I told her we should go live at my house. It would be fun because there were so many kids there. I admitted that sometimes we did have to work hard outside in the community gardens and do other work-type stuff, but I told her that even part is not so bad because it's nice to be outside and we have nice big red-colored mountains not too far away and they're nice to look at.

She asked me if I'd ever gone and hiked up in those red mountains. I told her that some of the older boys did it sometimes, and that I'd always wanted to do it too, but the Prophet told us God said girls shouldn't be doing things like that.

Rosie made a funny face when I said that. She said when we got back there, we'd go right straight up into those red mountains together just to show them that girls can do fun stuff too.

I still wasn't sure the Prophet would let us do something like that, but I didn't tell Rosie that. I told her it would be nice there even if we didn't get to go up into the mountains.

Then Rosie asked me why that prophet guy should be able to tell us what we can or can't do. Wasn't he the man who made me take off all my clothes and did that bad thing to me? What if he wanted to do that to me again?

I had to admit I didn't like thinking about that very much. I told Rosie maybe we should both just stay away from him.

She said or maybe we would teach him a lesson.

I wasn't sure what she meant about that, and it confused me, but I didn't ask her what she meant because I really did want her to come back home to live with me and like being there.

When we got to the big city it was named Phoenix, and I never imagined a city could be so big. We drove past a lot of houses, and then we drove past a lot of buildings, and then Bella stopped the car and she went into a store that sold liquor. While she was in that store, I nudged Rosie and nodded toward the street. Maybe if we ran away right then, Jobe would let us go.

I think Rosie knew that I was suggesting that this might be our best chance to run away, but she shook her head no. That must mean she has a better plan. I'll just have to be patient and wait for her to tell me when it's the right time to escape.

After Bella came back out of the liquor store, she started driving again and she was drinking out of a bottle at the same time. That made Jobe mad at her and they got into a big argument about it. Bella started calling him Papa Jobe, saying all he cared about was me. That made me feel good that he cared about me, but I wasn't sure why Bella was saying that. I looked at Rosie, but she just put her finger up to her lips, which by now I know means I should just keep quiet and not get involved.

After that, Jobe told Bella she had to get us some more food, and she did, some cookies and some potato chips. I ate some of the cookies and Rosie did too. I'm glad to see Rosie eating. She's too thin and she needs to be strong when it's time for us to run away together.

Bella drove us into the downtown part of Phoenix city, and we went out onto the sidewalk in front of a big building where Jobe started asking people to give us money. He did it by quoting things from the Bible. He told the people that the money was to get some kind of special treatment for Rosie, but while Bella was busy talking to Jobe, Rosie told me not to pay any attention to that. She said she didn't need any special kind of treatment. She said it's only an excuse Bella uses to get money out of people.

While we were there, some police in a car came by and Bella made Rosie and me run away. I got Rosie aside and told her maybe we should talk to the police. I said we could tell them who I am and that way we could get away from Bella.

Rosie said no, that would get Jobe in trouble. The police would lock him up in jail for a long time. She said it would be better to wait for a chance to get away without getting anybody in trouble.

I didn't want Jobe to get put in a jail, so I said maybe we should wait until Jobe isn't looking and then just run away real fast. Bella wouldn't be able to catch us. But Rosie said that wouldn't work either. Bella would just yell to Jobe to catch us, and then they'd watch us a lot closer. But she said I shouldn't worry because she was working on a plan. She said I had to be patient, and she reminded me of our blood oath to stick together. I said I would try to be patient, but I'm starting to wonder how long this is going to go on.

We stayed out there on the hot sidewalk all day while Jobe got money from the people. Then Bella bought us some more food, and then she drove us to a place out at the edge of the city that's sort of like being out in the desert again except the lights of city are still pretty close. There was a trail up into the hills to a place that Bella already seemed know about. We slept on the ground there, like we did before, but this time it was different because there were other people sleeping not too far away, down the hill. When we passed by those people, I saw that a lot of them were sleeping all over the place, and some of them had made themselves little cardboard houses. They looked kind of mean and dirty so it felt scary having those kinds of people camping so close to us.

Bella had us sleep just like we did when we where way out in the middle of the desert, with Bella and Rosie on one blanket and me and Jobe on another blanket. Jobe still wanted to be close to me and touch me while I'm sleeping, so I talked to him about that. He seemed very sorry that he keeps on trying to touch me, and he promised not to do it anymore. I can tell he really likes me, so I asked him if he'd help me and Rosie get away from Bella. He said he would, and that made me really happy. I'm not sure Rosie will want him to come along with us, but I'll tell her that after Jobe helps us get away, we can tell him we want to be on our own. In fact, we can tell him he'd be better off not being with us because the police might not believe he helped us get away from Bella.

After our little talk, I let him touch me while I was sleeping as long as he didn't touch me in my special girl places. Rosie said that would make him want to do bad things to me because that's just the way boys are. Jobe is a little bit older than me, but sometimes he doesn't seem all that old. Sometimes he tells me what it was like when he was little, and that makes it seem like part of him is still a little boy.

But he sure does know a lot about what is in the Bible. That must mean he really is a good person. He told me his mother taught him to read using the Bible, and she made him memorize every part of it. But he said his mother is dead now and he really misses her. But from the things he told me about her, it doesn't seem like she really was a very nice person. He said sometimes she'd beat him and lock him up in a closet. He said she did that to get the devil out from inside of him. I feel sorry for him. He doesn't seem as bad as Rosie says all boys are. Now that he says he'll help Rosie and me get away, I'll have to tell to Rosie about that tomorrow. She'll be glad.

Jobe 10

The sun is not even up yet when Bella comes to wake Jobe and Chrissy. "Nice to see the two of you all wrapped up together. One big happy family, right?"

Jobe quickly moves away from Chrissy and sits up. He doesn't want Bella to get the wrong idea and think he did anything bad to Chrissy during the night. And he especially doesn't want her to think he and Chrissy might be planning anything together.

Bella feeds them cold hot dogs again, but she lets them have as many cookies as they want for desert. Then she leads them back down the hill to the car.

And then it's right back to that same place downtown to try to get money from people. Jobe is now more eager to get people to give him money because he's slipping some of it into his own pocket instead of giving it to Bella every time. He feels bad about telling a little lie about needing the money for Rosie's treatment when he's actually pocketing some of the money for when he and Chrissy get away. But he knows it's for a good cause, getting Chrissy away from Bella. He promises himself that he will pray and ask God for forgiveness for lying. Still, it worries him. After you lie to people once, does it make it easier to lie again? Maybe this is what happens from being around a real liar like Bella. Is it yet another sign that the Devil is lurking nearby, trying to draw him in? Jobe promises that as soon as he gets Chrissy away from Bella, he will never again tell anybody a lie, no matter what.

Bella yells at him, "What's the matter with you, Jobe? Why are ya just standin' there? People are goin' past ya. Get busy."

Jobe shakes off his worrisome thoughts about lying and the Devil, and concentrates on his job. He knows his little lies are working even better as he learns how to read people. He's figured out that you can get money out of some of the men in suits by appealing to their main worry that someone is going to take their money away from them. He tells the men in suits what the Bible says, *Value only that which does not fail, that which no thief can steal, that which no moth can destroy.*

One older woman stops and seems friendly. She says, "I can't give you any money, son. I lost it all at the casino."

Jobe is not sure what a casino is, but he says, "I understand. But remember, the Bible says you should not set your hopes on the uncertainty of riches. Set your hopes on God who will richly provide you."

She must have liked something about that idea because she immediately digs into her purse and gives him a handful of quarters.

He gives her a little bow and says, "The Lord will bless you for helping those less fortunate."

Spending the day out there on the sidewalk is hot and tiring, but Jobe doesn't mind because he's getting better at getting money from the people, and he knows the faster he gets money, the sooner he and Chrissy can get away.

Bella likes it that he's getting so much money, and she keeps on encouraging Jobe by telling him what a great job he's doing.

The girls aren't paying much attention; they both mostly just sit still and stare straight ahead, but Jobe knows Chrissy will be happy when he tells her he's been getting money so they can get away on their own.

As the day goes on, Jobe learns he has to use a lot of different kinds of Bible verses, depending on the person. He's learned to examine each person coming down the sidewalk before he decides which Bible verse will work best on them. And he has to modify some of the Bible verses a little to make them work even better. A Bible quote that often works well with older people is *Provide yourselves with money that does not grow old, the treasure you will find in Heaven.*

One that works well with a lot of other people is *Give, and it will be given to you. Good measure, pressed down, shaken together, running over, will be put into your lap. For with the measure you use, it will be measured back to you.* Some of the people seem confused by that one, but it often works anyhow.

For a certain type of woman, those that look sympathetic, he learns a good Bible verse is *Value the treasure in your heart, not the treasure in your pocket.*

For another type of woman, those who are better dressed and wearing shiny shoes with tall heels, a better verse is *If you would be perfect, go, sell what you possess and give to the poor, and you will have treasure in Heaven.*

None of the Bible verses seem to work with young people, especially not with people as young as Jobe is. They often laugh at him, and one tall boy pretends he's going to hit Jobe before he walks away laughing. After that, Jobe decides not to talk to young people at all.

When the sun gets low in the sky, Bella says they might as well knock off and go back out to their camping spot.

By the time they get there, it's almost dark. Bella passes out the food and says she's bushed. "Get some sleep, everybody. Our boy Jobe here is finally gettin' his head on straight and gettin' us some money. Tomorrow, we'll get even more."

Jobe crawls under the blanket with Chrissy and whispers, "I got some money for us. For when we get away."

She turns to look at him. "You did? A lot?"

"Not enough, but it won't be long now. Trust me, we'll be away from Bella before you know it."

Chrissy is quiet for a moment, and then says, "I'm really starting to miss my mom and my little sister, but I'm worried about what everybody will think of me when I go back."

"What do you mean? Won't they be happy to see you?"

"Oh, sure, my mom will. But the community might not."

"The community? What's that?"

"Well, I live in a kind of a special community. We have a . . . sort of leader who tells us what to do, and he says we have to stay away from people who don't believe in the same things we do. So I don't know what he'll think about me going off with people who aren't part of our community."

"Can't you just tell him what happened? Just tell him Bella took you away even though you didn't want to go. He'll understand."

"Maybe. But maybe he'll think I did something wrong to make it happen. And some of the other people in the community might not understand either. They might say unless I was actually tied up, I should have tried harder to get away. They don't know much about the outside world. Everybody was born in the community, or at least they've been there for a long time. The important thing is that they don't like associating with people who don't believe what we believe."

"You mean people who don't believe in the Bible? My mother was like that too. She didn't want me to associate with people who didn't believe everything that's in the Bible."

"Well, Jobe, it's not only that. We have other things we believe in too, not just the Bible. There are other holy books besides the Bible."

Jobe isn't sure what she might be referring to. "Uh, other holy books? What books?"

"Well, there's several, but the main one is . . . I mean haven't you ever heard of the Book of Mormon?"

"I've heard of Mormons. You mean they have their own book?"

"Yes, but not all Mormons believe everything in that book. For example, some people don't believe a man should have more than one wife and that you can't get into heaven without doing that. The Prophet told us that a lot of latter day saints up in Salt Lake City have forsaken the truth that's in the holy books. He says they've been led astray by worldly desires. He says that's why kids in our community aren't allowed to watch television, and why we can't have any pets, and why we can't play with red toys. He says we could get tainted."

"You know, Chrissy, my mother used that word too. Tainted, I mean. My mother always said we have to be careful to not get tainted by contact with the Devil. She said the Devil will tempt you with worldly desires. Is that like the same thing?"

"Sort of. Actually, I'm not sure. All I know is that we aren't supposed to associate with people outside of our own faith. It's like a rule, and when I get back there, they might think I broke that rule. Maybe they'll think I'm so tainted now I can't get salvation anymore."

Jobe isn't sure Mother would like the people in Chrissy's community. She didn't like Mormons. She always called them "the weird Mormon's." But she never said why they were weird. Now he's learning there are other kinds of Mormons that maybe are even weirder, Mormons that have all kinds of special rules about how many wives they can have and what kind of things their kids are allowed to do. They even have their own holy books. He's pretty sure Mother wouldn't like hearing that. Maybe it would be better if he and Chrissy went away together somewhere else besides her community.

"Are asleep, Jobe?"

"No, sorry. I was just thinking about what you said. Tell me more about what your community believes in."

"I'm not sure I can tell it right. The rules seems to change all the time. It's up to the Prophet."

"But how do you tell if the prophet is always right? I mean, like why does he think there's something wrong with toys that are red?"

"Well, he's supposed to be in direct contact with God. He says he's only telling us what God told him to tell us. You know, like what the rules are."

Jobe wonders if God really does tell this prophet guy what the rules should be. "Tell me more about this prophet man, Chrissy. What kind of person is he?"

Well, he's just . . . you know, the Prophet. He's the one who everybody looks up to because he's God's messenger to us."

"Do you like him?"

"Well, it doesn't matter what I think."

"Of course it does. You're a person, just like he is."

Chrissy is quiet for a few moments, then she says, "Well, one thing I don't like is when he says we girls have to get married as soon as we're able to have kids. And he gets to decide who we marry. And it's always to older men."

To Jobe, that's important news. It means that in her community, Chrissy is maybe almost old enough to get married, and young girls like Chrissy get married to older men. Jobe is older than Chrissy is, so maybe if he went back to her community with her, he could talk this prophet guy into being the older boy who gets to marry her.

Jobe decides to tell Chrissy a secret. "God talks to me too. Sometimes. I mean maybe not in words, but he sort of . . . guides me."

"Really?"

"Yes, but not to tell other people what to do, only to tell me what to do."

"Is that how you ended up with Bella and Rosie? He told you to?"

"Uh, well, that's what I thought, But now maybe I'm not so sure. Usually I feel His hand guiding me, and at first I didn't think I should go along with Bella, but then I knew He was telling me Rosie needed my protection. I still wasn't so sure, but then Bella led me to you, and then I knew God really was guiding me."

Chrissy is quiet for a minute. Then she says, "Do you really think God led you to me?"

"I sure do. I knew it right away. I knew you and me were meant to be together. And we will be too, as soon as I get enough money. We'll run away and be together."

"But, Jobe, we have to go to my home. I really do miss my mother, and my little sister too."

"Oh, right. I know that. I'll take you back home. I will."

Chrissy snuggles closer to him and whispers. "That would be the best thing. You can go with me and help me explain to them how it was Bella that took me away. If you want to, you should stay there and live with my family too. With Rosie and me."

Jobe isn't happy to hear that Chrissy is still wanting Rosie to go along with them, but maybe after they get away, Chrissy will forget all about Rosie.

Jobe is still thinking about that when, all of a sudden, Bella jerks the blanket off of them. "All right, you two. Unwrap yourselves. It's my turn." She grabs Jobe's arm and roughly pulls him to his feet.

"But Bella, me and Chrissy were just getting to sleep. You said it was time for us all to go to sleep."

Bella doesn't reply; she just pulls Jobe away. Jobe isn't sure what she wants. Did she figure out that he's been keeping some of the money for himself? Does she suspect he's going to run away with Chrissy? Was she close enough to hear what they were talking about?

Bella doesn't say a word as she leads him up the hill, and then over a smaller hill into another little valley. She flops down onto her back and pulls down her pants. "Come on, boy. Let's go. I'm horny as hell."

Jobe pulls back. Didn't she believe him when she tried to get him to do this the last time? He's not going to get caught in lust anymore, especially not now just when he and Chrissy are getting along so well and are almost ready to get away. Why can't Bella just leave him alone so he can stay with Chrissy? He looks back in the direction where Chrissy is. What did she think when he went away with Bella just now? Did she think he's still willing to do whatever Bella wants him to do? He should go back right now and explain to Chrissy that he'll never do that kind of thing with Bella anymore. In fact, he'll promise her not to do that kind of thing with anybody else but her, not ever. He turns to go, but Bella yells at him: "Oh, so now I'm not good enough for ya. Now that you got your own hot little pussy, this old girl who taught you everything is not good enough for ya anymore."

Jobe looks back and sees that Bella is pulling her pants up. She's got an angry look on her face.

Jobe shakes his head. "It's not that Bella. I'm not doing anything to Chrissy. It's just that . . . well, I've decided it's just not right to . . . I mean to do what we did before. I don't want to get caught in lust anymore. It could be the work of—"

"Are you shittin' me about not doin' it with Chrissy? What the hell's the matter with you, boy? Here I grab her and serve her up to ya on a silver platter, and you don't take care of business? So what the hell do the two of you do over there all night?"

Jobe shrugs. "We just sleep. And sometimes we . . . talk."

"Talk? What the hell kind of man are you? That little dolly is hot to trot for ya, and all you wanna do is talk? You got to take care of that girls needs, boy. I know what she wants, woman to woman. Girls like her can't say it out loud, but it's what she wants. Take it from me. I know."

Jobe can't believe what Bella is saying. Could it be true? "Chrissy never told me that, Bella. I don't think you're telling the truth."

"For Christ's sake, Jobe. Are you that dumb? I can tell it from the way she looks at you. She wants it bad."

"Do you really think she . . . uh, wants it?"

Bella laughs. "Damn straight she does, boy. A woman can tell when another woman is hot to trot. Get your ass back over there and give her what she wants. Be a man."

"Do you really think so?"

"I know what I know, kid."

"Well, okay. I guess I'll go back now."

"You do that. And that means I'm gonna hafta hike down the hill and get my own. Fact is, I'm pretty sure I can find somebody better'n you anyhow."

She stomps on down the hill.

Jobe heads back to Chrissy, trying to decide if what Bella said is really true. Maybe if in the place where Chrissy lives, girls as young as Chrissy get married because they're ready for it, ready to do the thing that gives them babies. Maybe if he gave Chrissy a baby, then he would get to be her husband.

Jobe hurries back to their campsite, excited about the idea that he could get married to Chrissy and have a baby they could take care of together.

He slides back in under the covers next to Chrissy and lies very still, trying to tell if she is awake. She's breathing regularly. Maybe she went to sleep. He carefully puts his arm over her, intentionally letting his wrist rest against her wonderful little breasts. He waits to see how she reacts.

She murmurs something and snuggles closer to him.

Jobe decides to move his hand, just a little, so he can feel roundness of her perfect little breast under her shirt. He feels a surge of excitement when she doesn't move away.

Chrissy pushes even closer to him, so close that he feels his excited boy part pressing up against her wonderful little bottom. So maybe Bella is right. Maybe Chrissy does want it, but she just doesn't know how to say it. He carefully lets his hand move down until it's between her legs. He touches her there very gently.

She murmurs in her sleep, but she doesn't move his hand away.

Jobe decides she's ready for the next part. He cautiously reaches down into the top of her pants and moves his hand down very, very slowly until he finds the elastic top of her underwear. He slips his hand inside, and when his fingers find the top edge of her fine public hair, it sends such heat through him that he can't resist putting his fingers down just a little farther into her warm dampness.

Chrissy jerks. Then, she grabs his wrist and pulls his hand out of her pants. She sits up and looks at him. There isn't much light, so Jobe isn't quite sure what that look means. Maybe she didn't really mind what he did, but was only surprised by it.

She lies back down and turns away from him.

Jobe isn't sure what she wants. Does her pushing his hand away mean she doesn't want him to do anything to her? But she didn't tell him not to. And she didn't get out from under the blanket.

Jobe moves up against her and presses his boy part tighter against her bottom. He again reaches around in front of her and again pushes his hand down inside the front of her panties.

This time, she doesn't react. It must mean Bella was right: she does want him to do it to her.

He keeps his hand where it is, and uses his other hand to push down his own pants. He whispers, "Chrissy, I know you've never done it before, but trust me, you'll like it. And it will prove that we should always be together. Just let me show you how."

"No!" she says, and she pulls his hand out of her panties.

Jobe is surprised how firm her voice was. Maybe she really doesn't want to do it. Maybe Bella was wrong, and some girls don't want it.

But he still has his pants down, and he's still pushed up against her bottom. He whispers, "Just lie still and let me show you, Chrissy. I know what to do. Just let me pull your panties down a little farther, and I'll get on top of you. It'll prove that we're meant to be together."

He turns her over onto her back and pulls her panties down to her knees. She just lies there, looking up at him. He looks at the girl part of her. It's dark, but he remembers how nice it was back at that little river seeing how beautiful that part of her was with the water running down there between her legs.

He gently crawls on top of her, but she squeezes her legs together tight. "No, Jobe. Please don't."

But Jobe can't seem to make himself stop. He's so close now, and she must want it too, or she wouldn't have let him get this far. He squirms around trying to force open her legs. He remembers how good it felt when he did it with Bella, and he knows it will be much, much better doing the same thing with beautiful, wonderful Chrissy.

But then he feels the most terrible pain in the back of his head. He knows it's some kind of terrible hurting, but he doesn't know what it means. Maybe it's only part of the powerful feeling he's having by becoming one with his wonderful little Chrissy. He's almost able to ignore the pain and keep going, but then the pain comes again, and this time it's much worse.

Somebody pushes him off of Chrissy, and he finds himself on his back seeing a zillion stars in a black sky. For a moment, he's not sure if he's seeing stars in the desert sky or stars from inside of his head.

After a few seconds, he hears some whispering. He sits up and sees Chrissy and Rosie standing close together. They're looking down at him, and Rosie has a big rock in her hand.

Jobe feels the back of his head where the pain is. It's wet. He takes his hand away and looks at it. The distant lights of the city are only giving off enough light to see that whatever it is, it's something dark. Is it blood?

He turns back to look at the girls. "Rosie! Did you hit me?"

She doesn't answer, and she keeps the rock in her hand as she leads Chrissy away to the other blanket.

Jobe again feels the back of his head. Now he's sure of it: his head is bleeding. But he doesn't care about that; he doesn't even care about the pain. What he does care about is that he was totally wrong about what Chrissy wanted, and now he's maybe driven her away for good. It's all Bella's fault. He has to explain that to Chrissy. And he has to explain quick, before Chrissy decides to hate him forever.

He stands up and pulls up his pants. He hurries over to the other blanket where Chrissy and Rosie are sitting, hugging together. He doesn't want to cry in front of the girls, but he can't stop himself. He gets down on his knees, and between sobs, he begs for Chrissy's forgiveness. "Listen to me, Chrissy. It's all Bella's fault. I would have never done that to you if she hadn't said it was what you wanted. You have to believe me, Chrissy, I love you. I really, really do. I would never do anything to hurt you. I will never do anything like that to you again. I promise. You have to believe me."

Chrissy hides behind Rosie, and they both just stare at him.

"Please, Chrissy. Tell me you forgive me."

She won't respond. She continues to hide behind Rosie, and Rosie still has the big rock in her hand.

Joe reaches out his hand toward Rosie. "Please, Rosie, make her understand. It's all Bella's fault. You know what Bella is like. She tricked me. I promise I'll never do anything like that again. You have to convince Chrissy that I really do love her, and from now on, all I will do is protect her. And you too, Rosie. I'll protect you too. I'll get both of you away from Bella so we can be on our own. I'll make money so you two can have anything you want."

He waits for Rosie to respond, but she just stares at him.

"Please, Rosie. You have to believe me. I'll never do anything like that again. I don't need sex. Sex is unGodly and unclean. I just wanted to show Chrissy how much I loved her. But now I know it was wrong. I just got all confused for a minute. It must have been the Devil leading me astray. But now I've rejected Him. Now I understand it was a very, very wrong thing to do. For just a minute, I got confused and turned my back on God. I let the Devil get ahold of me. But I'm over that now. You have to convince her, Rosie. Help me convince her that I love her. I really do."

Rosie turns to look into Chrissy's eyes. Then, she draws her fingernail across her own wrist.

Jobe doesn't know what that means, but Chrissy seems to understand. She points at a nearby low-lying cactus plant. "Go get a big thorn off of that cactus."

Jobe wipes away the tears with the back of his hand. "A thorn?"

Chrissy nods.

He does as he was told and goes to the cactus. He manages to break off a long thorn. He brings it back and tries to hand it to Chrissy.

But it's Rosie that takes the thorn. She jabs the thorn into his wrist, and wiggles it around, pressing down hard. Blood spurts out.

Jobe is shocked to see so much blood, and it hurts, but he doesn't care. If this is what it takes to get Chrissy to forgive him, then it's worth it.

Next, Rosie lightly draws the thorn across Chrissy's wrist. It barely makes a scratch. Then Rosie puts their two wrists together and says, "Swear."

Jobe almost thinks he heard wrong. Did Rosie say a word? He's sure she said "Swear." Does it mean Rosie can say words when she wants to?

"Say it!"

Rosie talked again, and Jobe is startled into action. He uses his other hand to press his bleeding wrist tight against Chrissy's. He closes his eyes and says, "Yes. I swear. I promise." He opens his eyes and sees that Chrissy is looking at him. She doesn't seem to be too mad at him, and that gives him hope. "Listen, Chrissy, I do swear. I really do. I would give my blood for you anytime. I promise I will never do anything like that to you again. I will only do whatever you want me to. Please believe me."

Rosie points at the other blanket and says, "Go away."

Jobe scurries back to the blanket, still amazed that Rosie said even more words. So she can talk, when she wants to.

Jobe lies down on the blanket and looks up at the bright stars in the very black sky. At least now he has a chance that Chrissy will forgive him. Maybe Rosie making his wrist bleed and putting it together with Chrissy's wrist means it is some kind of blood oath that proves that he'll never try to do that to Chrissy again. If that's what it means, then he's happy he did it. He vows to lie awake all night praying that she'll understand that it was only his love for her that made him try to do that bad thing to her.

As he looks up toward Heaven, the pain in the back of his head feels like a warning from God; it's telling him he'd better stop and rethink what he's doing with his life. He's been forgetting to ask God for guidance, and that led him astray. Bella got him so confused he hasn't been looking for the signs that God surely has been sending him. Like it says in the Bible, *The Lord himself will give you a sign. You will see signs and wonders, for prophecy is a sign not for unbelievers but for believers.* Jobe now realizes there were probably signs and omens all over the place, and probably dire warnings from God, but he got so caught up in lust, he missed them all. He clutches his Bible to his chest, grateful for its advice. He must always remember the words of the Bible and never let himself lose track of God's signs again.

Most important, now he knows he can't believe anything Bella says. Bella is the one who led him astray. It was Bella that led him to sin in the first place, got him to start thinking about lust, got him to start thinking about what he wanted instead of thinking about what God wanted of him. Bella lured him into becoming a sinner. How could he have allowed that to happen? The Devil must have invaded Bella and through her, lured him into His evil domain. He must vow that from this very minute he will keep his focus on the Lord above and turn his back on the sinful desires of the world here below. He'll be like those priests Mother told him about, religious men who never had sexual relations with women. He'll be Chrissy's protector, and that is all.

But then, as he stares up at the stars in the dark sky, he can't stop thinking about how it felt to be touching her down there between her legs, how it felt to lie on top of her, how it felt when their bare flesh was touching.

No! He should not even be remembering that. No matter how good that felt, he must always remind himself that lust is the work of the Devil. The Devil must still be hiding somewhere inside of him, trying to convince him that learning about sex is only part of his necessary learning about the world. But now he knows better. God is telling him he has to escape the clutches of the Devil. Like the Bible says, *Put on the whole armor of God, that you may be able to stand against the schemes of the devil.* The Devil must have gained access to him through Bella, and now he has allowed the Devil to slip inside of him. Is He still in there, just waiting to strike again? Jobe knows there is only one solution: he has to drive the Devil out. Whenever Mother suspected the Devil might be creeping into him, she'd beat him until the Devil would flee.

Jobe jumps up and goes stumbling up the hillside, looking for a suitable bush. When he finds one, he breaks off a willowy branch. He takes off his sweatshirt and his T-shirt and angrily throws them to the ground. He kneels in front of the bush as if it was the burning bush of the Lord, and using the branch like a whip, he begins to whip himself on the back, striking over his shoulder as hard as he can, again and again. He strikes his own bare flesh harder and harder with his whip of

God. And the more he does it, the more it hurts, and he knows that is good. He hits himself faster and faster until it becomes a rhythm that's like a repeated prayer. It hurts so much he has to clench his teeth tight together, but he won't let that stop him. If God will give him the strength, he'll be able to keep it up until he's sure the Devil is driven out. Eventually, his arm begins to get tired, but he still doesn't stop. The pain is starting to fade, and Jobe knows what that means: it means God is approving of what he's doing to himself. God is helping him have the strength to continue to drive the Devil out. With each stroke of the Holy Whip, he repeats the prayer Mother taught him, "Forgive me, Father for I have sinned.." He whispers it over and over until it becomes a chant, and the feel of the cleansing pain and the sound of whip striking his back brings Jobe so much happiness, he can hardly even imagine ever stopping.

But after an unknown amount of time, he finally does stop. The feeling on his back is no longer pain; it has become an old familiar feeling of pure joy. How could he have ever forgotten something so wonderful?

Still on his knees and panting like a dog, he feels the coolness of the night breeze gently drying the blood on his back. He hopes it's a lot of blood, and he's proud that he could bring forth so much blood. How long has it been since he did that to himself? Too long. No wonder the Devil was able to sneak back into him. He realizes he's grinning. He's almost as happy as when Mother used to whip him like that.

He remembers one joyous time like that when he and Mother were both naked because it was his job to wash her when she was in the bathtub. She was very stoned on whatever drug she had injected into her vein that night, and in the middle of washing her with soap, she began to guide his hand down there between her legs. It was not something she had ever done before, and Jobe wasn't sure what he was supposed to do, so he let her move his hand wherever she wanted it. She moved his hand faster and faster down there between her legs.

But then, Jobe got worried and asked her, in a very apologetic whisper, if this is what God would want.

She instantly smacked his hand away and jumped up out of the bathtub. Dripping water, she ran to get her whip. She came back into the bathroom and made him kneel with his head on the rim of the toilet. She whipped him and whipped him until he could feel the blood running down this back and into the crack of his bare butt. With each strike of her whip, she'd scream, "Devil, get thee away from my son, Devil get thee begone." And it worked. Jobe could joyfully feel the hand of God helping her, and that's when he knew the Devil was draining out of him along with the blood.

After it was over and Mother ran out of the bathroom in tears, he stood in front of the mirror and turned to see his back. There were many crisscrossed red stripes, and each stripe was emitting a trickle of blood. It was not the first time Mother had done that to him, but this time the stripes were deeper and more plentiful. He was proud that this time, for the first time, he hadn't cried at all. It meant he was becoming a grown-up person, brave enough to endure such a hard whipping without shedding a single tear.

Now, kneeling on the sharp little rocks of the desert, Jobe assumes his back must look like that again. It must be crisscrossed with bleeding stripes. Imaging what that must looks like again makes him feel satisfied: the Devil won't be able to look at his bleeding back and still think he has a chance of invading such a brave person.

Jobe picks up his T-shirt and his sweatshirt, but doesn't put them on. He doesn't want to get them all bloody because it's the only thing he has to wear.

As he walks back down the hill to their campsite, he's feeling really angry at Bella for lying to him about what Chrissy wanted and for leading the Devil to him. Now he's really ready to run away with Chrissy, and the sooner the better

That brings back a thought that has always troubled Jobe: why does God sometimes allow the Devil to get inside of him? Was it another lesson?

He stops to think about it. Why did God bring him together with Bella in the first place? Was it the only way to bring him to Chrissy? But if that is so, why did God let the Devil lure him into trying to do that bad thing to Chrissy? God always has a reason. Jobe knows that, but it's always been hard to understood why God allows bad things to happen. Once, when he was little, he asked Mother why God made them live in such bad places and why he had to be hungry all the time. She just said God works in mysterious ways.

But now God has helped him drive the Devil out, and that means he will find the will to get Chrissy away from Bella and her temptations. He will never again try to do anything like that to Chrissy. That kind of thing should only happen between a husband and a wife.

Like the Bible says, *Let marriage be held in honor among all, and let the marriage bed be undefiled.*

Jobe tries to imagine what it would be like to be married to Chrissy. It would start with the two of them walking down the aisle of a church. Chrissy would be dressed all in white because she would still be pure.

Yes, that is the answer! Marriage is the answer. He will ask Chrissy to marry him, and she will say yes. The Bible, as always, has the answer: *He who finds a wife finds a good thing and obtains favor from the Lord.* It also says *A man shall leave his father and his mother and hold fast to his wife. They shall become one flesh.* And that is the way it will be with him and Chrissy. Once they are married, it will be fine for them to lie together naked and be together in a real bed and take pleasure from each other's bodies. The Bible says it: *Because of the temptation to sexual immorality, each man should have his own wife.*

Despite the pain in his bleeding back, and the pain in his head from where Rosie hit him with that rock, Jobe is overwhelmed with happiness. He did what the Lord commanded, and he drove the Devil out. And it led to a solution: as soon as the time is right, he'll ask Chrissy to marry him, and they'll go off together to have a baby and make a home of their own.

Jobe starts walking again. He'll go back and make sure Chrissy is no longer mad at him. If he keeps on showing her how sorry he is, she'll have to forgive him.

But then he hears something. A sound of shouting from farther down the hill. He stops and listens. The shouting is coming from down there where the homeless men are camped out. He's heard the sounds of fighting from down there before. Maybe they're fighting again.

Jobe puts his T-shirt and sweatshirt back on and walks a little ways down the hill toward the sounds. He hears a woman screaming. He doesn't remember seeing any women down there. Could it be Bella She went down there because she wanted to find a man to have sex with. What if she got herself in trouble? And if she's in trouble, maybe he should he go down there and try to help her. But why should he? She's the one who lied to him about what Chrissy wanted. She's the one that made him do something that made Chrissy mad at him. If Bella has got herself into trouble, then it's her own fault.

But if something bad happens to her, what would become of Rosie after he and Chrissy leave to go get married? He did promise to help and protect Rosie as well as Chrissy. Maybe he should at least go down a little farther to see what's going on. Now, he's hearing loud laughing. Those men down there must be drunk. The sound of the woman screaming has stopped, but why was she screaming before?

As he get closer to where the homeless men's camp, he sees a group of men gathered in a circle next to a big campfire. They're all looking down, and they're all laughing. A bottle is being passed around.

Jobe creeps a little closer. And then he sees what's going on: the men are gathered around a couple making love on a blanket. The men in the circle are watching and laughing and drinking, as if the sex is a kind of entertainment. It's such a blatant orgy of sin, it takes Jobe's breath away. How could a couple allow themselves to be watched when they were engaged in such a personal act?

The man gets up off of the naked woman, and amid applause and laughing, another man takes his place on top of the woman.

Now, Jobe can see that the woman *is* Bella, and he can tell she's not at all happy to be the center of the show. She's totally naked and her wrists are tied to stakes, stretched out on each side. They've stuffed a rag in her mouth, but despite the rag, she's still managing to make muffled screaming sounds. It sounds like she's cursing the men.

Jobe is frozen in indecision. He's watching a gang of tough looking men rape Bella over and over again. How did this happen? What did Bella say or do to make so many men want to rape her? Was it her fault, or did they just grab her and decide to have some fun at her expense?

Most importantly, what should he do about it? Should he even do anything? Maybe they'll soon get tired of doing it to her and let her go. And even though Bella looks angry, Jobe knows she likes sex. Maybe she really doesn't mind all that much.

But then Jobe sees her do something that tells him she *does* mind. She smacks her forehead up into the forehead of the man who is raping her.

The man is surprised by it and leans back away from her.

The laughing stops. One of the men says something Jobe can't hear, and then the man who is on top of Bella slaps her face. She says something that's muffled by the gag in her mouth, and he slaps her again, even harder this time. That gets the other men to start laughing.

Jobe decides he has to do something. He can't allow a woman to be hit and raped at the same time, even if it is Bella. He can tell Bella is really angry, but the man continues to rape her, and he's laughing really loud as he continues to slap her face over and over again. The other men are still laughing too.

Jobe finds himself running down the hill. He hardly realizes what he's doing, and although he stumbles over rocks and bumps into low-lying cactus plants, he somehow stays on his feet until he gets close enough to jump on the man's back. He knocks the man off of Bella and sits on him.

The man is surprised, but not for long. He strikes out at Jobe, and his fist glances off of the side of Jobe's face.

This is the second time Jobe has been struck by a man he doesn't even know, and he doesn't like it one bit. He is seriously thinking about hitting the man back when he feels hands grab onto arms. They pull him off of the man, and as Jobe lies on his back, two of the men start to kick him in his side. Jobe tries to struggle to his feet, but then somebody with dirty boots kicks him in the face, and that knocks him back down again.

That's it. Jobe is no longer willing to turn the other cheek. His hand feels a good-sized rock on the ground. He grabs it and jumps up and uses the rock to hit the kicker right in the face. To Jobe's surprise, the man falls down. Jobe realizes he must have hit the man harder than he meant to, but now that it's done, he's not sorry, not sorry at all. The man deserved it. And when another man comes at him, Jobe uses the rock to hit him in the face too. That man goes down, just like the first one did. Jobe spins around, ready to hit anyone else who comes at him, but he sees that the rest of the men are backing away. Even one of the men he hit in the face is up and running away. The other man he hit is lying on his back groaning. He's got his hands up to his face and blood is running out between his fingers.

Jobe is very surprised at how this is turning out. He's never hit anyone before, but it seems as if he's not all that bad at it. These grown men are all afraid of him.

He kneels down and takes the rag out of Bella's mouth.

She yells, "Untie my hands, Goddam it!"

Jobe unties her hands, and she jumps up and starts kicking the man who is still lying on the ground. The man frantically crawls away into the darkness, trying to get away from her.

Bella picks up a large rock and chases after him. The frightened man flops over onto his back and holds out his hands as she raises the rock high above her head.

Jobe realizes she's going to kill the man, so he jumps forward and takes the rock away from her.

She turns on Jobe. "Why did you do that? Now the son of bitch is getting away."

"Well, jeez, Bella. You don't want to kill him do you? You'd get in a lot of trouble."

"Screw that," she says. She takes the rock away from Jobe and starts to chase after the man again.

But a voice comes out of the darkness, quite close. "You'd better get your fuckin' boyfriend out of here, Bella. We catch either one of you around here again, and you're both dead. You hear me, Bella?"

Bella stops and throws the rock in the direction of the voice. "Yeah, I hear you, asshole. But I am gonna come back, and when I do, we'll see who ends up dead."

The voice laughs. "Okay, sweetheart, we'll be waitin'." The voice makes kissing sounds.

Bella turns back to Jobe and says, "Let's get the hell out of here." She starts up the hill, still totally naked. But then she stops and yelps and starts hopping around on one foot.

Jobe says, "What's the matter now?"

"What the hell do you think is the matter? I stepped on a damn cactus. She sits down in the dirt and looks at the bottom of her foot. Go back down there and get my shoes. And my Goddamn clothes too.

Jobe picks up another rock and heads back down. He keeps his eyes on the darkness beyond the campfire, but if the men are still out there, they're keeping their distance.

When he gets back to Bella with her clothes, she's still sitting on the ground. She puts her shoes on hurries up the hill. She's still totally naked, but she doesn't seem to care about that.

Jobe follows, carrying her clothes.

When they get back to their camping place, Jobe sees that Rosie and Chrissy are huddled together under the same blanket.

Bella yells at them: "Get everything together, you girls. We gotta go. And I mean now!"

Chrissy sits up and stares at Bella. "Uh, why don't you have any clothes on, Bella?"

"Never mind about that. Just do what I said and pack up. Now!" She starts to get dressed.

Chrissy looks at Jobe, but he isn't sure how to explain Bella's nakedness to her. He sure doesn't want her to think Bella being naked has anything to do with him, so he says, "It was some bad men. They were hurting her." He points. "Down there."

Rosie seems to understand right away. She jumps up and starts stuffing the bedding and the food into the plastic bags.

By the time they make it back down to the car, there's a little bit of light in the east. Although Jobe can hardly believe it, the sky is getting lighter. The whole night seems to have somehow gone away, and the sun is about to come up.

When Bella tells them to get into the car, Jobe opens the back door for the girls. Rosie slides in first, followed by Chrissy. Jobe is about to close the door when Chrissy reaches out to touch his hand. She whispers, "Thank you, Jobe."

He carefully closes the door and stands there looking at his hand where she touched it. She touched him and she thanked him. It means she's forgiven him. It means that she still wants to be with him. He'll get some more money from the people, and then he and Chrissy will go away together and they'll get married. It means God is again looking after him, and that means from now on everything will be fine.

Chrissy 10

Dear secret diary. After another day of Jobe getting money from people in downtown Phoenix, Bella took us back to the same camping out place. When Jobe and me were sleeping under the blanket together, he told me he'd been keeping some of the money for when we got away from Bella.

I told him he should come and see the community I live in, but I said the people there might not like me anymore because of my going away with Bella.

He said he didn't think that was fair. He said he didn't understand what kind of people would be mad at me because it wasn't my fault.

That's when I told him what it's like to live in a community where everybody believes the same thing and where we have a Prophet who tells us what God wants us to do.

He said I should just tell the Prophet and everybody else in my community that it wasn't my fault.

I only wish it was that easy. Jobe probably thought our community didn't sound like a very nice place to live, especially after I told him the Prophet won't let us girls do anything except get married and have babies. I didn't dare tell him about what the Prophet did to me. I almost did, but then I thought he wouldn't understand because to tell you the truth I still don't really understand it either. Maybe the Prophet was preparing me for marriage. Maybe he prepares all the young girls for marriage like that, but if that's true, none of the other girls has ever talked about it. Maybe they're afraid to, like I'm afraid to.

After me and Jobe stopped talking about that, I got worried that when I get back home maybe the Prophet will try to do that to me again. If he does, this time I don't think I'll let him. Does that mean I've changed? Will he kick me out of the community if I don't let him do whatever he wants?

It's all so confusing. Being with Bella and Jobe, and especially being with Rosie, is making me think about things in a different way. Maybe something inside of me is changing, and I'm worried that it's making me think about the Prophet and our community back there in a bad way. I think I'll try to get Rosie alone and ask her about what to do if the Prophet tries to do that to me again. Maybe she can tell me how to stop him.

Then later, Bella came and got Jobe up and they went away somewhere. But pretty soon Jobe came back alone, and he got real close to me under the blanket and touched me. And then he tried to do to me what Rosie had warned me all boys want to do to us girls. He put his hand down into my panties and touched me down there in my girl place, and that's when it started. Jobe got on top of me, and I tried to make him stop, but he seemed different, like he couldn't stop himself. Luckily, Rosie saved me by hitting Jobe on the head with a rock. Then Rosie and me ran away from him and hid under the other blanket.

Jobe came running right over to where we were and he said he was real sorry. I was still mad at him and so was Rosie, but he kept on saying how sorry he was, and he was crying, so I finally started to a little bit sorry for him. After all, he's only a young boy, not all that much older than Rosie and me, and like Rosie said, I guess maybe young boys like him just can't help themselves.

I guess Rosie finally started to feel sorry for him too, because she made him get a cactus thorn and she cut his wrist with the thorn and made it bleed and then she put his wrist together with my wrist and made him do a blood oath that he would never try to do anything like that to me ever again.

He did promise, over and over again, and I believed him. He said it was Bella's fault. I guess she got him all confused and it was like he didn't know what he was doing. And then, dear diary, guess what else he said. He said he loved me. It was amazing. Nobody has ever said anything like that to me before, and it made me realize that I kind of like him too. But I don't think I love him. At least not as much as I love Rosie.

After that, Rosie made him go away, and that meant Rosie and me got to be under the same blanket and take all of our clothes off and rub the girls part of each other like we did that time before. It was fun. She was calling me her little kitten, and we were kissing each other on the lips, and everywhere else too, even down there. I got my finishing feeling before Rosie did so she had to finish herself, and I said I was sorry that I didn't know how to do it better but she said not to worry about it, I would get better at it with more practice. She said we would have plenty of time to practice after we ran away from Bella and Jobe.

I didn't tell her that Jobe had also said he wanted me to go away with him without her. I just asked her if she already had a plan for us to get away.

She said she was still working on it.

I asked how long it would be before she had her plan worked out.

She said not too long. We would just have to watch for the right opportunity and then we would run away and be together for ever and ever.

That made me very happy.

But then, we heard Bella and Jobe coming, so we hurried and got our clothes back on just in time.

When Jobe and Bella got there, Bella didn't have any clothes on. She didn't say why, but Jobe said some bad men had hurt her. This time I knew exactly what had happened. It was just like Rosie said, all men will try to do what they want to do with us girls if they can, and that must be what happened to Bella too.

It wasn't even light yet, but Bella said we had to leave right away.

By the time we got back to the car, the sun was just coming up, and I could see that Bella's face was all beat up. I guess it was those bad men Jobe was talking about, but I don't know why they would want to hit her along with that other bad thing they were probably doing to her.

Anyhow, when we drove away, it was me and Rosie in the back seat as usual, and Bella and Jobe in the front seat as usual, except this time Jobe kept on looking back at me. His eyes seemed very sad.

Even though the four of us are together all the time, Jobe seems like he's lonely. I feel sorry for him and I bet he's still real sorry about what he tried to do to me last night. If I get a chance, I should tell him I really do forgive him.

I don't think he knew what he was doing, not really. Rosie says all boys want to do that kind of thing to us girls, and they can't help themselves, so that's why we have to be careful to never let them get us alone. I'll tell him that I understand why he did what he did, but I also need to make sure that if we ever end up under the same blanket again at night, it will be okay if he just hugs me, but that's all. He took a blood oath, so I'm sure he won't ever try to do anything like that to me ever again.

Jobe 11

As they pull out of the desert park's parking lot, Bella guns the car's engine and takes off so fast it sprays dirt and gravel out behind them. That tells Jobe that Bella is still really angry. He worries what she might do, so he asks her where she's going in such a big hurry.

She won't answer, and once she gets to the highway, she drives really fast back toward town.

Jobe turns to look at the girls in the back seat. They're huddled together, very silent. Rosie is staring out the window, but Chrissy is looking back at him. He hopes that means she's not so mad at him anymore. Maybe the blood oath that Rosie made him take with Chrissy is working. Maybe if he's especially nice to her from now on, after they get away she'll begin to trust him again.

Bella seems to be heading back toward the downtown area of Phoenix, so Jobe assumes it means she's going back there so he can get more money from the people. She says it's supposed to be for Rosie's special treatment, but now he's pretty sure Rosie doesn't even need treatment, at least not for not talking because now he knows she can talk if she really wants to. Maybe she isn't really retarded, or whatever that autistic thing is. Maybe she's actually a lot smarter than she seems to be.

When they get back into the city, Bella turns off the highway. But it doesn't look like she's heading for the downtown area where the tall buildings are. Instead, she drives slowly through an area of Phoenix that's mostly small businesses. Jobe pays close attention: he's not going to make the mistake again of not noticing things that might be a sign of what God wants him to do. He sees a Chinese food place, a music store, a pet supplies store, and a shoe repair place. But Bella drives right past all of them, slowing from time to time to carefully look at each store.

Jobe decides to break the silence that's settled over the car. "Uh, Bella, where are we going?"

Bella says, "It's along here somewhere. I noticed it a few days ago when we went past it."

"Noticed what, Bella? Do you want me to help you look?"

"There it is!" she shouts. She pulls the car to the curb in front of a store that has a glass front on it. The words "GUNS - BUY SELL TRADE" are written on the glass in big black letters.

Jobe is pretty sure this is not a good thing. Does it mean Bella wants to get herself a gun? It must mean she's still mad at those men who raped her. He touches Bella's shoulder. "Uh, Bella. I don't think getting a gun is a very good idea."

Bella ignores him. "Damn. They're not open yet. No problem. We'll wait."

Jobe decides he'd better try harder to talk her out of this. Who knows what she might do if she gets herself a gun. "Bella, didn't you hear me? I said I don't think this is a very good idea."

She gives him a mean look. "You don't, huh? So you're still tryin' ta be the man of the family, and that means you think you can tell me what to do? Maybe you didn't hear those guys last night. Didn't they say if they find us, we're dead? That means both of us, buster. We got to protect ourselves, don't we?"

"Well, yes, I heard them. But maybe they were just mad because I hit them. Maybe they'll calm down . . . uh, later."

Bella frowns at him. "You think? Now you're gonna be the one doing the thinkin'? Is that right? Well, screw that. Maybe they'll calm down, but I won't. You saw what they did to me."

"Well, yes, but I hit them to make up for that, didn't I? I knocked two of them down, and that one man was bleeding out of his nose. Maybe that's enough."

"Enough for a you maybe. Enough for a Bible thumper like you. But not enough for me. This old body may be a bit worn, but it's the one thing I got that's my own. What I do with it is up to me, not up to some homeless jerkoffs who think they're hot shit just because they did a few home robberies when nobody was even at home. Those assholes were laughing at me. You saw it. They said I was fat, and they laughed at me. Nobody laughs at me. They'll be sorry they laughed at Bella the bell. Damn sorry. I'll take care of 'em, and then we'll blow this burg. There are plenty of other places twice as good as here. Maybe Texas."

She turns to look at Rosie who is still huddled together with Chrissy in a corner of the back seat. "You remember Texas, don't you sweetie? You liked it there, didn't you? Bunch of country hicks, but not such a bad place, eh?"

Rosie turns to look out the window and doesn't respond. But she must be paying attention, because she points at something.

Jobe looks to see what she's pointing at. It's two men approaching the front door of the store. One of them looks pretty old, but the other one is much younger, maybe not all that much older than Jobe himself. The surprising thing is that they both have guns in holsters at their sides. That surprises Jobe, but as he thinks about it, he remembers that time he and Mother stayed for a short time in a motel room that was paid for by an old man. There was a television in that room, and while Mother slept, Jobe got to watch a TV movie about cowboys who had guns on their sides just like these two men do. He's pretty sure he remembers that movie was about a place they called Tombstone, Arizona. Maybe Arizona is still that kind a cowboy place, where men get to wear guns to pretend they're cowboys like in that movie.

The older man unlocks the door, and they both go in. Soon, an "OPEN" sign appears in the front window.

Bella opens her door. "Lets go, kids."

Jobe grabs her arm and whispers. "Bella, don't you think the girls should wait in the car?"

Bella grins at him. "Well, damn. You really are startin' to play the papa of this little family, aren't ya? Well, I'm still in charge here, and I'm not leavin' them out here alone. Let's go girls. Out of the car."

The girls get out and the four of them go inside the store.

If the older man who's now behind the big glass display case is surprised to see their odd group entering his store, he doesn't show it.

Jobe wonders where the younger man went. He looks around and sees a big mirror high up on the wall. It seems like an odd place for a mirror. Could the younger man be hiding behind that mirror, maybe looking at them right now?

The man behind the display case says, "Welcome. Welcome. Always nice to see a family sticking together. Teenagers these days need to stick with their momma. Right, missus?" He winks at Bella. "What can I do ya for today?"

Bella leans both hands against the glass display case and looks over all the different kinds of handguns inside the case. "I need me a gun. Personal protection."

The man breaks into a smile. "Well, you came to the right place, missus. We got the best selection in town. What'd you have in mind?"

"I think I want an automatic. How many bullets do these things hold?"

The man opens a sliding door at the back of the case and takes out a gray pistol. "Well, how about this nice Ruger? Holds ten bullets. Forty-fives. Real stopping power. Believe you me, this little baby'll stop any bad guy who might be chargin' right at you, no matter how big he is." He winks again and hands the gun to Bella.

Bella feels the weight of the gun in one hand and then switches it to her other hand. "How much?"

The man is still grinning, and Jobe wonders why he's so happy.

"Well, I can let you have it for only four fifty. Today only."

Bella looks up at the man. "Four hundred and fifty bucks? You got to be kidding."

The guy abruptly stops grinning. He leans across the counter and speaks very seriously: "You know, lady, I think you're right. Ruger overprices their pistols. The name, you know. I got one just as good for half the price." He takes the Ruger back from Bella and puts it into the case. He takes out another gun and hands it to Bella. "Feel how much lighter this one is? Perfect for a woman who needs personal protection."

Bella looks the gun over, again switching it back and forth from one hand to the other. "I guess this one'll do the job. How much?"

"Normally, three hundred, but today only, I can let you have it for only two hundred. How's that for a great deal?"

"Well, let's see. I only got maybe . . . one sixty. Would you take that?"

Jobe knows she has more money than that from all the money he's been getting from the people on the street. But he hopes that the high cost of the gun will make her change her mind about wanting one.

The man shakes his head. "Sorry, missus, no can do. But tell you what, you give me the one sixty now, and I'll hold the pistol for you until you come back with the rest."

Bella frowns at the man. "Okay, okay. Maybe I can cough up a little bit more. Two hundred it is. I'll take it. Wrap it up."

The man stands up straight and again breaks into his broad smile. "Now we're talkin'. Let's do the paperwork and its yours."

"Paperwork?"

"Right. Only take a few minutes." He holds out his hand. "Let's see your driver's license."

"I have to have a driver's license?"

"Well, yeah." The man laughs. "Actually, the feds don't care if you know how to drive. They just need to know you're a legal resident of Arizona."

"I got to be an Arizona resident?"

"You're not? Oh, you're a snowbird, eh? Just here for the winter. We get a lot of that this time of year. No problem. All I got to do is see a driver's license from your home state. Then I can ship this fine pistol to your home address."

"Ship it? What? You mean I can't have the gun right now? Listen, man. I got serious problems here. I need this gun to protect me and my little family." She gestures toward the girls who have retreated and are standing arm-in-arm against the far wall.

The man is no longer smiling. He shrugs. "Sorry, missus. Them's the rules. They're touchy about gun sales these days. You know, after all the mass shootings. The anti-gun nuts have been putting the screws to the politicians, and they've got real strict about it."

Bella hands the gun back to the man. "Well, I'll just have to find another store."

"Well, you'll get the same story at any other store. Like I said, them's the rules now. Besides, I got the best prices in town." The man leans across the counter again, and talks very softly. "But there's a real easy solution if you really do need the pistol right away. I shouldn't be tellin' you this, but you got that car out front, right? All you got to do is go down to the DMV right now and take the driver's test. Get yourself a temporary Arizona driver's license and bring it back here. I'll call it in to make sure your name isn't on the feds list, and you'll walk out of here with this fine new automatic pistol. How about that?"

"What you're tellin' me is I got to have an Arizona driver license just to have a gun. What kind of state is this?"

"Yeah, I think it's crazy too. But it's the law. It's the only way. I guess they don't want you snowbirds comin' in here and shootin' the place up." He laughs. "Just kiddin'. Why don't you just hop over there to the DMV and get me a temp license. We'll have this deal finished up in no time."

Bella stares at the gun in the man's hand.

Jobe hopes she isn't going to try anything tricky. After all, the man does have a big silver gun in a holster on his side, and the younger man might be hiding somewhere.

But Bella just says, "Damn," and turns away. "Come on girls. We're leaving."

On the way out of the shop, Bella stops in front of a poster that's stuck to the wall. It announces a gun show, with new and used guns. It says the gun show will be going on all week at the fairgrounds.

Bella points at the poster, and turns back to the man. "How about this gun show? Maybe I can get a gun there?"

The man shakes his head. "They'll tell you the same thing. Those damn anti-gun nuts will make sure the cops are there watching to make sure all sales are done by the book. Your best bet is to get me that temp Arizona driver's license. Take my word for it."

Bella says, "I'll think about it. Come on, kids."

Back in the car, Bella tells Jobe, "I'll betcha that guy is wrong about gun shows. He just didn't wanna lose a sale. And I know right where that fairgrounds is." She starts the car and pulls away from the curb fast, almost sideswiping a passing car. The man in the car honks and Bella does her usual thing, waving her middle finger at the man.

As they speed down the street, Jobe decides he's got to put a stop to this madness right now. "Listen, Bella, you have to stop this. That man said they won't sell you a gun at that gun show either. Let's just do what you said and leave this town. If we go somewhere else, those bad men won't be able to find you. Come on, Bella. I'd like to see some different places, and I bet Chrissy would too." He turns to look at Chrissy, but she doesn't respond. She and Rosie are huddled together, both staring out the window. Jobe wonders if Chrissy is starting to take on Rosie's approach to things—just ignore it and look at nothing.

"Sure, sure," says Bella, we'll get the hell out of this stupid state. But no matter where we go, there's gonna be assholes like those men you saw last night. I shoulda got myself a gun a long time ago."

Jobe touches her arm. But, Bella, we haven't even had breakfast yet. I'm hungry, and I bet the girls are real hungry, aren't you, girls?"

Both of the girls just continue to stare out the window.

"Right, right. We'll get somethin' to eat soon as I check out this gun show deal. Only take a few minutes."

Jobe is pretty sure it's going to take a lot longer than a few minutes, but Bella seems so determined he doubts if there is any way he can talk her out of it. Maybe if she tries one more time and is unable to get herself a gun, she'll give up on the idea.

As they head for the place where the gun show is, Jobe thinks about how crazy Bella is acting. Maybe this is the right time for him to get away with Chrissy. If Bella gets involved in buying a gun, maybe they could get away quick without her seeing them go. They could get so far away Bella would never be able find them, and then they could go somewhere and get married and never have to think about Bella again. Jobe knows that sooner or later, he'll have to take Chrissy back to her home, but now, after what she told him about the community she lives in, he's thinking it would be better if they got legally married first.

When they arrive at the fairgrounds, the parking lot next to the building where the gun show is being held is crowded with cars. Bella finds a place to park and gets out.

Jobe says, "Uh, Bella, why don't just you and Rosie go in. I'll stay here with Chrissy."

Bella turns back. "The hell you say. You and Chrissy alone? Not a chance. We're all goin' in."

Rosie responds by hopping out of the car and reaching back to pull Chrissy out. They head for the entrance, and Jobe obediently follows.

Once they are inside the building, Jobe is amazed at the size of the place: the ceiling is really high up, and there are rows and rows of tables with guns laid out on them.

Bella wanders down the aisles, looking at the guns on every table.

She doesn't stop at any of them, and Jobe wonders what she's looking for. Is she sizing up each of the sellers, hoping to find one she can manipulate? To Jobe, the gun sellers all look like pretty tough guys.

Bella stops in front of a table that's manned by a great big bald guy who's wearing a black T-shirt with a picture of a pistol on it. Under the pistol are the words "I Don't Dial 911 - I Dial .357"

Jobe isn't sure what that means, but he assumes it must have something to do with guns.

Bella is carefully looking at the guns on the man's table. There are some long guns with worn wooden parts, and a few pistols that also seem to be about used up.

Jobe wonders why she picked this table out of all the others.

Bella picks up one of the pistols. "How much for this one."

The bald man says, "That one? You won't find another one like that it in this whole show. I can let you have it for only five hundred. Long as you got the cash."

Bella puts the gun down. "Five hundred for that old thing? I can get a brand new one for half that."

"It's an antique, lady. But I take it you're not lookin' for an antique gun, right? Let me show you what I got." He takes out a fancy-looking silver gun. "How about this one?"

Bella shakes her head. "I can't afford a new one. Listen, mister, let's cut to the chase, what's the cheapest used automatic you got?"

The man reaches under the table and brings out a pistol that looks even more beat up than the others. "How 'bout this beauty? I can let you have this good old classic for only a hundred bucks." He hands it to Bella.

Bella looks the gun over, and again does her routine of switching it back and forth from one hand to the other. "It looks pretty old. Does it work?"

"You bet it works. Probably works a hell of a lot better than some of the new ones they make these days."

"Okay. I'll take it."

For the first time, the bald man smiles. "Fine. Just show me your Arizona driver's license and we'll do the paperwork."

Bella is aiming the gun at the lights high above in the ceiling. "Well, that's a problem. My wallet got stolen. That's why I need a gun, don't ya see."

The man leans closer to Bella and whispers, "Not a problem with me, lady. But you won't get out that door without showin' them your Arizona driver's license." He points toward the front door, the only door in the whole place.

He reaches out to take the gun from Bella, but she pulls it back. "Now listen, buddy, I got to have some self defense to protect my family here." She gestures toward the girls who are standing back and apparently not paying any attention to what Bella is doing.

"I'm right with ya, lady. If it was up to me, you could walk right out of here with any gun I got for sale. But they've cracked down on these gun shows since that shootin' down in Tucson. Maybe you heard. Supposedly, the gun that the guy used was bought at a gun show."

Bella hands the pistol back to the man. "Well, hell with it then. If you won't sell me a gun, I'll find somebody who will." She gestures vaguely at the rest of the building.

The man shakes his head. "Never happen. Somebody might sell you a used pistol, but it's gotta be done right. The paperwork has got to be filled out proper. Those state men at the exit door know what they're doin'." He again points toward the door.

Bella looks at the guy for a long minute, and then leans forward. "Listen, buddy. If you were in my shoes, and you had a family to protect like me, what would you do?"

The man looks at her, nodding. He also leans forward. "If it was me? Well, this is only hypothetical, you understand. I'd buy a prop gun."

"A prop gun? What's that?"

"You know. A gun for bein' in a play, or maybe in a quick draw contest. They shoot blanks."

"Blanks? What the hell good would blanks do me if some guy grabs me and . . . I mean if my family was in danger?"

The man again whispers: "You said if it was me, right? If it was me, I'd take that prop gun to a gunsmith and have him fix it up to shoot real bullets."

"That can be done?"

The guy nods. "Sure can. But hey, you didn't hear it from me, right?"

Bella also nods. "Okay, you got one of them? One of them prop guns I mean."

The guy grins. Just happen to have a couple." He reaches down under his table and takes out a pistol.

Bella takes the gun from the man and handles it. "Looks real," she says.

"That's the idea. In a play, you want it to look like the real thing."

Bella again switches the gun from one hand to the other. "Even feels like a real one. Okay, how much?"

"Just for you, I can let you have it for a hundred fifty. Long as you got the cash. I'll even throw in a few blanks. No charge."

"A hundred fifty? You said that real gun was only a hundred."

"Well, that was a used one. This is brand new. And it comes with a certificate that says it's a non-functioning prop gun. It'll get you out the door, no questions asked. If they ask, you can say your boy there is gonna be in a school play." He points at Jobe.

Bella begrudgingly pays the man the money, and he puts some flat-nosed bullets into the gun.

Bella quickly leads Jobe and the girls toward the front door. There's a line to get out, but after Bella shows the man at the desk the prop gun and the paperwork, they're soon out of the building and heading for their car.

Back in the car, Jobe is happy Bella wasn't able to buy a real gun. Now, if he can just talk her out of getting the gun converted to shoot real bullets, maybe she'll be satisfied with something that looks like a real gun. Maybe all she really wants is a gun to scare away men who might try to take advantage of her.

Back in the car, Bella drives straight back toward the downtown area. As she drives, she can't seem to stop talking about how dumb the state of Arizona is not to let people have a gun to protect themselves, and how stupid it is to have to pay more for a fake gun than a real one. "Oh well, guess we'll just have to rustle us up some more cash. Ready to do your thing, Jobe?"

Jobe looks back at Chrissy. She looks right back at him, and the scared look on her face tells him she too must be worried about Bella wanting to get a gun. It's now more important than ever that he gets some money so they can run away quick. He'll do the money getting thing this one more time, and then they'll go.

But then, Bella spots a public phone and pulls over to the curb.

She gets out, and Jobe watches her as she leafs through a big book that's attached to the phone by a wire. Soon, she tears a yellow-colored page out of the book and comes back to the car.

Jobe says, "I thought we were going back downtown."

"One thing to do before we go."

Jobe hopes she's not going to try to buy a gun again.

But when she stops the car, Jobe can see it isn't a gun store; the sign on the front says, "Gunsmith."

Jobe immediately understands: she's going to try to do what that man at the big gun show said: she's going to get her fake gun "fixed up" to shoot real bullets.

Bella again insists that they all have to go inside, and she won't take no for an answer. She leads them in and walks right up to an older man who has long gray hair and a big gray beard. He's wearing thick glasses, and he's sitting at a desk, leaning over, doing something to a gun that's been torn to pieces.

Jobe hopes Bella isn't going to do something that will get them all in trouble. He glances at Chrissy and Rosie. They are standing against the wall, and Chrissy seems to be whispering something to Rosie.

Bella pulls the fake gun out of the back of her pants, and that surprises Jobe. He didn't even know she had it hidden back there under her shirt.

She shows the fake gun to the man at the desk. "Hi there, mister. I got this here gun. Prop gun is what the guy who sold it to me called it. He said you could fix it up to shoot real bullets."

The man looks at Bella over the top of his glasses. "He did, did he?"

"Yep, that's what he said. How much to do that kind of fix on this here gun? I got to protect my little family here, ya see."

The man doesn't even smile. "No way, lady. Can't do it. I could lose my license doin' something like that."

Bella acts surprised. "But the man said—"

The man takes off his glasses. "I don't give a shit what the man said. You aren't gonna get anybody in this town to do that. You shoot somebody with a gun that's been altered and guess who it's gonna come back on. Me."

Bella points at the girls. "But how'm I gonna protect my kids? I got enemies. Serious enemies."

"Just point that gun at 'em and that should do it. Did the guy sell you any blanks for it."

"Yeah. A few."

"Well then, shoot a few shots into the air. That should scare away your so-called enemies. That gun looks exactly like a real one, and if it goes off, it'll sound just like a real one too. Now, if you don't mind, I got work to do."

Bella leans close to the man. "Listen, mister. Maybe we can work somethin' out." She points toward the back of the shop. "I bet you got a room back there, don't ya, old fella? Let's go back there and make, uh, a sorta trade. I bet I can make what you got in your pants jump up like it used to. What do ya say to that?"

The guy takes off his glasses, and sits back to look at her. He laughs a short laugh and says, "Well, maybe I would take a chance on you. That is, if you were twenty years younger and at least thirty pounds thinner." The man laughs again.

Jobe knows the man is not really laughing because of anything funny. It's a mean kind of laugh.

Jobe can tell the man's words and his mean kind of laughing are making Bella really mad.

She says, "Watch your smart mouth, asshole." She points the fake gun at him. "If this was a real gun I'd shoot your damn balls off."

The man laughs his mean laugh again. "Well, it ain't, is it?" He opens a drawer and pulls out a big pistol. He aims it at her face. "But this one is, lady. Now I want you and your brood out of my store. Right now."

"Fine with me, mister. You're way too old for me anyhow. But as soon as I walk out that door, you're gonna regret what you missed out on."

This time the man doesn't laugh. He just waves his big gun toward the door.

Bella heads for the door. "Come on, kids. This asshole says he's a gunsmith, but it's obvious he doesn't know how to do the simplest job. He ain't the only gunsmith in this town."

Before they make it to the door, the man calls after them. "You're right, lady. There are a few other gunsmiths. And I know 'em well. Soon as you walk out of here, I'm gonna call 'em to warn 'em about you. You'll get the same answer from them as you got from me"

Bella collects the girls and hurries them out the door. Jobe follows, but he looks back, and sure enough, the man has picked up his phone.

"Stupid jerk," says Bella as she herds the girls into the car.

Jobe jumps into the front seat as Bella starts the car. She roars away from the curb, still mumbling to herself.

Bella drives back downtown to the same place they got money from people before. She parks the car on the same side street as before and leads them out to the front of the building. She gets the girls seated on the sidewalk, takes out her begging sign, and tells Jobe to get going doing his Bible thing.

But Jobe doesn't move. "Listen, Bella, you said we were supposed to be getting the money for some kind of special treatment for Rosie, but instead you went and spent it all on buying a fake gun. And besides I'm not even sure Rosie actually needs any kind of special treatment. She seems to be doing fine just like she is."

Jobe expects Bella to get mad at his words, but she doesn't . Instead, she puts her arm across Jobe's shoulders and pulls him close. "Now don't be that way, Jobey old boy. It's only that now that I got me a nice little family, I needed to get me a gun to protect us all. And you're wrong, Rosie does need special treatment. I know she's doing a lot better now that she has a friend, but she's still not talking, and that means she still does need special treatment."

Jobe is about to protest that Rosie really can talk, but he glances at Rosie who is shaking her head at him.

Bella doesn't seem to notice. She pats Jobe on the shoulder. "Now don't get all grouchy on me, Jobe. I know what I'm talkin' about. After my Rosie stopped talkin' and wouldn't do anything I told her to, I took her to a free clinic. It was a man there at that clinic that said my girl might be having that autistic thing. He examined her, and then he told me she was not only not talking, she was unresponsive. That's the word he used, unresponsive. I asked him what kind of pill you could get for that. He said there wasn't any kind of pill for being autistic. He said she'd need some kinda special therapy. He said she'd hafta go into a special clinic for autistics. Said it would cost a lot of money. I told the man I didn't have no money at all, and that was when he said there was places run by the state that she could go into. Some kind of hospital where she'd live in there all the time. Well, I caught on to what he was sayin' right away. They meant to lock her up somewhere and never let her out again. No way I was gonna do that to my Rosie. So you see, that's why we have to get money, Jobe? To get her that kind of special treatment where they don't have to lock you up." She turns to point at Rosie. "Come on, Jobe. Look at her. You don't wanna see our poor little Rosie locked up forever in one of those place do ya? You want her to be out here with us learnin' about the world, right?"

Jobe has to admit he wouldn't want to see Rosie locked up. Maybe Chrissy is right, maybe they should take her along with them when they run away. He and Chrissy could be sort of like Rosie's mother and father to make sure she gets taken care of.

Jobe says, "Well, okay, but you have to promise to quit thinking about shooting anybody. You promise?"

Bella pats him on the shoulder. "Well now, that's up to you, isn't it, Jobe? If you can get us enough money, we can blow this town, and then we won't have to worry about those that might wanna hurt us. Now, how about you get your ass out there and grab onto some of those people. Tell 'em about what I just told you. Tell 'em Rosie needs special treatment, and it costs a lot of money. Right?"

Jobe begrudgingly goes out onto the sidewalk and begins to stop people.

For some reason, most of the people coming along on the sidewalk are older people. Not so many men in suits. That makes Jobe wonder if today might be a Sunday.

He soon learns that it's hard to get old people to give up their money. He decides these people will need different kinds of Bible verses. When an old lady walking with the help of a cane comes along, Jobe points to Bella who is now sitting next to the girls with her begging sign on her lap. Jobe tells the woman about the Bible saying that says *Each one must give as he has decided in his heart, not reluctantly or under compulsion, for God loves a cheerful giver.*

The woman just says "Hmmf" and goes on her way.

Another couple comes along, and they won't even stop long enough to listen to Jobe. They hurry away as if they're afraid of him.

After several more failures in a row, Bella calls Jobe over and shakes her finger at him. "You're not doing it right, Jobe. They ain't coughin' up any damn money at all. Get serious about it. Threaten 'em if you have to. We ain't got all day to sit out here in this hot sun."

Jobe shrugs. "But I'm doing what I always do. I tell them what the Bible says, but these people just don't seem to want to give us any of their money. They don't seem to be worried about what God's going to do to them when they die."

"That's the trouble. You're just doing what you always do. You're just spouting Bible verses at 'em. These people can tell when your heart isn't in it."

Jobe turns to look. There are more old people coming, but he's starting to wonder if he really should be bothering them. Maybe these old people have their own troubles. Maybe they're on their way to a church to pray, maybe praying for their own help. They're not like the men in suits. In fact, maybe these people just don't have any money to give him.

Bella gets up and grabs the front of his sweatshirt. "Hey, boy. You listenin' to me? Pay attention to what I'm tellin' ya. Just spouting Bible verses at these people isn't working. You got to look these suckers in the eye and figure out what kind of person they are. Then you tell 'em what they wanna hear."

Jobe doesn't know what she means. "How can I do that? I don't know anything about them."

"Well, you gotta act like you do. You gotta act like you're their best friend. Figure 'em out, Jobe. That's the whole trick about bein' out here workin' the street. You got to work 'em, boy. Work 'em. Each one is different. Now get out there and get us some bucks."

Jobe has no idea what "working them" means. All along, he's just been assuming they would want to help a poor little girl like Rosie. With the men in suits, all he had to do was remind them that the Lord smiles down on those who help the less fortunate. Maybe these old people are also the less fortunate. "But Bella, I can't tell people to give us money if they don't have much money themselves. It wouldn't feel . . . right."

"Right? Right? Shit, boy, there ain't no right or wrong is this damn world. It's dog eat dog out here. We gotta eat don't we? The girls gotta eat, don't they?" She again points at the girls. "Lookit how skinny our sweet girls are. You want them to starve? That what you want? "

Jobe looks at them. Chrissy and Rosie are holding hands, both of them just looking straight ahead, like they don't care about what Bella is saying.

"You know, Bella, I think that's the problem. They just look like a couple of nice little girls sitting outside on a nice sunny day."

Bella turns to look at the girls. "Ya know, Jobe. Maybe you're right. I'll take care of that. She whispers something to Rosie, and Rosie responds by slumping her shoulders forward and looking at the ground. Rosie jabs Chrissy with her elbow, and right away Chrissy also slumps forward.

Now Jobe is sorry he said anything. It isn't right that Bella is making them look unhappy. But he knows the best solution would be to try harder to get some money from the people passing by. The sooner he does that, the sooner he'll have enough money to get way with Chrissy.

The next person who comes down the sidewalk is a man wearing a white shirt and a red tie. Jobe thinks maybe that means he's a worker in some nearby business, and he's going out for lunch. That gives Jobe an idea. He steps in front of the man and says, "Good afternoon, sir. May I please ask a favor of you." He points at Rosie. "I'm asking people to donate to a fund to help get treatment for the poor little girl."

The man looks at Rosie, and Bella responds by holding up the cardboard sign that says Rosie is retarded.

Jobe touches the man's sleeve. "We're asking everyone if they would just give up half of what they'd normally spend on lunch, the poor girl's mother could afford to pay for treatment. As the Bible says, *'Give, and it will be given to you. And in Heaven, you will inherit a kingdom prepared especially for you.'*"

The man stares at Jobe for a moment, but then he gets out his wallet. He hands Jobe two one-dollar bills.

Jobe profusely thanks the man, and as he walks away, Jobe calls after him, "Your righteousness will endure forever, your horn will be exalted in honor."

The man waves his hand in the air without turning back, and he goes on down the sidewalk.

Jobe slips one of the dollar bills into this pocket and takes the other bill to Bella. She takes the bill and grins at him. "Now you're getting it, Jobe. Keep it up. But try to get a little bit more out of the next one. A dollar's not gonna get us very far."

For the rest of the afternoon, Jobe continues to examine the people that come along before he decides how to talk to them. Some of them give him money, some of them don't, but he keeps at it.

Soon, a very old couple comes along. They're leaning on each other for support. Jobe decides to modify some of the Bible's words about leaving the gleanings of the harvest for the poor. He reminds the old couple that they won't be able to take their money to the grave with them. He tells them that once they are dead, they will be measured by the good deeds they left behind. The old man seems confused by Jobe's words, but he does pull a wad of bills out of his pocket. Jobe can see it is mostly one-dollar bills, but there are a couple of five-dollar bills mixed in, so Jobe takes those two five-dollar bills, and leaves the rest in the man's hand.

Bella doesn't seem to be paying any attention, so he pockets both of the bills.

But then he's startled to see that Rosie is staring at him. She must have seen him pocket the money. For once, Jobe is happy Rosie doesn't ever talk to Bella.

When a man wearing a kind of worker's uniform that has dark stains all over the front of it comes along, Jobe tries the Bible saying that says *Whoever is generous to the poor lends to the Lord, and he will repay him for his deed.*

The man laughs and walks on shaking his head.

Jobe can hardly believe that man had so little respect for the Bible. Maybe that man doesn't believe there is a Heaven, so he didn't think he really will be rewarded after he dies.

After several hours of hard work, Jobe has managed to get quite a few people to give him money. He's talking to a man in a dark suit, trying to get him to at least cough up a little money when he hears Bella whistle. He turns to her and sees that she's pointing toward the street. A police car is pulling up to the curb.

A short policeman with a red face gets out and approaches Jobe. He takes off his hat and wipes his forehead with a handkerchief before he speaks: "Whatta ya think you're doing, bub?"

Jobe tries to act calm, even though inside he's not feeling calm at all. "Well, uh, we're trying to get people to give us money, sir. It's for Rosie's treatment." He half turns to point at Rosie.

The policeman looks at the two girls. "That right? Which one is Rosie?"

Bella jumps up and goes to pat Rosie on top of her head. "This is my Rosie, officer. She's got the autism."

"Autism? Is that right? Well, why don't you take her to a hospital or something?"

Bella nods. "Oh, we're gonna do that, officer. That's why we're trying to get some money. Those places cost a lot of money."

The policeman looks at her, frowning. "Listen, lady, if you don't have any money, they hafta treat your kid for free. That's the law. What I think is that you're just using her to get money for yourself. Why don't you go and get a job?"

Bella shrugs. "Man, don't you know how hard I've tried to do that. But what kind of job can I get when I got to take care of my kids here?"

The policeman looks at Jobe. Looks like this one is old enough to get his own job. Why doesn't he go get a job? Flippin' burgers or somethin'? Or construction. He's a bit thin, but he's a pretty tall fellow. He could probably carry boards or whatnot. Lotta construction jobs around here these days."

Bella nods again. "He does work. Odd jobs, you know. And you're right, construction jobs are good. Whatever work he can get. He's a big help to us, but I need him with me now 'cause we're just passing through. On our way ta Texas, ya see. Got relatives down there that'll take us in."

The policeman says, "Well, you'd better go there then. Better than hangin' around here. Now, I'm gonna have to see some ID."

Bella scratches the back of her neck. "Well, that's the problem officer. Another reason we're here. We got robbed. Took everything we had. Look here at my wrists. See the bruises?"

The policeman looks closely at her wrists. "Looks like you been tied up."

"That's right. They tied me up while they stole all our stuff. We're lucky they didn't kill us, me and my girls. Now we're just trying to get enough money to get to Texas. I got relatives there. They'll help us."

The policeman glances at Jobe. "Your boy here doesn't seem to have any bruises. Why didn't they tie him up too?"

"He wasn't there. He came back from looking for work just in time. Chased 'em off with a rock."

The policeman stares at Jobe for a long moment. "A rock, eh? And if I check, I'll find a police report on this so-called robbery?"

Bella shrugs. "Naw. Do you think the cops . . . I mean you police won't usually do anything about homeless people stealing from each other."

"Homeless, eh? Well, you should have reported it. We take every case seriously. But I'm gonna give you a piece of advice. You said you were heading for Texas where your relatives are. My advice is to git goin'. I see you around here again, I'm gonna have to check up on you all. You get me?"

Bella is again nodding her head. "Yessir. Just what we plan to do. You won't see us here anymore. We were just about to leave town."

The policeman again takes off his hat and wipes his forehead. "Besides, it's too hot out here for kids to be sitting in the sun. My advice is to pack your crap up and go. Now!"

"Right, right," says Bella, smiling. "Too hot here anyhow. Time for us to move on." She turns to the girls. "Come on, kids. Let's get you out of this sun. What say we get us some ice cream? Then we'll hit the road."

The two girls stand up, still holding hands. Jobe holds his breath and watches Chrissy closely. Is she going to say anything to the policeman? Is she going to tell him who she really is?

But no, she just looks down at the ground, so Jobe can finally let his breath out. It has to mean she really does want to stay with him. It means she's ready to go away, just the two of them.

After the cop leaves, Bella shakes her head. "Damn. That was close. Now we got to get outta here. Too bad. Just when we were finally makin' some real money." She points at her big plastic bag. "Grab my stuff, Jobe. Let's get out of here before he comes back."

Jobe picks up Bella's bag and follows her and the girls back to where they parked the car. As he lags behind, he uses the opportunity to grab the fake gun out of the bag. He hides it in the back waistband of his pants, like he saw Bella do, and he makes sure it's completely hidden under the back of his sweatshirt. As soon as he can, he'll find someplace to get rid of it.

As Jobe walks, he thinks about what that policeman said about running them in. If that policeman would have taken them to the police station, it would be all over. They'd find out about Chrissy being taken away from Utah, and they'd blame him. He can't take a chance on that happening. It means he and Chrissy should get away from Bella, and right away. That policeman might tell his policeman friends about seeing them trying to get money from people. That means they can't be seen out on the sidewalk trying to get money anymore. Jobe hopes Bella understands that.

Back in the car, Bella says, "Guess we got to find another place. I know another business area a little ways from here. Good pickin's there too, as long as Jobe does his job." She turns to Jobe. "Ready to do your thing again, Jobe? Do as good as you did here, and we'll be on the road to Texas before dark."

Jobe can't believe Bella is acting like nothing has changed. As soon as Bella gets the car started, Jobe grabs the steering wheel. "Wait a minute, Bella. You heard what that policeman said. What if he tells somebody about us?"

"Aw, the cops don't give a shit about us. He forgot about us the moment he drove away. Let's just get a bit more money, and then we'll be on our way."

Bella puts the car in gear, but Jobe won't let go of the steering wheel. "No, Bella. Me and Chrissy are going to have to go away by ourselves. It's time."

Chrissy leans forward and says, "But Jobe, me and Rosie—"

Rosie pulls her back, and Chrissy stops talking.

But Jobe knows what she was going to say. She wants Rosie to go too. But that won't work. It has to be just him and Chrissy together, and no one else.

Bella laughs. "You and Chrissy. Don't make me laugh."

"I don't think you should laugh, Bella. I love her and I think she loves me too. We're going to go away to be together. We'll get married and then, after a while, we'll go back and tell her mother what happened." He turns to look at Chrissy, but she won't look back at him.

Bella laughs again. "Well now, sounds like mister big pants has got it all worked out. But I got some big news for mister big pants. Remember when I went into the store to get you all some food. Well, guess what I saw in there. A newspaper with your picture in it."

"My picture?"

"Yeah. They probably took your picture off of that surveillance camera they caught you on outside that Walmart store back up there in Utah. The newspaper said you kidnapped poor little miss Chrissy, and they've expanded the search for ya everywhere. And that's not all. Turns out you offed your poor old mother too. They found your fingerprints on the hypodermic needle that killed her, and some neighbors saw you sneakin' away in the middle of the night. Didn't think they'd catch you for that one, did ya?"

Jobe stares at her, not even sure he can believe the words she is saying. His fingerprints on Mother's drug needle? She never let him near her precious drugs. But now that he thinks about it, maybe he did touch that needle, but only to take it out of her arm where it was still stuck in after she died.

"What's the matter, mister big pants? Cat got your tongue?"

"No, Bella a cat doesn't have ahold of my tongue. And I didn't hurt my mother. I would never do that. She just liked her drugs too much and one night she took too much. I didn't know what to do, so I just left her in the hands of the Lord."

"Ha! A likely story."

"I don't care what you say, Bella. Me and Chrissy are leaving. You and Rosie can do whatever you want, but me and Chrissy are going to go our own way. Then, later, after we're married, I'm going to take her back to her mother, and then I'll explain everything. I'll tell them it wasn't me that stole that car and took Chrissy away, it was you. And I'll tell them that my mother just loved her drugs too much, and that's why she died. I didn't do anything to her. They'll understand."

"Bullshit. They won't believe you for a second. I Goddam guarantee you, if you leave me, they'll track you down. I'm the only hope you got. And don't forget, it'll be dangerous for Chrissy too.

You're a wanted man, Jobey old boy. You might as well face it. They got nuthin at all on me. It was your picture they had in that newspaper, not mine."

Jobe refuses to talk to her anymore. He just looks straight ahead.

Bella shakes her head. "All right, mister big shot. Tell you what I'm gonna do. We're goin' to this other place I know, not far from here, and I expect you to raise some bucks for us. Then, the four of us will sit down and decide what to do next, okay? We'll work it out. You and Chrissy can still sleep under the same blanket, like always. We'll go down to Texas, and things will be a lot better down there. You'll see."

Jobe doesn't answer. If she thinks she can talk him out of taking off with Chrissy, she's wrong. His mind is made up. And when he said it, Chrissy didn't say a word. That proves she's ready to go too.

As they head for Bella's other begging place, Jobe can feel the gun pressing against his back. He's tempted to throw it out the window, but he knows Bella would see him do it and just go back and get it. He'll have to find a place to throw it away later. The important thing is that now Bella knows he and Chrissy are going to leave. He knows Chrissy really likes Rosie, but Bella and Rosie will do just fine on their own. In fact, they'll be better off without him and Chrissy. It's a problem that his picture was in that newspaper, but Bella made Chrissy look completely different from what she used to look like, so maybe he can do that same kind of thing to himself.

As Bella drives, Jobe makes a plan. He'll get as much money as he can from the people on the street, enough to get away to somewhere else, a place a long ways away where the police won't even think of looking for them.

Bella parks next to some tall buildings that look a lot like that other place downtown. She leads them out in front of one of the buildings, and parks herself and the girls against a low wall in front of the building and tells Jobe to get busy.

This time Jobe really puts his heart into the task of getting money from people because he knows any money he makes with only be for him and Chrissy.

There are a lot of people on the sidewalk, and Jobe stops every single one of them. He shows them his Bible and tells them that Jesus is coming soon, and that when he arrives he will reward those who have been generous to those in need.

He stops a man in a fancy black suit and tells him, "Do not lay up for yourselves treasures on earth, where moth and rust may destroy or where thieves might break in and steal, but lay up for yourselves treasures in Heaven by helping those in need."

The man laughs, but he does hand over a twenty-dollar bill.

Jobe stuffs it into his pocket without even looking at Bella. He's got almost enough now for him and Chrissy to get away.

He stops another man who's dressed in green pants and a white shirt that has shiny yellow buttons. He tells the man, "Do not set your hopes on the uncertainty of riches. Instead, set your hopes on God who will richly reward you in Heaven if you have lived a life of generous living." The man gives him a handful of bills, but they're mostly ones. Jobe stuffs the bills into his pocket and thanks the man.

An older couple comes along, and Jobe tells them, "Those who are generous in this lifetime will sit at the right hand of God." The woman opens her purse and is about to give Jobe some money when a police car pulls up to the curb and stops. Two policemen get out and approach Jobe.

Jobe is trying to decide what to do. Should he run, or just act normal?

But before he can decide what to do, Rosie jumps and runs to one of the policemen. She grabs the policemen's arm and says, "Help us, officer. Please help us. She points toward Chrissy. That is Christine Barlow, the little Mormon girl who was kidnapped up in Utah." She points at Jobe. "He's the man who kidnapped us."

Both of the policemen turn toward Jobe.

Rosie shouts, "Look out, the kidnapper has a gun!"

Both of the policemen take out their guns and point them at Jobe.

Rosie yells at Jobe. "Show them the gun, Jobe. Quick. Before it's too late."

Jobe has never heard Rosie yell before, and he's surprised at how loud she can yell after being quiet for so long. He decides he'd better do what she says before they arrest him and find the gun for themselves. He reaches back and pulls the pistol out of his waistband.

Both of the cops react by ducking down and yelling, "Drop the weapon!"

Jobe is surprised by their actions. They must not understand that it's not a real gun. He says, "No, it's not what you think. Look. He points it at them and pulls the trigger to show them it doesn't shoot real bullets. The sound of the blank bullet going off is very loud. It scares Jobe so much he accidentally pulls the trigger again, and this time the blank bullet going off seems even louder.

Rosie yells, "He's trying to kill us. He's going to kill all of us."

Both of the policemen start shooting their guns, and Jobe feels something hurt his stomach. It feels like something very hot went right though the middle of him. He only has time to think that the feeling of something going right through you is a very strange feeling before he hears more gunshots and he feels another very bad pain in his chest. He sits down hard on the sidewalk, and again, tries to show them that the gun is fake. He wants to tell them that even though it made a very loud sound when he pulled the trigger, that was only the sound of the blank bullets going off. But he can't seem to make his mouth work, so he just sits there, holding the gun out to them, trying to make his eyes focus on Chrissy who for some reason is sitting on the sidewalk screaming and crying, and she has both of her hands up in front of her beautiful face. He looks for Bella. Maybe she can explain to these policemen about why she bought the gun and that it's only a fake gun, not a real one. But Bella is somehow gone. Where did she go? He looks back at the two policemen who are slowly coming toward him. Both of them are sort of leaning forward and their guns are still pointed at him. If only he could make his mouth work, he could explain it all to them. He wants to look at Chrissy again, but his eyes don't seem to be working right. He's sure he has both of his eyes open, but what they are seeing is getting darker and darker.

Chrissy 11

I'm back home now, and I have to tell you that things got really really bad down there in Phoenix. After we left the camping spot, Bella drove all over town trying to buy a gun. Rosie said she was probably trying to get revenge on the men that had hurt her. I said if she got a gun we should get away from her quick, and Rosie agreed. She said she would figure out a way, and soon.

But Bella wasn't able to buy a real gun, so she bought a pretend gun that looked real.

Then we went back to the downtown part of the city and Jobe was getting money from people by talking to them about what the Bible says when two policemen came. Rosie yelled at the policemen and told them my name and said we'd been kidnapped. She pointed at Jobe and said he was the one who kidnapped us and she told Jobe to show them the gun that Bella had bought. He did that, and the policemen shot him because they didn't know it was only a pretend gun.

After that, the police made Rosie and me stay in a room at their police station while they asked us a lot of questions. They said we were safe now because the man who had kidnapped us was in a coma and was probably going to die. And even if he didn't die, they said he'd be put in prison for a very long time, so we girls didn't have to be afraid anymore.

They said they found my cut off red hair in Jobe's pocket. They said he must have hacked off my red hair and kept it for himself. They said he was "a real wacko."

Rosie told the police that I was autistic and couldn't talk hardly at all. She told the police that Jobe had kidnapped both of us up in Utah, and then he made us get into a car and took us down to Phoenix. She told them he was getting money from people by showing them his Bible and threatening that he'd hurt them if they didn't give him money. She said he was some kind of "religious nut" who had made us hide out in the desert at night where he made us take off all of our clothes so he could do bad things to us. She said the kidnapper hardly gave us any food at all and she was so happy that the police had come along in time before he could kill both of us.

The police had a lot more questions. They looked at the pictures I'd drawn in my notebook, and even though they saw that I'd been drawing a lot of different kinds of pictures, the only ones they cared about were the pictures of Jobe. They tried to ask me a lot of different kinds of questions, but I did what Rosie had told me to do and didn't talk at all. I just cried and cried. After a while, my dad showed up and said I had to go back to Utah with him right away. The police let me go, but Rosie had to stay behind.

Once I got back here at home they locked me in a room all by myself. My mother was the only one allowed to come in and see me, and she told me the Prophet was deciding what to do with me. She said he might have to kick me out of the community because I had been "tainted" by the man who kidnapped me and did bad things to me. I didn't say anything to anybody because while we were at the police station in Phoenix, Rosie had whispered to remind me that we had a blood oath not to tell anybody anything. She said I should act like I had been "traumatized" and couldn't talk hardly at all anymore.

No sooner did I get back here when something else happened. I started to bleed down there. My mother said it was normal, and it only means my body is ready to have children now. She gave me a pad to cover it up and to catch all the blood that was coming out of me.

After several days of being locked up, I got taken to the Prophet. He sat behind his desk just like he did the last time I got called in, but this time he didn't make me take off my clothes. I did that myself, just like Rosie had told me to do. I took off all my clothes right in front of him and told him he could do anything he wanted to me. I told him we could start with a thing my kidnapper had taught me, a trick I could do with my mouth on his private part. If he would take off his pants, we could do that and all kinds of other things.

He came around from behind the desk real quick and took off his pants. I got down on my knees in front of him and reached down between my own legs and got a lot of blood on both of my hands and real quick I spread it all over his private MALE part and all over his big fat stomach. Then I grabbed his pants and ran out the door screaming that he was trying to rape me.

The women in the outer office got all upset and ran into his office and I ran in after them and we all saw the Prophet trying to hide behind his desk and trying to cover up his bloody private parts with his hands. I screamed over and over that he tried to rape me. I yelled, See there, that's my blood all over him.

After that, two of the women led me out of his office, and helped me get dressed. Then they took me back to that same room and locked me in again.

That's where I am now, and so far nobody has come in to try to talk to me. I know they'll want to kick me out of the community now, but I'll be gone before they can do that. Tonight, when everybody is asleep, I'll sneak out the window and head for the highway where Rosie will be waiting for me. She says she knows a place in Las Vegas where men will pay a lot of money to see me naked. She says they'll also want to do other things to me, but I won't have to do that. She says she'll take care of that part herself, and we'll make so much money we can get an apartment by ourselves and be together forever and ever.

www.ingramcontent.com/pod-product-compliance
Lightning Source LLC
Chambersburg PA
CBHW070844120626
46556CB00002B/877